Raymond Large, a man dedicated to observing the intimate interplay of others, was glued to the image in the two-way mirror.

Therese was undressing and the other two were helping her. She stood by the bed while the man levered the dress up past peach-coloured knickers and over her rounded hips The redhead was busy unfastening the back of the garment. The pair of them pulled the dress over the big woman's head.

Full, voluptuous breasts, deeply separated, were outlined through her thin camisole which was whisked away to reveal a pink corset, severely laced, compressing the buttocks and pushing up the heavy breasts. Eager hands seized her knickers and pulled them down over black silk stockings. Between the taut suspender straps gleamed a glossy triangle of pubic hair.

In the secret room, Raymond uttered a small gasp of delight . . .

The Wild Party

Aaron Amory

First published in 1994
by HEADLINE BOOK PUBLISHING

A HEADLINE DELTA paperback

10 9 8 7 6 5 4 3 2 1

ISBN 0 7472 4566 5

Typeset by Keyboard Services, Luton

Printed and bound in Great Britain by
Cox & Wyman Ltd, Reading, Berks

HEADLINE BOOK PUBLISHING
A division of Hodder Headline PLC
338 Euston Road
London NW1 3BH

The Wild Party

PART ONE

The Guests

PARIS – NICE

September, 1933

Mark

Mark Harries hadn't expected the chambermaid at his small hotel in the Latin Quarter to be as pretty and pert as the chambermaids in a French bedroom farce; nor had he anticipated a girl as eager to jump into bed with strangers as the randy, frilled-apron doxies featuring in smutty stories told by commercial travellers in the north of England. He was not in fact *expecting* anything at all.

The female who brought coffee and hot croissants and honey to his room on the morning following his arrival at the hotel was not, as it happened, French at all. She was Portuguese and her name was Incarnita Morales.

He sat up in bed, knuckled the sleep from his eyes, and looked at her a little blearily – he had returned to the hotel late the night before, after a visit to the Folies Bergère and a not too satisfactory romp at the hustling flat of a B-girl he met in a Montmartre nightclub. He saw behind the breakfast tray a woman of about forty, wearing a starched white apron over a pink-and-white check dress. She was quite short, with a close cap of dark hair, a mouth emphatically outlined with very dark red lipstick, and no other make up as far as he could see. Her figure, partly concealed by the stiff apron, was compact: big-breasted, broad-hipped, a little more in the hourglass direction than the boyish silhouette favoured by the Paris fashion magazines.

At the time he paid her not much attention: a murmured good-morning and a polite thank-you before she left the room. It was not until nearly midday, when he came back to the hotel after a small shopping expedition, that he looked closely at Incarnita Morales. She was just completing the 'doing' of his room. The bed was made, towels in the bathroom had been replaced, the porcelain washbasin shone. As Mark passed the stack of fresh laundry and the mop and brush leaning against the wall outside, and walked through the open doorway, the chambermaid was running a duster over the bedside table. She turned and smiled as he came in and laid his purchases on the bed.

Was this, she asked, the first time he had been in Paris? No, he replied in fluent if accented French; he had been a number of times before, but never as often as he would wish.

Ah. He was here on business then, and not perhaps just for a holiday? He was, Mark replied, although the business itself was in the South, on the Riviera coast. The Paris part was just for meetings and the signing of contracts.

'Oh, but how fortunate, how lucky!' Incarnita exclaimed in a husky voice even more accented than his own. 'You are to return to the *Midi*, to the sun! How I miss the sun in this cold city!' She turned again to close the shutters and drew the curtains halfway across the window. 'What business is this, that takes you all the way from England to the Mediterranean?'

'I am what they call a landscape gardener,' Mark said. 'Someone with a lot of money – more money, perhaps, than sense, as we say – someone wants me to design a *parc à l'anglaise*, an English-style garden, for a château down there.'

She nodded, looking at him approvingly. Mark was chunkily built, trim in a pale grey suit, with dark hair, a pink face and large brown eyes. She picked up her duster and prepared to leave the bedroom. As she passed him, she laid a hand briefly on his sleeve. 'You are very lucky,' she said.

When she had gone he remained staring at the closed door. In the darkened room, he realized, she had looked . . . well, certainly not glamorous, but definitely attractive, alluring even, in some indeterminate, subtle way that defied analysis. Beneath that slightly staid exterior, there lurked a nascent sexuality, he was convinced; a particularly sensual persona which needed no more than a positive touch to flower it to life. She was like a loaded pistol waiting only for the right hand to tighten on the trigger – or, to put it more vulgarly (as he was inclined to do), she was what the Americans called a sex bomb, lacking the right person to pull the pin.

The firm breasts, the powerful hips and small waist, that decided mouth and the guarded complicity of the woman's gaze would, he was sure, combine to produce a lusty package worthy of any man's bed. Even if the bed was a hired one in a Paris hotel.

He put the thought from his mind. It was almost lunch-time and the most important of his business meetings was at two-thirty.

Mark was a man for whom all appetites were important. He was a bachelor, an individual who would have been termed, thirty-years ago, a philanderer. He liked to play the field – three engagements already had foundered on the reefs of his infidelity – and had by now accepted the fact that his wandering eye was sufficiently all-embracing to have scotched any desire he might have for a permanent relationship.

It was however for the celebration dinner he proposed to award himself that his appetites yearned when he came back to the hotel after the success – the unexpectedly lavish success – of his conference with the owner of the château on the Riviera and his lawyers.

Until Incarnita Morales tapped on his door and came into his room to draw the curtains and turn down the bedcovers.

She was wearing a plain black dress beneath the starched apron this time. Otherwise she looked exactly as she had when he had seen her at midday . . . except, wait, there *was* a difference! The dark red lipstick still emphasized her mouth, but now there was rouge tinting her cheeks and make-up around her eyes: kohl-fringed, they would say in *La Vie Parisienne*, or was it just mascara? Perhaps the hotel management liked the staff to look a little more sophisticated in the evenings?

Mark doubted that. He travelled a lot, and in his opinion hotel managements took no interest whatsoever in the outward appearance of their hired help: servants were there to do as much work for as little money as possible, and the more inconspicuous they were, the better.

There was something, nevertheless, about that darkened mouth . . . a tiny quirk, perhaps, to the rather full lips? A hint – no more than that – of humour lurking in the depths of those deep brown eyes?

The slightest, subtlest rumour of a possible – what? – availability? If the right approach was made.

He had been sitting in a chair by the bedside table when Incarnita came in, reading the early edition of *Paris Soir*. A French production of Wilde's *The Importance of Being Earnest* was to be transferred from Nice to the Comédie Française in Paris. The American aviator Wiley Post had completed a round-the-world flight in *Winnie Mae*, his Lockheed Vega monoplane, in 187 hours. All fifteen members of the Riberac rugby football team had perished when their char-a-banc plunged down an embankment in the southwest and caught fire.

Mark folded the newspaper, laid it on the bed, and stood up.

The chambermaid smoothed down the triangled sheet and blanket on the far side of the bed. The curtains were already drawn. She withdrew Mark's violet-and-tan striped pyjamas from beneath the pillow and placed them on the turned-down corner. Then she straightened up and met his gaze.

She smiled. 'A good day?' she enquired.

Deliberately, he interpreted the phrase as a statement. 'Yes, wasn't it?' he said easily. 'Splendid weather for the time of the year – though it was a little chilly out of the sun.'

'No, no – I meant . . . the business. This of the gardens. It went well?'

'Oh . . . well enough.' He smiled in his turn. 'I would much rather have had the time free, though. So that I could enjoy the city. But still . . . we all have to work, don't we?'

'*Eh, oui.*' Incarnita walked slowly around the foot of the bed. She stood quite close to him. 'It is the same for everyone: there is no escaping the call of duty.' Absently, she brushed a speck of dust from his lapel with two fingers. 'Is there, Monsieur?'

'It is not always impossible,' said Mark. 'Escape, I mean. How long have you been doing this kind of work?' He nodded towards the bed and the curtains.

'Since the children were old enough to look after themselves when they come home from school. Before I was married, I worked as a *vendeuse*, a shopgirl, at the Galeries Lafayette.'

'You don't mind your children being on their own in the evening?'

'My husband,' she said, 'is with them until eleven o'clock. He works for the railways. A signalman. He is on the night staff at the Gare St Lazare – and in any case my evening work here is only twice a week.'

'Don't you miss your husband – if he works nights, I mean? Aren't you lonesome sometimes after dark?'

She heaved a Mediterranean shrug. Beneath the stiff apron, breasts sheathed in black rose and fell. 'In Portugal, we have a proverb: All experience, however displeasing, is good.'

'I'm pretty sure,' Mark said, 'that we have a similar model in England.' He reached out and placed his hands gently on her upper arms. 'The good thing about experiences, *n'est-ce pas*?, is that they can be shared.'

She tilted back her head and looked up at him, an unfathomable expression in her eyes. She made no move to evade his grasp. The red lips pursed very slightly in what might have been a repressed smile.

Mark drew her towards him. He bent his head and kissed her.

The result was electrifying. She flung herself against him as forcefully as an iron bar drawn to a magnet. The whole length of her compact, voluptuous body was plastered against him and her breath jetted through flared nostrils as violently as if she had received a blow in the solar plexus. He could feel her knees trembling against his legs.

He felt cool hands lock behind his head. The woman's mouth was open wide: between wet clinging lips, a hot tongue thrust far into his own mouth, exploring teeth, gums, palate and the warm hollows inside his cheeks.

She was eating him up! Mark ground the erection stiffening abruptly in his loins against the body whose soft flesh he could feel against him through the layers of shirt and jacket and dress and the crisp white apron she wore. His hands were clenched over the taut, muscular mounds of Incarnita's buttocks. Now he moved them around, over her padded hips and up the rib cage to the fleshy weight of breasts thrusting out the apron bib. As he had thought, no bust bodice or brassière constricted the heavy globes moving so easily to his touch.

The kiss lasted a long time. When at last the wild beating of his heart threatened to stifle his breath, Mark disengaged himself. Holding her by the shoulders, he propelled her towards the bed. 'Come,' he said hoarsely.

But she broke quickly free and stepped away. 'No, no,'

she panted. 'Is not possible. Please. Not now.'

'B-but I thought,' he stammered. 'I mean, why . . .?' His hands were shaking.

Incarnita Morales shook her head. 'Not now,' she repeated. 'I have other rooms to do. The housekeeper is much – how do you say? – strict. Each thing must be completed at the correct time.'

Mark cleared his throat. 'You said you worked late two evenings a week – and this is one of them. Right?'

She nodded, moving towards the door.

'What time do you finish work? You don't stay the night in the hotel?'

'No. I must be home by eleven. I told you. My work stays until eight o'clock, sometimes later if there are many guests.'

'And tonight?'

Incarnita smiled. A small smile, one corner of the mouth only, but promising. Her lips were still wet, Mark noticed, and her eyes were bright. 'Tonight not many guests,' she said. 'Perhaps nine o'clock.'

'Later, then? You will come here after nine and have a . . . a . . . you will drink champagne with me then?'

The smile broadened. 'Later,' she said in a low voice. She nodded once, went out of the room, and closed the door softly behind her.

She returned at five minutes past nine. There was no discreet tap at the door: it opened and closed noiselessly, and she was in the room. Holding a finger to her lips, she whispered: 'Housekeeper thinks I have gone home already; when I leave, I must take back stairs.'

Mark opened his mouth to say something, but she shushed him into silence. She was indeed, he saw, dressed for the street: a dun-coloured, lightweight duster coat that reached halfway down her calves; low-heeled, sensible shoes. There was no make-up on her face, and little trace of the sophisticated and sensually liberated creature plastered against him earlier that evening. She looked in fact like a little woman employed as an upstairs maid at a hotel on her way home after a day's work. For a moment, helping her off with her coat, he wondered if he had made a terrible mistake. As she slipped the garment on to a hanger and hooked it into the wardrobe, he turned away and busied himself with the champagne and glasses he had bought before the shops closed.

Mark poured two drinks and turned again. The start of surprise that he gave was enough to spill wine from one of the glasses and soak his sleeve.

Incarnita hadn't stopped with the removal of her coat. Like a clockwork toy programmed to complete a particular routine, she had continued methodically to strip. She had already peeled off a shapeless jersey dress and enough underclothes to bare herself to the waist. Now, matter-of-facty, she bent forward to unlace her shoes, pushed down an underskirt and oyster-coloured French knickers, and stepped out of them all.

She was naked, standing unselfconsciously before him with one hand held out for her champagne and, at last, a small smile on her face.

Seeing her there beside his bed, Mark forgot at once the titillating fantasies of gradual disrobing which had excited his imagination since the early part of the evening. The subtleties of inch-by-inch exploration, the breathless suspense of successive and ever more revealing discoveries, were put firmly from his mind. To him, every woman was a new woman – and this one was a prize.

She was quite heavily built – almost thickset by the standards of the current fashion arbiters, whose boyish models posed like drooping flowers. But the curves and the hollows were in all the right places. The ankles were slender, the calves shapely, and the thighs, muscular though they were, a perfect introduction to fleshy hips and a small, smoothly sculpted waist. The breasts above this were slightly pear-shaped, but firmly swelling and widely separated. Staring at the soft curve of the woman's belly where it swooped down into a triangle of thickly clustered, black pubic hair, Mark thought at that moment that he had never seen a sexier sight in his life.

He walked up to her and raised his glass. The rims of the two glasses touched. They drank.

Once again Incarnita laid a finger across her lips to prevent him saying something. She giggled suddenly. 'We must be very quiet,' she whispered. 'The housekeeper patrols!'

He grinned back. The unspoken complicity excited him. Two children, hidden beneath the stairs, sharing a naughty secret! He felt his penis lengthen, stiffening against the stuff of his trousers. 'You are very beautiful,' he whispered.

Her smile was radiant. 'Tell me with your body,' she murmured. 'But first' – she sat on the edge of the bed and reached out her hands – 'you must let me make you bare like me. Then we can be together, no?'

The tension in Mark's loins abruptly increased as she unbuttoned his jacket and he felt expert fingers thread the tip of his belt out through the buckle. The waistband of his trousers loosened. Cool air played on the heated skin of his belly as the buttons of his fly were undone, one after the other.

Remembering the practised way she had removed her own clothes, the sureness of her touch now, he was beset by a sudden doubt: wasn't it all, perhaps, a little too pat? Could she be a pro – a hustler using the hotel as a cover?

That was another thought chased from his mind. Soft fingers brushed against the outline of his iron-hard cock. Through the silk of his underpants he could feel them probing, measuring, tracing the length of its pulsing shaft and then firmly closing around it. He caught his breath: the sheathed stem had been tweaked roughly sideways, pulled free of the clinging garment, and brought out into the open through his gaping fly.

Holding it between the forefinger and thumb of her right hand, Incarnita leaned forward and closed velvet lips over the throbbing tip. Her left hand reached in to fondle the wrinkled sac pouched beneath.

Mark was panting with excitement. He wrenched off his jacket, loosened his tie and pulled his shirt over his head. He flung away shirt and tie, and shoved the unfastened trousers down over his hips.

For a moment he stood there trembling, while she sucked gently on the acorned tip of his penis. Then, without taking any more of the veined staff into her mouth, she pulled away, thrust trousers and underpants fiercely down to his ankles, and said in a hard, hoarse whisper: 'Come to me now.'

She swung her legs up on to the bed and stretched out on her back.

Stepping out of the discarded clothes and kicking them away, Mark realized for the first time that the woman was not one hundred percent nude: she still wore black silk stockings rolled down to the knee; the film of sheer, dark material harmonized so perfectly with the black bush, the contrasting white flesh and the deeper, purplish tint of the nipples tipping her heavy breasts that the fact had failed to register with him before. He lay down on the bed beside her.

For a moment she looked approvingly at his compact figure – the muscled, flat plane of his belly, the deep chest and the black hairs downing his forearms and running out along the backs of his fingers. Then, with a final stare at the stiff and dark-fleshed cock jutting lewdly from the tangle of pubic hair shadowing his loins, she reached for him once more.

Mark's breathing quickened as her hand closed over him. He raised himself up on one elbow and feasted his eyes on the naked length of her body. Incarnita too was breathing fast now. Her fleshy thighs had parted slightly when her fingers wrapped around his aching hardness. Now, amongst the thicket of dark hairs above, a thin scythe of pink flesh showed – and at the top of this pale, intimately folded crescent, a pearl of moisture already gleamed. He stretched his free hand eagerly towards her.

The pubic mound was hot beneath his palm. His fingertips touched springy hair, brushed hair that was damp, sank suddenly into warm flesh that was silkily sliding wet. His questing index brushed against a small rubbery button that stiffened at once as Incarnita uttered a stifled cry and jerked her hips up off the covers. It was time, he thought, to kiss her again.

The effect, the instant his mouth closed over hers, was as electrifying as it had been the first time. Her breath snorted through her nose as those avid lips clung greedily; her body arched up to press against him; the moist and muscled tongue invaded the cavern of his mouth as savagely as the fingers of his free hand now rummaged between the wet lips of her cunt.

It seemed to him that they remained like that for an eternity, the tongues jousting, wrestling in the hot dark, the woman's loins trembling each time his caress coaxed a start of ecstasy from the throbbing bud of her sex. She had begun a slow, dreamlike massage of Mark's rigid staff, milking the distended skin over the stiffened core, palming at the end of each stroke the seeping tip. Her other hand stole across her belly now, gently, gently to squeeze his testicles in their tender pouch.

So compelling was the exquisite agony of his fluttering nerves that he saw for a long time no reason to progress the scene any further: it was enough to remain there, motionless except for the most economic of small movements, lazing in a tide of sensual bliss.

But nothing in life remains static: one advances or

retreats; the more a situation gains in intensity, the more it must develop and elaborate if it is not to dwindle away to meaninglessness. Gradually Mark became aware, through the insistence and urgency of the insidious tiny squelching sounds stimulated by his hand and hers, that the scenario demanded a change of pace.

Instinctively, Incarnita reached the identical conclusion at the same time. 'You are right,' she breathed, breaking away from his devouring kiss. 'In Portugal we have this saying that to be doing hastily does not always make for more rapidity—'

'More haste, less speed. Yes, so do we.'

'—but there comes nevertheless a time, *amore*, when changes must be made – so come close to me now, when I am all ready for you and waiting.' She clamped a hand over his hip and pulled him towards her.

In a single swift movement, he rolled over and lowered the length of his body between her suddenly spread thighs. At once, as if pre-set to this particular routine, their four hands busied themselves with new tasks. Supporting himself on his elbows, Mark leaned over the satined skin of her rib cage, pushed up the swelling mounds of her two breasts, and lowered sucking lips to each of the stiffened nipples in turn. She kept one hand on his hip, kneading the tautly muscled flesh over the pelvic bone. With the other, she grasped the blue-veined, oiled and glistening wand spearing from his hairy loins and wagged it gently through the dark, damp thicket at the base of her belly, nudging aside the sexual lips to position the distended tip at the entrance to her love canal.

Incarnita increased the pressure on his hip, forcing him down.

Breath hissed from her open mouth as Mark's cock bludgeoned through the hot, wet labial folds to tunnel up to the hilt in the scalding clasp of her secret inner flesh.

He raised his head from her breasts and groaned aloud,

revelling in that absurdly triumphant elation he felt each time his throbbing and eager shaft was swallowed in the voracious depths of a woman's belly.

Now, as the imperatives of lust drove them to renewed, more forceful movement, the couple were transformed into a unity: they became what a Welsh poet once described as the 'two-backed beast of love'.

Twined together on the hotel bed, they moved easily and at once into a slow reciprocating rhythm, action and reaction silkily married as Mark's powerful hips forced the thick, hard cock repeatedly into her, and she arched up each time to meet each pistoned thrust.

The two hearts hammered as one within their welded-together chests.

He forced his two hands beneath her, seizing the pliant half-moons of her buttocks so that he could lever the woman's sweating loins closer still to his pounding hips. On either side of those hips, her thighs spread wider, wider, the knees bent and the legs drawn suddenly up to scissor across the small of his back. She wrapped her arms around him, raking his strong back with frantic nails, lacing her fingers behind his head to drag his mouth down to her out-thrust tongue in a third ferocious kiss.

Slowly, imperceptibly, the speed of their lubricated coupling increased. What had started sedately as a walk became a trot, a canter and finally a gallop.

Inside the shuttered room, hoarse exhalations of breath pounded from the thrusting couple overlaid the rhythmic and accelerating creak of the bedsprings. From time to time, provoked by an extra-deep penetration, a particularly heavy thrust, a small mewling cry escaped the woman. A single petal detached itself from a bowl of roses on the dressing-table and floated to the floor.

Outside, footsteps passed down the corridor. In the distance, the gates of a lift clanged shut. Wind gusting against the closed window brought closer the noises of night-time Paris: a rumble of traffic, klaxons blaring, the far-off strains of an accordeon. In the street below, a voice shouted something unintelligible into the night.

Oblivious of all these sounds Mark Harries and his partner, driven to the very zenith of physical excitement, floated at last up on to that onrushing wave from whose rearing, thundering crest there is no drawing back.

The wave broke.

A strangled cry burst from Mark's lips as Incarnita shuddered into a galvanic release and the rapid contractions of her vaginal muscles milked him relentlessly into his own climax. The aching, distended staff buried deeply within her erupted at once into pulsating action, spurting the hot, white proof of his desire far up into her receptive belly.

Later, when the small sobbing cries in his ear had died away, and the hammering of his own heart had subsided, he levered himself off her and sat up on the bed. 'Incarnita,' he said, 'I think you are wonderful!' He leaned down and kissed her on the nose.

She smiled lazily, sleepily. 'What is the time?' she murmured. He picked his wristwatch off the bedside table, 'Ten-fifteen,' he said.

'Marvellous! So we do have time for more!'

Mark reached for the champagne bottle. He poured two more glasses. 'I did say wonderful!' he enthused.

Their second bout of lovemaking was less tempestuous, more reflective. It was an affair of exploration, of slow caresses, of the tingling thrill induced by the play of lips and tongues and fingertips on secret places. But when at last the acrobatics of oral and manipulative stimulation gave way to a second straight fuck, and he took her from behind as she kneeled beside the bed, their shared orgasm was even more shattering than the first.

It was then – the bottle was empty; she was putting on her clothes – that he wondered again whether or not he should offer her . . . no, not money; a 'present' was the tactful way of putting it.

But the dark head was shaken decisively when, after a few awkward attempts, he finally came to the point. 'It is kind,' she smiled, 'but not. Most definitely not. In Portugal—'

'Don't tell me,' Mark said. 'In Portugal you have a saying?'

'We do. It is never to mix together business and pleasure. My business is to work here at the hotel. My pleasure . . . well, it is only on Saturdays that my husband and I are at home at the same time, and then the children are there. So my pleasure, or at least some of it' – she looked, still smiling, around the room – 'my pleasure is like this, with you.'

He kissed her on both cheeks as she stood by the door. 'My pleasure,' he said.

Raymond

The house was in the Avenue Kléber, three hundred yards from the Arc de Triomphe at the eastern end of Paris's snob 16th *Arrondissement.* It had once belonged to a Belgian countess who had been a leading figure among the *Amázones* – the notorious Lesbian cult so fashionable in Paris at the turn of the century. But the lady had migrated, with advancing age, to the South – where there was a higher proportion of unattached females, due to the death rate among rich businessmen, and the weather was sunnier too. The present owner, Raymond Large, was a wealthy Englishman who had just acquired a vineyard in Provence. It was around the château attached to this property that Mark Harries was to design his *parc à l'anglaise*.

Mark arrived for the second meeting with his client on the morning after his encounter with Incarnita Morales. He paid off his taxicab just before midday, and walked through the archway leading to the house. It was one of those city mansions known in France as a *hôtel particulier*, built around a courtyard with each of the severe, three-storey façades topped by an attic floor beneath steep slate mansard roofs.

There was a huge Delaunay-Belleville limousine parked next to a Citroën runabout in the cobbled yard. Mark passed between the cars, skirted a line of tamarisk and oleanders in green tubs, and climbed the steps to the glassed-in porch. The double doors were swept open by a liveried manservant.

Large received him in the study, a vast panelled room on the first floor, with French windows overlooking a walled garden bright with geraniums. He was a tall, lean man of about sixty, with crimped silver hair and alert blue eyes behind hornrimmed spectacles.

Mark found him easy enough to get on with so far as business was concerned – he was matter-of-fact, decisive, and willing to be told, a rare quality in a rich man. But on the personal level there was a certain reserve he found it difficult to penetrate: Large's hatchet face, with its blade of a nose, was seldom raised enough to meet his gaze directly, and the thin-lipped mouth was slow to smile. It was not until the paperwork was finished, the contracts signed, and the French notary sent back to his office with the completed files that the owner of the château allowed a hint of his more private nature to appear.

The manservant, assisted by a parlourmaid wearing a frilly white apron and a lace cap, had set up a buffet lunch on a gatelegged *directoire* table spread with a white cloth. Large was standing by the open French windows with a glass of champagne in one hand and a smoked salmon sandwich in the other. With his back to Mark, he was staring down into the garden – a neat pattern of flowering shrubs interspersed with classical figures, and the geraniums in stone urns on either side of a flagged pathway.

'Very successful.' Playing the polite guest, Mark stood just behind his shoulder. 'It's an admirable design, in line as well as colour. I particularly like the blue of that ceanothus against the white wall of the summerhouse.'

Raymond Large swung around to face him. 'Thank you, Harries. I would have expected you to appreciate the thought that went into it. Not everyone, alas, has the talent and sensitivity to enjoy fully the *purely visual*.'

Mark's eyebrows raised: the emphasis on the last two words had been very marked. 'Well, of course,' he began, 'the visual impact of any design is one of the most important—'

'Not just in the matter of design!' Large interrupted. He strode across to the table and snatched up another sandwich. 'In the whole of life . . . nature, things, the universe, *people* . . . it's not what they say: that means nothing; it's not what they are: that can be misleading; it's what they *do* that counts! *Seeing* is believing – that's the truest of all our sacred maxims!' Behind the thick lenses, the man's blue eyes were gleaming.

'It's good to meet someone prepared to credit the visual arts,' Mark smiled. 'It's not always that—'

'Not just the arts, not even the crafts, but the whole of life. The whole of it! Vision is by far the truest of our five senses.' The enthusiasm animating Large's once reserved features was becoming manic. He drained his glass and pulled the silver ice bucket across the table towards him. Twirling the bottle, he jerked it out and slopped champagne into Mark's glass and then his own. 'A man in your profession, Harries, is in a *unique* position to appreciate the visual aspect. You earn your *living* making things look good.'

'Yes, I guess I do. But—'

'Take sex, for instance.'

'I beg your pardon?'

'Sex. A young chap like you is going to be interested in sex. Bound to be, eh? Of course you are.'

'I imagine my interest is as strong as the next man's,' Mark said defensively. What was the old boy getting at now?

'Well, there you are!' Large said triumphantly. 'But have you ever thought – how right he was, the fellow who said sex was only serious to those actually doing it! For the rest of the world it's not serious: it's *entertainment*. Think of the Folies Bergère; think of the smutty magazines on sale along the *quais* and those novels with green jackets in the

Shakespeare bookshop; think of Greta Garbo and Fifi d'Orsay.' He paused, shaking his head. 'Think of the *Bible*, Harries!'

Mark grinned. 'Yes, of course: the success of all those things – except perhaps the Bible – is certainly based on sex appeal. Just as many of the advertisements in fashion magazines and the cheaper newspapers are.'

'Have you ever actually *read* the Bible?' Large demanded. 'No matter. You are of course right to use the word "based". These . . . phenomena . . . merely *suggest* or imply the sexual component in their quest to entertain. But think, man, how much more successful the quest would be if the sex was actually *there*!'

'You mean . . . ?'

'I mean if you had reality instead of nothing more than a reminder of it; I'm saying what if you can *see* the sex.'

This time Mark made no reply. While he was speaking, Raymond Large had wolfed another sandwich, a slice of pumpernickel garnished with dressed crab, and half a lobster patty. Now he refilled his glass, the eyes brighter than ever, and asked: 'What kind of sex are you interested in, Harries?'

'Any kind really,' Mark replied. 'I'm kind of an enthusiast!'

'Splendid! A man after my own heart. Fill your glass, then, and follow me: I propose a little demonstration which I think might amuse you.' Seizing his own glass and the bottle, Large led the way out of the room.

Mark shrugged. Wondering what he was letting himself in for, he followed his host along several passages and up a narrow stairway leading to the attic floor. 'The servants' stairs,' Large confided, 'but they are not allowed to use them in daylight hours. Come – we shall install ourselves in here.' He unlocked a door and switched on a low-powered light in a small room with a sloping ceiling. Mark followed him in.

The floor of the room was thickly carpeted. One wall, the highest and longest, was covered by fitted bookshelves, and there were piles of magazines neatly stacked on a central table. Judging by the covers, the magazines were all pornographic or of the nude-photo type marketed as art. A quick glance along the shelves told Mark that most, if not all, of the books stored there were in the category of erotica. A large magnifying glass lay on the table beside the periodicals.

Had he, Mark wondered, been brought all the way up here to lust over a collection of dirty pictures? The only other furniture in the room – two deep-seat leather armchairs – faced what appeared to be a curtained window.

Before he could make any comment, Raymond Large indicated the chairs and said: 'Take a seat. Make yourself comfortable. I don't think we have arrived too early.' He strode silently across the carpet and twitched aside the drapes.

Mark gasped aloud, instinctively shrinking back into the chair. It was a window all right – but instead of the expected Paris rooftops, the view was of a brightly lit bedroom. And the bed was occupied by a naked man and woman.

Large chuckled, observing his guest's reaction. 'Don't worry,' he said. 'It's a two-way mirror: we can see them but they can't see us!'

Staring wide-eyed, Mark took in the couple. The girl was a *rouquine*, a redhead, maybe eighteen years old. She was lying on her back on the bed with her knees drawn up. The splayed thighs were no more than five or six feet from the mirror, and the two men in the secret room were gazing straight at her obscenely exposed genital area, at the tawny thatch covering her loins, and the scarlet-nailed fingers even now parting the moist pink lips nestling there.

The man was further away, kneeling up just behind the girl's head. He was a muscular fellow, sallow-skinned, with dark hair matting his chest and a stout erection spearing from the thick bush at the base of his belly. Mark recognized him as the manservant who had showed him in.

'I told him to take the afternoon off,' Large said. 'He thinks I don't know he's made himself a little love-nest up here. In fact I tempted him to do it, showing him over the house when I first employed him.'

'And the girl?'

'She's a new kitchen-maid. I let him hire the female staff, you see: it ensures a continuous supply for me in here – because naturally he employs the pretty ones, and those he's sure he can seduce.'

Large's voice had become husky and a little strained during this explanation; his eyes remained avidly fixed on the couple as he spoke. By then of course the penny had dropped for Mark. All that concentration on the visual, the fancy dialogue and the 'academic' approach, cloaked one single fact: the man was a voyeur. It was as simple as that.

Raymond Large got off watching other people do it.

Most people, Mark reflected, would find such a sight stimulating – if they were honest with themselves. The difference with Large was that this was his sole, his only satisfaction. He was an obsessive, and this was his thing. A quick glance stolen at the rigid bulge thrusting out his crotch seemed to prove the point. 'Your man doesn't know about . . . this?' Mark said, indicating the two-way mirror.

'Certainly not. The door has a special lock and I have the only key. He was told it was a disused store-room and the key was lost. The mirror itself,' Large said conversationally, 'has an interesting history. It was once installed at the Chabanais, one of the most famous and the most luxurious brothels in Paris. I was able to buy it when the place was refurbished five or six years ago.' He shook his head. The voice was definitely hoarse now. 'God knows what scenes of flagellation and debauch have been witnessed through this glass; what randy, lascivious archdukes and industrialists and high-priced whores have been spied on from this side!'

Mark's attention was riveted on the young woman lying on the bed now. The exploring fingers had spread vaginal lips wide, stirring the folds of flesh to moisture, teasing the stiffened bud at the apex of her open cunt. Her hips, gyrating slowly against the covers, arched up from time to time as a special thrill tingled her nerves. Behind her, the kneeling manservant had taken his hard cock in one hand. He was staring straight ahead, massaging the loose foreskin back and forth over the bulbous, distended tip.

'That's one of the advantages, you see,' Large said. 'Being an ordinary mirror on the other side, I mean. Everybody likes to watch themselves in a looking-glass. As a result they expose themselves as lewdly and lustfully – and as near my side of the glass – as they can!'

Mark cleared his throat. 'Remarkable!' he said.

The manservant was now leaning forward over his companion, supported by a hand on either side of her waist. The dark wand of his penis hovered just above her face. As the two men on the far side of the glass watched, the girl reached up her free hand and grasped the shaft. A pink and glistening tongue stole from her open mouth to lick the tip. Her lips pursed to suck in the blood-engorged knob . . . and then, as the man lowered himself further, almost the whole of his rigid cock was swallowed up.

He bent his arms, sinking his head until it was poised above the redhead's rotating loins. She freed the fingers titillating her clitoris and clamped her hand over the back of his neck, forcing his head savagely down into her crotch.

The manservant was stretched out along the length of the girl's body now. He reached his hands around her drawn-up thighs, dabbling raping fingers in the hairy cleft between them to drag open the outer and then the inner lips of her cunt. His head began to bob frantically up and down as his protruding tongue lapped the dark opening between them.

'Wonderful!' cackled Large. 'Marvellous! What a performer!'

There was already, Mark saw, a darker patch staining his brown pinstripe trousers just to the left of the fly.

At three-thirty, Mark regretfully took his leave of Raymond Large. 'I'd love to stay,' he said – the couple on the far side of the two-way mirror were still lasciviously entwined – 'but I'm catching the night train so that I can look around your property undisturbed, before you and your guests arrive at the weekend. And I have to pack up my kit, check out of my hotel, and do one or two things before I head for the station.'

'My dear fellow! I understand,' his host said without taking his eyes from the screen. 'But since, clearly, you appreciate the little charade laid on so unsuspectingly for our special benefit, I am wondering if you could see your way to extending your own visit to the weekend? You will, after all, be staying in the château anyway.'

'I don't see why not,' Mark said. 'What had you in mind?'

Large turned for an instant towards him. 'My guests,' he said significantly, 'have been . . . carefully selected. It will be rather a special party . . . a party with . . . entertainments . . . that might, I fancy, amuse you. For the moment, I'll say no more – except that I hope, sincerely, we shall see you there.'

'It will be a pleasure,' said Mark. 'I'm not sure, though, that I shall be able to submit proper landscaped plans by then: it depends a lot on the existing layout of the property.'

'Good Lord, no! I wouldn't expect you to!' Large expostulated. 'That's business; you submit your plans when you're good and ready, and not a moment before. That's understood. The weekend will be devoted entirely to pleasure – and if there's one thing we must never do . . .'

'We must never mix business with pleasure?' Mark supplied with a reminiscent smile. 'But how right, how very right you are!'

When Raymond Large returned to his secret room after he had seen his visitor out, the scene on the far side of the two-way mirror had changed in detail but it had lost nothing in intensity.

It was the manservant who was lying now on his back. The red-haired kitchen-maid, facing the mirror, was straddling his hips, impaled on the thick, fleshy staff springing from his loins. Flexing and relaxing her knees, she rose and fell in a slow dreamlike rhythm, the gleaming and rigid penis appearing in all its veined splendour, almost to the throbbing tip, on each upward movement . . . and then vanishing again between the splayed lips of the girl's cunt as she sank back on to his prone body.

She herself seemed far away, remote in some no-man's-land of lust: her two hands cupped small, pointed breasts; her lips were slack; her eyes, glazed with some private ecstasy, stared fixedly at her image in the mirror – although to Large, hidden on the far side of the glass, she appeared to be gazing straight, with who knew how much erotic complicity, at him. His right hand stole down to his crotch, fingering open the buttons of his fly.

For a little while longer, the set-piece continued: the redhead, a salacious rider, rising and falling (as Large imagined it) in invisible stirrups, the manservant flat on his back, arching up his hips only occasionally to bury his pole even deeper in his partner's belly. But then, as her rhythm became hesitant, sporadic, signalling the approach of a climax, the man lifted her bodily off him and rolled her over onto her back. Swiftly, he changed his own position, springing across to knee apart her thighs as he positioned himself between her legs. He took his cock in one hand, spread her vaginal lips with the other, and sank down to force the stiffened cudgel fiercely into her.

Both the love-nest and Large's secret room were soundproofed, but the girl's suddenly opened mouth, the galvanic upthrust of her hips as the penis rammed into her, were as evocative to the voyeur as if he had physically heard her cry out.

Very soon afterwards – the couple had only just settled into an easy, long-stroke copulating rhythm – the orgasm forecast became a reality. The girl's body convulsed. Her heels drummed on the bed. Still with that soundlessly screaming mouth, her head rolled wildly from side to side on the pillows. Then, as the climactic spasms seized her pelvis, she wrapped both legs around the manservant's waist, raking his back at the same time with blood-red fingernails.

A moment later it was the turn of the stud. The muscles of his pounding buttocks tensed, hollowed. His hips ground the girl ferociously down into the bedclothes, and his head jerked up with bared teeth as he shot his load of white-hot sperm into her trembling belly.

It was while the couple lay spent in one another's arms that the door of the love-nest opened and an older woman walked into the attic room.

She was perhaps fifty years old, heavily built with a large bust but fairly narrow hips and trim ankles. Her dark hair was worn in a bun on the nape of her neck.

Raymond Large exclaimed aloud, clapping his wet hands with excitement.

The woman was his housekeeper, Thérèse Paquin. Although he had tried once or twice, not very successfully, to spy on her when she undressed or walked scantily attired to the servants' bathroom, he had never seen her naked, and he had certainly never seen her in the attic room before.

What was she going to do?

Would she berate the manservant for daring to seduce a young girl who was theoretically in her care? Would she upbraid him for abusing his master's amenities, for behaving in a scandalous fashion, for misusing his afternoon off? Or would her reaction be more in sorrow than in anger? Had she herself at one time or another been in a similar situation in that very room? Was it possible that she could actually be *jealous* . . . ?

For the moment, certainly, it looked as though some kind of altercation was taking place. Clearly, Thérèse was speaking vehemently, with expansive hand gestures. The expression on her face could have been anger. Or it could have been something else. Excitement perhaps? For the first time since he had installed the two-way mirror, Raymond regretted that he had made no provision for *hearing* what went on in the love-nest.

He couldn't see the manservant's face: he was sitting up on the bed now with his back to the mirror. Once or twice he shrugged. He spread his hands wide. Was he making excuses? Was he angry because she had walked in? There was no way of telling. As for the redhead, she too had pulled herself up into a sitting position. She was looking up at the older woman with an expression that could have been defiant. Or just interested.

Not one of the three, it seemed to Raymond, showed the slightest trace of embarrassment. He craned forward suddenly, his blade-like nose almost touching the mirror. Thérèse had reached behind her; she was fumbling with the fastenings at the back of her black dress. There was a sly smile on her face.

Good God – was she going to *undress*?

Had they invited her to join in? And Thérèse, the stiff and starchy, disapproving Thérèse, had agreed? Just like that?

What did it matter? She *was* undressing. And the other two were helping her. She stood by the bed while the man levered the dress up past peach-coloured knickers and over her hips. The redhead, smiling too now, a conspiratorial smile, was busy at the back of the garment. They stood up then, pulling the dress off over Thérèse's head.

Big breasts, deeply separated, appeared within a voluminous, similarly peach-coloured camisole. Thérèse crossed her arms and pulled that off too as the others seized the waistband of her knickers and pulled them down, down past hips and buttocks and thighs, past black silk stockings to the floor.

In the secret room Raymond uttered a small gasp of delight. The stockings were drawn up tight by clipped suspenders. And the suspender straps stretched down from a pink corset, severely laced to constrict the woman's waist, compress her buttocks and push up the heavy, swelling breasts. Between the straps a thick tangle of wiry pubic hair only partly concealed prominently pouting vaginal lips.

The man behind the mirror watched in fascination as the naked redhead stood behind Thérèse, wrapped bare arms around her, and pushed those breasts up so that the manservant could bend forward and suck the oversize, wrinkled areolas and nibble the stiffened brown nipples at their centre.

Smiling still, Thérèse raised a stockinged toe to tickle the glistening sexual equipment bulging from the manservant's loins. The cock, flaccid and limp after his exertions on the bed, lengthened again at once and began to harden. He dived his hands down to dip probing fingers in among the hairs beneath the corset. Sheathed hips jerked suddenly below the kitchenmaid's embrace.

A moment later the lewdly posed trio had changed position. They were all on the bed, the man prone on his back and the two women manipulating, stroking and milking his now rigid shaft with all four hands . . . Thérèse was on all fours while he pulled apart the milk-white globes of her fleshy bottom and took her from behind . . . The redhead cupped her small pointed tits, offering them to the older woman to suck . . . Now the positions were reversed once more and the redhead was on her back.

Thérèse bent over her, slack breasts hanging above the tightly laced corset. Placing her hands behind the girl's knees, she pushed her bent legs back and up until the knees almost touched her breasts and the whole tawny furrow between her legs was exposed. The girl squirmed, reaching for the man. The housekeeper lowered her head then. Greedily, she sucked up into her own mouth the tender lips shielding the redhead's clitoris. Her tongue snaked in, seeking the sensitive bud.

She found it as the girl's lips closed over the manservant's throbbing penis head.

Raymond Large took a gold hunter from his waistcoat pocket and sprung open the lid. He sighed. Such a thrilling situation under his very own roof! He'd got used to the manservant's occasional bouts in the attic room with one girl or another, but this . . . this was beyond his most treasured dreams! And with Thérèse of all people! What treats might the future hold in store if he could be at the right time in the right place . . . in this place in fact!

He sighed again. Too bad there was an important wine merchant coming to see him at five. He would have to hurry down to his office to be there in time to greet the man . . . and leave the lustful trio to complete their exploits on their own.

With a last lingering and regretful look at his coupling employees – they had moved yet again and the man was between the two women – Raymond drew the curtains over the glass and tiptoed from his secret room.

Back in his study – the wine merchant had not arrived yet – he lifted the earpiece from a brass and ivory telephone set and twirled the handle to summon an operator. 'Hallo?' he said into the trumpet mouthpiece. 'Mademoiselle? This is Kléber seven five two three . . . Yes, that's right: seven five two three . . . I would like to make a call to the *Département* of Alpes Maritimes, a personal call to Mademoiselle Séverine Rouffach . . .'

Séverine

Raymond Large's Riviera property lay in the hills a few miles north of Nice. The château, which dated from the time of the Knights Templar, was perched on a hilltop near the village of Courmettes-les-Rochers; the vineyard attached to it was spread over forty-four acres of sunny, terraced slopes below.

These vines had once produced an elegant, pricey and much admired Côtes de Provence red wine. But a succession of careless, absent owners and crooked managers had disastrously lowered the quality of the product and the domaine had lost the right to use that registered *appellation*. When Large bought the château, half the terraces were abandoned and the small amount of wine that was produced was taken away to a local co-operative in tankers, to be blended into a cheap red table wine. It was the new owner's aim to restore the property to its former glory and once more acquire the right to label his wine 'Château Courmettes – Côtes de Provence'. But before this could happen a great deal of money would have to be spent – new stock would have to be planted, new systems installed, new capital injected and the whole place modernized. And although Large was rich, it did not suit him so soon after the Great Depression to release that much money from his other interests. His September house party, just before the vintage, was designed – very carefully designed – to impress and eventually sweeten a possible investor.

The success or failure of this plan would depend on the vineyard manager. And the manager was a woman, Séverine Rouffach.

She had been brought up in the wine business: her father was a grower, with vines on the lush slopes of Alsace, at the eastern extremity of the Vosges. Now she was Raymond Large's confidante as well as the expert he had employed to bring the Courmettes domaine back to life.

Séverine took his Paris call in what was euphemistically termed 'the Proprietor's Bureau', a ten by ten foot office sandwiched between the first-year and second-year *chais* – long, low, pantiled outbuilding designed to mature the new wine in wooden casks before it was bottled. The office was furnished with two chairs, a scarred, flat-topped desk, and an ancient oak filing cabinet. A yellowed chart on one wall showed the distribution of the buildings and different 'parcels' of vines around the property. Many of these strips were scored through with red crayon to denote areas no longer under cultivation.

The telephone was old-fashioned: a wooden box, sprouting a black bakelite mouthpiece, screwed on the wall. Séverine unhooked the receiver and held it to her ear, perching herself on a corner of the desk. She was a tall, fair woman of thirty, with short, bobbed hair and wide grey eyes.

After he had dealt with a number of points concerning the modernization of the vineyard, Large said; 'There will be an extra guest at the weekend. Harries, the landscape gardener, will be staying on. Can you manage?'

'I think so; I can put Kirk in the boxroom when he comes up from Antibes.' the young woman's voice was slightly husky and agreeably low in pitch. 'This extra man, he is . . . shall we say in the same field?'

'Oh, I think so! You don't need to worry. I have – ah – personal experience, but you can sound him out yourself if you like.'

'Very well.'

'As for the other guests ... well, you're my hostess. Everything going according to plan?'

'Yes.'

'The boat arriving on schedule?'

'Due at Golfe Juan tomorrow afternoon.'

'Good. And the – ah – merchandise? I can't say more as this is a party line. You *will* make sure Kirk delivers it in plenty of time?'

'Of course. He's bringing Margaret along. A girl that crews for him. I suppose that's all right?'

'Certainly. I told you, you can ask whoever you like, as long as they fit in . . .'

'Margaret will.'

'. . . and as long as there are no *locals* . I'll go as far out on a limb as you like to square the investor, but I won't have village rumours exaggerating "goings on" at the château.'

'Understood,' Séverine said. 'The nearest we have to that is a couple of actors from a play running in Nice. One of them is Margaret's brother. But they transfer to Paris at the end of the month, so they should be safe enough.'

'I hope so, Séverine. I trust your judgement anyway. What's the final tally?'

'Fifteen, counting you and me. Sixteen if the investor brings someone.'

Large chuckled. 'She'd better be broadminded if he does!'

'From what I hear of the gentleman,' Séverine observed, 'he'd be unlikely to bring anybody narrow – in any sense of the word!'

'So much the better. Now that journalist from Marseille and his wife, the Joneses – he's not likely to *write* anything, is he? I mean, they *are* . . . what shall I say? Well, our kind of people?'

It was Séverine's turn to laugh. 'If the gossip is true,' she said, 'it will be as much as any of us can do to keep up with them!'

When the conversation was over and Large had hung up, she went out into the sunshine and stood for a moment, staring from the *chais* to the buildings housing the hydraulic wine presses, the fermenting vats and the bottle stores. The owner, she reflected, couldn't have chosen a worse time to ask her to organize a weekend house party – a very specialized party which would call for lot of actual work in the château. The *vendange*, the wine harvest, was due in ten days' time; the grape-pickers would arrive at the weekend following the party; the broker who would make an offer for the final product was coming to inspect the crop a few days before. In the meantime this Englishman, the landscape gardener, had to be fed, housed and shown around the property. And of course the day-to-day running of the domaine, increasingly frantic as the harvest approached, must continue smoothly.

Séverine sighed. The tycoon Large hoped to interest in the property had to be in Cherbourg on Tuesday evening: he was returning to New York on the maiden voyage of the new British luxury liner, the *Queen Mary*. There was no other time when the party could have been arranged.

A tall tractor, with high, arched axles to allow the machine to straddle the rows of vines, trundled out of a shed. Two blue-overalled workers were stacking the wicker baskets used by pickers on the far side of the yard. Séverine called some instructions to the tractor driver and returned to the château.

It was separated from the farm buildings by a small valley – a complex massif of age-old, sun-scorched stone topped by shallow, tiled roofs at many different levels. From the windows of the Templars' tower a blue vee of sea was visible between two hills, and on a clear day the long, dark silhouette of Corsica, sixty-two miles away, could be seen on the horizon.

Séverine took a zigzag path, looping down between the terraced vines, the black grapes – syrah, grenache and carignan – thickly clustered beneath broad, spatulate leaves. She crossed a Roman footbridge spanning a narrow stream and climbed the flight of steps leading up to the terrace below the rear elevation of the château.

If Raymond Large was looking for outside capital to invest in the vineyard, he had not been afraid to spend his own, renovating and modernizing the ancient building. Modern bathrooms had been added and central heating installed. Panelling from one of the Loire châteaux graced the reception rooms. The roofs had been completely re-hung with antique tiles, and a ballroom with a new, sprung pine dance floor created between the walls of what had been an enormous hunting room and game larder. The inside of the château now was a picture of rich, polished woods, expensive materials and elegant period furniture.

Outside, facing away from the valley and the vineyard, the main elevation looked out over an arched entrance courtyard to a grassy plateau dotted with olive trees. The driveway curled away between these to penetrate a thicket of acacia and holm oaks, beyond which was the gate-house and the road leading to the village of Courmettes-les-Rochers.

Séverine skirted the château and walked through the arch into the courtyard. A dark, muscular man with tanned and weatherbeaten features was unloading cartons of champagne from the dickey of a prune-coloured Delahaye roadster with flared wings and a streamlined, sloping tail. She had heard the car arrive as she climbed the steps from the valley. It had clearly been driven hard because heat trembled in the bright light above the shield-shaped radiator and the tick of cooling metal was loud in the yard. 'Jean-Jacques!' she said. 'I didn't expect to see you here! Where's the party and when?'

Jean-Jacques Ancarani swung around. White teeth

gleamed in the dark face. His eyebrows were very thick, above piercing blue eyes. 'Séverine! I thought you'd be down in the *chais*, supervising the men hosing out the vats ready for the new vintage.'

'There's too much to do up here,' she said shortly. 'Gilles is capable of managing on his own.'

Ancarani was the *Maître de Chai*, the man responsible, ultimately, for the monitoring of every step in the production of the wine, from the length and temperature of fermentation to the sugar content of the must, from the percentage of alcohol to the time in barrel – the expert in fact on whom the quality of the contents of each bottle depended. He had been born in the town of Ocana in southern Corsica, the son and grandson of men in the wine trade. Apart from five years spent with the Foreign Legion in North Africa, he had himself worked in the trade all his adult life.

'Just getting in a few litres of joy to share with the lads during the vintage,' he explained, indicating the champagne cartons with a wave of his hand. 'But one bottle more or less won't be missed. It's a hot day. Why not split one with me now . . . just to give us the courage to go on?'

Séverine shook her head. 'Thanks, Jean-Jacques, but no: I haven't got the time. I told you: there's far too much to do.'

'All the more reason to take a break,' the Corsican said persuasively. 'Get your second wind and attack with new strength! Come on, Séverine, do.' He tucked a carton under one arm and reached for her hand.

She never quite knew why she allowed herself to be led up the steps to the château entrance and installed in a small sitting-room on the first floor. Perhaps it was just the relief, the momentary release from a schedule that was too charged, that changed her mind. In any case, she found herself sitting on an elegant but rather hard Empire *chaise longue*, expectantly watching the foil stripped off, the wire removed, and the cork expertly and soundlessly thumbed from the champagne bottle.

Ancarani poured into two cut-glass flutes and handed her one. '*Santé*,' he said. 'Your good health.' He raised his glass and drank.

Séverine smiled, raised her own glass, drank. The wine wasn't chilled, but it *was* refreshing. After the second glass, the many tasks weighing on her shoulders seemed perceptibly lighter. She smiled at Jean-Jacques.

They had been working together for almost a year now – she with the hiring and firing of the workforce, the paying of bills and other administrative duties, he with the improvement of the product itself. But she didn't really know him on a personal level: their respective duties had never brought them into direct contact – or opposition – and mutual respect, tinged with politeness, had been the only emotion shown an either side.

She looked at him now with new eyes. She supposed he was about forty – a very *masculine* man. He was deep-chested, with long arms. The dark hair curled in a way she thought of as particularly Mediterranean. His rugged features, stamped with determination, decision, and even a touch of ruthlessness, were nevertheless softened by a wide-lipped mouth that was surprisingly sensual. Séverine wondered what it would feel like to have those big hands with their square-tipped fingers on her body.

They had been talking in a desultory way about the vineyard, about the American who was supposed to invest in it, and about the house party which was designed to be a contributary factor influencing his final decision. Like Séverine herself, the Corsican had his quarters in a wing of the château, but she was as yet unaware how much – or how little – he knew of the *kind* of party it was to be. Or whether Large intended to invite him to the more ... well, specialized ... part of the festivities. She was unable therefore to enlarge on the details of her arrangements, and after a while a silence fell between them.

The bottle was empty. Ancarani reached in the carton for another. 'You don't look at all comfortable, perched on that thing,' he said. 'Why don't you came and sit over here, where there are proper cushions?' He unwrapped the gold foil, twisted off the wire, and eased out the cork with as little noise as before. He stretched out a hand for her empty glass.

'Oh, no, Jean-Jacques,' she said hastily. 'Thank you, but I really must not. There's so much to do . . . and I feel a little tipsy already!'

But she rose from the *chaise longue*, crossed the room and sank down on a heavily embroidered Persian divan strewn with brightly coloured silks and satins. He poured the drink anyway and placed her glass on an occasional table fashioned from a circular brass tray supported by spindly black lacquer legs.

Séverine was not a promiscuous person. Neither was she an innocent totally without experience. She had once been engaged to the captain of a pleasure steamer plying between Strasbourg and Koblenz, on the Rhine. She had emerged unscathed from one or two *affaires* when she was a student in Paris. But the skipper was uninterested in wine and wanted her to give up her career in the trade, the student excesses had been no more than youthful exuberance, and since then the vine and its products had taken up most of her time – in any case she had yet to meet a man with whom she felt sufficiently in tune to start a serious relationship. She was nevertheless a young woman with a highly developed sensuality – and this Corsican, this Ancarini, with his wide, slightly cruel smile, was *very* attractive indeed. Why had she never noticed before?

Her glass had no more wine in it. How odd. She could have sworn he had just refilled it. She must have drunk it. Had she? Now – look! – it was filled again. 'Thank you, Jean-Jacques. I w-w-was a little thirsty. It's a very hot day,' she managed to say. She swallowed champagne. 'You were quite right. It's m-m-much comfier here . . .'

The following half hour always remained a little hazy in her mind. The *Maître de Chai* was talking – it was very interesting – was talking about . . . what? Every now and then his voice, which was pleasantly deep, she realized, seemed to fade away, and she had to shake herself to bring reality back into focus. She too, of course, was talking. About the Foreign Legion? No, that must have been him. But it was fascinating and she felt *marvellous*.

She couldn't remember what on earth she had been talking about.

Outside her door – she had a suite on the second floor; his was on the third – outside her door he had said, yes, it *was* a bit late for a siesta, but what the hell . . . and she had said yes, she did feel a spot of shut-eye would be . . . and he had asked had she ever seen what he had done with his little nest under the eaves and she had said no and suddenly everything was crystal clear, hard and definite in the bright light, and she was standing in an attic room with a view, above terraced vines and olive trees, of the distant sea.

She saw heavy Provençal furniture, beautifully polished, a cheval glass, a wide nineteenth-century brass bedstead and Burgundian hunting prints decorating a white wall. Two heavy calibre shotguns and a rook rifle stood in a rack beside the door.

Reflected in the cheval glass, she saw a man and a woman, both of them smiling dreamily. The man's arms were around her . . . and, yes, my God! Jean-Jacques did have his arms locked around her waist . . .

His face was inches away; she could see the dark bristles on his chin in the late afternoon light filtering through the window. His warm, winey breath played on her brow. 'Séverine, you are beautiful,' he said. And then he kissed her.

That was when Séverine melted – or that's what it felt

like: she sensed the entire inner core of her body liquifying, draining down to fill her feet. Her hands, tingling, rose of their own accord to lace behind his head as his lips drifted onto hers, searched, tightened. The sudden hot bolt of his tongue spearing into her mouth made her shiver from head to toe. She was wet already; she could feel it.

A little timidly at first, her own tongue crept forward to meet his. He sucked it hard into his mouth, caressing it, licking, playing with it. He was breathing heavily, the air snorting in his nostrils. Crushed against him, she was aware of the thudding of her heart within its cage of ribs.

Ancarani snatched his head suddenly away. 'I want you!' he cried hoarsely. 'My God, I want you! This is no time for the niceties . . . the hell with all that foreplay crap, the lead-up-to-it-gently cant. I want you, Séverine, *now!*'

The rigid bulge thrusting at her crotch withdrew as he stepped away and tore his open-necked check shirt over his head. He flung it away and ripped open his belt, his waistband, shoving his trousers down over his hips, past his knees. He stepped out of them, kicked away shoes and stood before her naked.

Séverine thought she had never seen anything so uncompromisingly *male* in her life. Muscles rippled beneath the skin of his powerful shoulders and sculptured his strong arms. He had a flat belly, a lean waist and slim hips. Matted hair covered his chest and downed sturdy, athletic legs. Another line of hairs ran from his navel to where a short, thick cock, very dark in colour, jutted from the wiry triangle thatching his loins.

His desire, his lust for her was a palpable thing, vibrating in the stillness of the room. Panting now, he tore open her blouse, savaged away a bust bodice and lowered his head to her breasts. Faint thrills, rapidly gaining in intensity, swarmed like ants through the nerves webbing the upper part of her body as his lips closed over a nipple. She trembled, groaning aloud while he teased the sensitive buds, one after the other, into erection; her hips jerked involuntarily at the electric tremor coursing through her veins the moment her fingertips homed in on his bare skin.

Her hands clenched on the flesh of his waist, the taut, resilient flesh fluttering with muscular reaction at her touch. A current of air blew cool on the swelling slopes of her breasts where the skin was damp from his marauding tongue.

Ancarani stood upright. His eyes were very bright and his breathing still laboured and rapid. Methodically, as if it was the most natural thing in the world, he began to undress her. She stood stock still, her pulses racing, as he unbuttoned the rest of her blouse, easing it down over her shoulders and arms, removed the bust bodice and unhooked the waistband of her skirt. He crouched down to squat on his heels, peeling the skirt and then a pair of lace-edged, white silk knickers past hips and thighs and knees and calves until they were pooled around her ankles. His hot lips rested for an instant on the quivering curve of her belly, buried themselves in the softness below her navel, and then he rose, picked her up, and laid her gently on the bed.

The strong, hair-covered arms supporting her around the shoulders and behind the knees provoked another electric thrill which manifested itself in a faint shuddering deep within her. She lay staring up at him with wide eyes, acutely conscious of the moisture drenching her loins.

He leaned over the bed. His left hand traced soothing arabesques over and around the contours of her body, modelling her out of nothing, sculpturing a form from the hotbed of his desire. Séverine knew her figure wasn't perfect – a trifle thick at the waist perhaps, a certain heaviness of hip – but under the magic of his caress she felt as alluring as the Aphrodite of Milos. Her breasts were large and soft – but not floppy; no, certainly not floppy! – and now they felt exquisite, aching again for his touch.

She sucked in her breath. The Corsican's right hand had

closed over her mons. She felt the heel pressing there, warm on the silky blonde hair, the fingers curled over the entrance to her secret place. Imperceptibly, her hips arched up off the covers to snuggle closer, closer to that alien but reassuring touch.

The fingers moved, easing aside the folds of wet flesh, sliding, sinking, flooding her with waves of sensation that sent tingles of delight rippling up her spine. Slowly, in a rapturous, dreamy caress, then fast and feather-like, the stroking fingers smoothed.

A sharp cry burst from Séverine's throat. From softness to hardness, a foreign touch had tunnelled its way within her secret flesh; one raping fingertip obscenely slid around the stiffened bud that triggered such spurts of elation throughout her frame. Jerking now, her pelvis swayed and shuddered.

Ancarani was kneeling beside her on the bed. She moaned, reaching an involuntary hand for the nearest part of him, his penis. The short, stiff shaft was hard as a rod of iron. Milking the foreskin back from the throbbing, purplish glans, she saw that a pearl of moisture gleamed at the suffused tip. She massaged the dark-fleshed staff as he continued, his eyes half-closed, to stroke the lips between her legs.

For a timeless moment they remained that way, locked into a rhythm of mutual caress. Then suddenly the Corsican sprang into explosive action.

From the foot of the bed he clamped his palms to the inner surface of Séverine's thighs, forcing them back and up and wide apart. Then, with a low growling noise deep in his throat, he sank his head down to the gaping lips which glistened among the hair furring her loins.

Her cry was louder this time – a cry of surprise? of excitement? of joy? – and her hips swivelled from side to side in a lazy, languorous motion as his mouth buried itself in the bushy furrow separating her legs. His tongue bored eagerly between vaginal lips, exploring, probing; he nibbled, he sucked, he teased, lashing the hot, super-sensitive inner flesh with that tongue until she squealed with delight, writhing wildly on the bed and then draping her legs over his shoulders to drum her heels on his back.

Ancarani was ablaze with lust. He released her, dragging himself up between her lewdly spread legs until she could feel with a thrill of expecation the blunt head of his cock nudging against the quivering flesh at the entrance to her cunt.

He slid a hand between them, seizing the shaft and stirring it among the damp folds . . . and then, with a sudden savage lurch, he flexed his hips and drove the thick, rigid shaft forcefully into her.

The breath flew from Séverine's lungs as she felt the invading staff lunge past her flowering labia to spear fiercely up into her belly. She was open, she was vulnerable, she was at his mercy. He could do what he wanted with her. The heavy weight of his body pressed her down into the mattress; his barrel chest squashed her breasts, the wiry hair grazing her excited nipples. Beneath her, his hands clenched on her buttocks, prising them apart as he forced her hips upwards to meet his plunging thrusts and swallow his hard cock ever deeper into the sucking throat of her sex.

He was battering into her more ferociously with every stroke. Her hips arched furiously up to meet him. She wrapped her arms tight around his shoulders and scissored shaking legs over his back. Every nerve in her violated body was shuddering with ecstasy as the manic pace of their lovemaking increased. Yes, this was rapture, this was joy, and she loved it, loved it, loved it . . . *Oh!*

They came together and it was like a rocket bursting in the sky, drenching the dark with stars.

Later, as dusk thickened the golden light over the terraced

vines, they went back downstairs – there were still two glasses of champagne in the bottle – and sat talking quietly of nothing in the dazed afterglow of sexual complicity.

There was a telephone in the first-floor drawing room – a rococo ivory and gilt machine like the one Raymond Large had in Paris. When Ancarani returned to his car to bring in the rest of the champagne cartons, Séverine lifted the handset from its cradle and twirled the handle to call the operator. 'Mademoiselle?' she said when finally there was an answer. 'This is the Château de Courmettes . . . Yes, that's right. I want to send a telegram to Golfe Juan. It is to be delivered to the cruiser *Mackintosh*, which is berthed in the port, and it is addressed to Captain Kirkpatrick Munroe . . . I will spell that name for you, Mademoiselle . . .'

Kirkpatrick

Sir Kirkpatrick Munroe, Bart., known at sea simply as Kirk, was owner and skipper of the eighty-two-foot, fourteen-berth motor cruiser *Mackintosh*, the home port of which was Golfe Juan, midway between Antibes and Cannes on the French Riviera.

The *Mackintosh*, so-called not because it was weather-proof or because its proprietor was a fetishist, but because he had family connections with the Scottish clan of that name, was mainly used for charter work. In the summer months, Munroe would sail sun-starved families from the North to Marrakesh or Casablanca, around the Greek islands or down the deserted coast of Spain; in the winter he sometimes rented the craft to oilmen or mineralogists from one of the big chemical companies who wished to survey the Mediterranean sea-bed. For much of the time however, since the money was relatively unimportant to him, he pottered around with nobody else but his crew – an engineer and a girl who kept the boat tidy and looked after the galley – on board. On the day Séverine Rouffach's telegram arrived, *Mackintosh* was returning from a one-week trip taking in Sardinia and the North African coast.

The cruiser was long and slim with bows like a small destroyer. The foredeck was short, with a striped awning above it; immediately aft, a diminutive flying bridge projected from the wheelhouse; and behind that there was a small diesel funnel. The low stern seemed to go on forever. This was because the craft was a former German torpedo recovery boat, seized as part of the reparations demanded after the Great War and converted to luxury civilian use, at enormous cost, by Munroe after he had bought himself out of his father's stockbroking firm in the City. The long, low stern had originally been designed to house practice tinfish after they had been fired, without explosive warheads, at targets far out to sea, and then recuperated. It was now graced with clerestory-style skylights, a number of ventilators, and an expensive, swing-out, single davit supporting a sizeable ship's cutter. An Anzani outboard was lashed, bottom up, athwart the deck.

Golfe Juan is in fact the port for the ritzy, tourist-oriented Juan-les-Pins. The boardwalk cafés built out over the water, the tall, narrow houses with their shallow roofs and iron balconies, the faded shutters and striped sunblinds make an agreeable contrast with the organized promenades and palm-tree formality of the resort. In the harbour itself on that day, seething as it was with every kind of vessel from dinghies and speedboats to ocean-going yachts, there was an atmosphere of things getting done. This wasn't just a place for rich men to use, stepping ashore from their costly toys as they did in Monte Carlo. Real work was carried out here. Two men with blowlamps busied themselves about the hull of a twelve-metre drawn up on the narrow strip of shingle; $50,000-worth of teak and brass and engine with a cockpit like a racing car was being derrick-loaded on to a trailer drawn by a tractor; men and women swarmed over the decks of the hundreds of craft tied up, tinkering, polishing, checking, and on the hard several groups of mechanics worked on dismantled engines.

Mackintosh slid towards the mole from the glass-calm bay – drawing admiring glances as she always did, not only because she was elegant but because it was known that her twin supercharged diesels could push her up almost to forty knots.

The rakish prow was still several cables lengths from the beacon at the outer end of the breakwater when the helmsman swung the wheel hard over – perhaps to avoid a clump of dangerous-looking flotsam – feeding at the same time a short burst of acceleration to the diesels. The abrupt change of direction and the sudden heeling over of the hull took a young woman standing by the taffrail completely by surprise. Caught off balance, she lurched against the rail, threw up her hands, and pitched over the side into the sea.

Somebody ashore shouted. A woman sunbathing on the poop of a huge floating gin-palace stood up and waved furiously. *Mackintosh*'s skipper ran to the end of the flying bridge, took in the situation with a single glance, and unhooked a lifebelt from the rail. He called something to the girl overboard and flung the lifebelt out over the sea.

Treading water, she tossed wet hair from her eyes, raised a hand in acknowledgement, and swam slowly towards it with an amateurish breast stroke. Kirk Munroe waited until she had reached the lifebelt and started to paddle towards the sandy shore on the far side of the port. Then he returned to the wheel and coaxed the cruiser through the dense harbour traffic to its mooring.

A scarlet Alfa-Romeo 1750 sports two-seater was parked on the quayside by *Mackintosh*'s berth. Munroe jumped ashore once the vessel was made fast and climbed into the car. He started the high-compression, supercharged engine and drove as quickly as he could to the port entrance.

A uniformed customs officer was standing by the gates with the *Chef du Port*. Waving a greeting, the skipper slowed, calling out: 'Margot went overboard. I have to fish her out somewhere along the pleasure beach, before she catches her death.' He jerked a thumb over his shoulder towards his engineer, who was standing at the end of a gangway, holding a leather briefcase. 'Tam's got the ship's papers,' he added.

The officer nodded and waved him on. The Alfa sped away along the waterfront.

It was back outside the gates ten minutes later with the young woman, hair in rats-tails, sodden beach pyjamas plastered to her body, shivering in the passenger seat. Munroe waved to the officer. 'Safe and sound,' he said cheerfully, 'but I'm going to take her home to get some dry clobber. First, though, I must return this to the ship – must comply with the safety regulations, what!' He reached behind the bucket seats and produced the lifebelt.

'I'm going that way; I can save you the trouble,' the Customs man said quickly. 'I'll give it to your engineer.'

'Civil of you,' Munroe said. 'Thanks very much.' He handed over the lifebelt. The Alfa growled away and was soon lost to sight among the summer visitors' Citroëns and Renaults and Panhards thronging the narrow main street.

The Customs officer made a cursory examination of the lifebelt as he walked to the cruiser. Just in case. You never knew with folks arriving from North Africa. It was no more than a simple check, really: he wanted to satisfy himself that there was no hidden opening, no concealed zip fastener on the inner curve of the ring, no contraband stowed away inside it.

He found no opening. No pouch of uncut diamonds lurked within. The lifebelt was solid cork all the way through.

Had the examination been more detailed, the officer might have noticed a strange thing: the film of moisture covering the surface and soaking the rope zigzagging around the circumference of the belt was fresh water, not salt. For this was not in fact the lifebelt that Munroe had thrown to the girl and she had floated ashore. It looked the same, it had the ship's name on it, but it was a ringer. The original lifebelt – and its contents – were still in the narrow boot of the Alfa. The whole charade had been organized to this effect.

It was really as a favour to Séverine. Kirk Munroe didn't need the money, but he was not above an occasional smuggling escapade – just for the hell of it, the thrill of breaking the rules and beating the game, or, as here, obliging a friend. He was, in any case, with his smooth, pale hair, goldrimmed spectacles and bland expression, an unlikely lawbreaker.

To his neighbours a few miles inland near the pottery town of Vallauris, he was an equally unlikely sea captain: Munroe's mild manner and faintly disdainful aristocratic air accorded ill with the boisterous behaviour of the hard-drinking skippers they were accustomed to seeing in the waterfront bars.

There was a third discrepancy he was careful to hide from these neighbours: Sir Kirkpatrick Munroe, Bart., was what a young, shortlived housemaid had once tearfully described to his butler as 'a randy old goat'.

Flat-roofed and blinding white, his Californian ranch-style villa stood on a steep hillside, surrounded by steeply terraced gardens shaded by mimosas and phoenix palms, brilliant with oleanders and purple bougainvillea. The house covered a large space on several different levels, although it was in effect a single storey building – a place of picture windows and reeded glass room dividers and tubular chrome furniture, with Chagall lithographs and garish canvases by Mondrian and Rouault brightening the bare walls. When he was not at sea, Munroe contrived to pass a bachelor existence here with no more help than could be provided by the butler, a cook, a houseboy and two gardeners.

The garage was beneath the villa. Munroe coasted the Alfa-Romeo down a steep slope screened by a tamarisk grove and parked beside a dark green Lanchester limousine. He climbed out over the leather-padded rim of the cutaway cockpit and unstrapped the narrow boot lid in front of the twin spare wheels.

The lifebelt was beside a toolbox, beneath a carelessly folded steamer rug. It looked like the others hitched to the *Mackintosh*'s rails, but despite the rope zigzagging around the circumference it was in fact not made of cork but inflatable rubber.

Munroe had let the air out of it as soon as he had 'rescued' his crew member from the Golfe Juan beach. Now he took the limp rubber ring from the boot and fetched a knife from a neatly laid out workbench behind the Lanchester. He slit open a rectangular puncture patch about six inches long, and shook out a small, slim package wrapped in oiled silk. It looked exactly like a half-full tobacco pouch, and he slipped it into the pocket of his reefer jacket beside an ancient cherrywood pipe. You never knew, when you were near the sea.

'Well,' he said to the girl, smiling for the first time since they left the port, 'that should put a bit of beef into Séverine's party, what!' He took her by one wet arm and steered her towards the stairs leading up into the house. 'You'll find some dry stuff in the guest room as usual. Meanwhile, I fancy this calls for a spot of celebration. I'll have Mason bring in a bottle of bubbly while you change.'

'That would be nice,' Margot Fairleigh said. 'Perhaps with a touch of brandy added? These things' – she plucked at the sodden beach pyjamas – 'have left me cold. And the lack of sidescreens on the Alfa hasn't helped!'

'A champagne cocktail!' Munroe enthused. 'The very ticket! You get a move on, old thing, and I'll organize it right away.'

She nodded and left him at the top of the stairs – a tall girl, taller than him by several inches, with unfashionably long blonde hair, a boyish figure and small, firm breasts that even the wet stuff plastered to her body failed to emphasize.

She had been working on Munroe's cruiser for almost a year now. He had met her at a Chelsea party at a time when she was recovering from an unsatisfactory love affair with an actor who lived on a houseboat on the Thames. Since she knew something of boats and boating, the idea of a semi-permanent job in the Mediterranean sun had proved irresistible.

Of course Munroe had made a heavy pass the moment she arrived on the Riviera; and of course she was going to let him. A vicar's daughter from Milton Ernest, near Oxford, she had been educated at an expensive ladies' college not a hundred miles from Cheltenham, and apart from the normal desire to outrage her kindly but straight-laced parents, Margot had developed a longing for the adventurous and the unusual, anything that ran counter to her sheltered background. Crewing a boat on the fabled Côte d'Azur was the nearest she had come yet to realizing her private wishes. But she was not – or not yet – sexually oriented. There were far too many fascinating things to experience to waste time on messy emotional experiences like the one with the actor. She was not, however, anti-sex; just not very interested. If the skipper wanted her to open her legs while there was nothing better around, she wasn't going to complain: she wanted to keep the job, and Munroe paid well.

So far as she was concerned, the sex *was* part of the job.

Munroe was waiting with the cocktails when she returned after a hot shower and a change of clothes. As she sipped gratefully, he unrolled the oiled silk pouch. It contained one hundred grams of refined hashish, what the Latin Americans call marijuana – not the dried leaves that can be smoked but the concentrated resin of the cannabis plant. 'Not enough to bother selling on the street,' he grinned, 'but plenty to make a whizz of Séverine's little show!'

The telegram, when the engineer brought it up from the cruiser later that afternoon, read:

WAITING WITH CAKES TOMORROW PM PLEASE BRING YOUR OWN TEA – SÉVERINE.

Munroe smiled, showing Margot the scrawled English capitals between the lines on the thin blue paper form. She nodded, smiling too. They were both fond of the American jazz music which had become so popular ever since Josephine Baker and the *Revue Nègre* took Paris by storm in 1925. Each of them knew that the word 'tea' was musicians' slang for marijuana; a 'stick of tea' was a reefer or marijuana cigarette. The telegram, therefore, was asking Munroe to deliver the smuggled contents of his lifebelt to the château on the afternoon of the next day.

'Your wine-growing friend,' Margot said, 'certainly seems to be bang-on as far as communication is concerned!'

Her employer laughed. 'Ask me,' he replied, 'there's a great more to old Séverine than meets the bally eye!'

Kirk Munroe's bed was eight feet wide. It was supported by four chromium-plated chains hanging from oversize hooks set in an acoustically-panelled ceiling. A huge mirror framed in carved African ebony was fixed to the white wall facing the foot of the bed. The only other furniture in the room was a black glass night table with stainless steel legs and a wicker chair hollowed out like an egg-shell and suspended from another chain. Kirk's clothes, linen, toiletries and other personal possessions were concealed behind soundlessly sliding doors in a short passageway leading to his bathroom. The bath, which had gilded fittings, was sunken, naturally – and just as predictably fashioned from marble imported from Carrara.

Later that evening, when dinner had been served and Mason, the butler, dismissed, Kirk undressed his crew member in front of the big mirror and took her on to the swinging bed. Her skin was pleasantly tanned and her flesh firm.

For a few minutes, almost absently, he stroked the parts of her that you were supposed to attend to as a polite preliminary to the actual fuck: he massaged the flesh of her small, taut breasts; he licked, and then worried with his teeth a little, their rubbery nipples; he smoothed the lower part of her pliant belly and fingered apart the folds of dry flesh nestling in her pale pubic hair. At the same time he slid a hand beneath the girl's buttocks, probing with a sucked forefinger the tight, muscled ring of her anus.

Margot moved herself companionably this way and that, shifting her long body to give him the most favourable areas to explore, parting her thighs to facilitate access to what her mother persisted in calling her privates. With one hand, she grasped the skipper's cock, alternately milking and squeezing the stiffened shaft. She liked to do what was expected of her.

It was just – she reflected, staring up at the silver chains as they swayed to her employer's exertions – it was just a matter of cause and effect, of action and reaction, question and answer; an established routine, like taking a sounding or manoeuvring a vessel into a berth, in which each partner had a predetermined rôle to play. The techniques involved were a great deal less troublesome than, say, those required to serve a roast joint, with three separate vegetables, all hot at the same time, in a tiny galley in a rough sea.

The non-conscious organisms, Margot was always faintly surprised to discover, were apparently more susceptible to sex than she was; either that or stimulus and reflex were totally automatic, the sensuality of those zones enumerated in the *Kamasutra* switched on as efficiently, as inevitably, as a wireless receiver or a bilge pump. Why else, despite the fact that she felt no special thrill, nothing stronger than a pleasant tickling, should her nipples have become erect?

Why should her hips, of their own accord, arch up to meet Kirk's manipulating hand? And why, suddenly, as suddenly as a tap turned on, should she find herself wet, flowering open so that the fingers of that hand slid easily now inside her?

She drew in her breath sharply. Lubricated by the moisture seeping between her legs, another finger had slipped into 'the other place' – Mother again! – and a nail had grazed the sensitive skin.

Mistaking the result of this momentary discomfort for an expression of ecstatic excitement, Kirk Munroe abruptly sat up, seized Margot by the hips – he was astonishingly strong for his modest size – and spun her over on to her face.

Now it was time for the party to begin!

Munroe was very highly sexed, it was true – he hadn't been termed randy or described as an old goat for nothing – but the spectrum of his physical desires was narrow. Not for him the languorous, long-drawn-out, shared appreciation of the mutually manual *carezza*, the infinitely postponed delight of eventual entry. He remained unmoved by the more arcane transports of oriental invention. Such recondite pleasures as those offered by the lovers of group masturbation, fetishism, sado-masochism or even the more esoteric excesses of the simple sexual caress held no attraction for him. His sole and special aim was what had been euphemistically termed at school 'penile gratification'.

To put it bluntly, Kirk Munroe wanted it in, he wanted it in all the time – and he wanted to see himself while he was putting it in.

His whole erotic life was centred on his prick; the subtle and infinitely varied, fluttering thrills that could – and would – build to such shattering explosions of joy, shaking the very core of his being, were oriented exclusively around that long, veined, rather thin organ with its acorn-shaped, circumcized head.

Perhaps this was why he was unaware to such an extent of his partners' joy – or lack of it.

Right now, his prick was at its maximum length, as stiff as a plank, and throbbing with the need to be wrapped in female flesh. 'Come on, old girl,' he said. 'Let's start off with the jolly old kneeling thing, what! You've got such a trim little bum that I can practically see the whole thing going in and out.'

By 'see' he meant see in the mirror: that large area of glass offered a more global view than he could arrive at, looking in close-up down the length of his own body.

Margot was obediently on her hands and knees, sideways-on to the mirror.

'A spot nearer the end of the bed?' he suggested. 'Don't want to miss anything, do we? Must have the image as large as poss. You don't mind?'

'I don't mind,' Margot said. She shuffled as far as she could. He came up behind her at once, steadying her with a hand on each hip, drawing apart the buttocks with his thumbs, and then lunged forward to allow his rigid, lengthy cock to find its own way between the now gaping pink lips glistening amongst her furrowed pubic hair. Head turned to watch the mirror, he thrust the hard shaft firmly into her.

She gasped again as the blunt head, plowing through her quivering flesh, nudged forcefully against the neck of her womb.

'Ah!' Munroe was pleased. 'Thought that would make you feel good, eh?'

Kneeling behind her, he lay along her back, hinged from the hips as he started a slow and rhythmic pumping movement, pistoning the stiff cock to and fro with steady strokes. He caught his lower lip between his teeth. The reflected image in the mirror was too much – the slender girl on her hands and knees, head hanging, the face covered by the long blonde hair . . . the small tits swinging and the hips aquiver each time his gleaming tool withdrew and slammed in again . . . all her bared genitals vulnerable to his repeated assault.

After a while, he tired of the position: after all, it was hard work keeping up with the hardworking man in the mirror. He sat on the edge of the bed, penis spearing up from his loins like a flagstaff, and had her straddle his thighs while he moved her up and down his staff with his hands on her pliant waist. In the glass he could see his aching cock appear and then vanish as her bottom rose and fell. Her small pointed breasts bounced before his face.

She lay on one side, her knees drawn up, offering the man in the mirror the whole lewd perspective of her exposed and hairy anal and genital area, the plundered lips of her cunt pouting and then compressed inwards as he withdrew and slid back within her.

She was impaled on his jutting rod, arms around his neck and legs scissored behind his waist when he asked her conversationally: 'You'll come with me to the château tomorrow?'

'Oh, yes' – the pelvis flexed and relaxed, the vaginal muscles tight – 'So long as it's not too late: I have to see my brother backstage before six' – a pause as Munroe's breath quickened, his rhythm became more jerky – 'He's in a Wilde revival at the Opera House in Nice.'

Later, as he was shafting her vigorously while she lay on her back with her knees so far drawn up that they touched her breasts, she caught sight of their reflection in the mirror. The suspended bed was swinging from side to side with the skipper's efforts . . . and the couple in the glass, too, were swaying this way and that: left and right and left again, as the naked skipper's buttocks rose and fell. 'What's the difference?' she thought dreamily. 'It looks just like lovemaking on a boat!'

'You're a sailor, after all,' Kirk told her sometime before midnight. 'Maybe you should go the whole hog, old thing, and have it the sailor's way?'

'I don't mind,' Margot said sleepily. 'What do you mean?'

'From behind,' Kirk told her, glancing towards the mirror. 'You know . . . the other way.'

'Whatever you like,' she said. 'I don't mind.'

It was still later when at last his thirst for sex reached satiation point – 'It's a question of power,' one of his ex-fiancées said once. 'I think it makes up for the fact that he's not very tall.' He had thrown Margot back down on the bed and was battering into her in the so-called missionary position, every nerve of his body singing as it relayed the relentless, now unquenchable excitement focused on his pounding cock. His release, when it came, threw them both half across the giant bed, the skipper's mouth wide open and yelling as he spurted the scalding milk of his lust deep into the darkness of her belly.

Some time afterwards, when the hammering of his heart had quietened and his breath was approaching a normal rate, he rolled off her and said; 'Topping! I hope that was good for you too.'

'Oh, yes thank you,' Margot said. 'That was lovely.'

Margot

'Tell me what you're going to use it for,' Margot said to Séverine. 'If you don't mind, that is. I mean, are you going to crumble it into little bits and roll it into fags and offer them around? Suppose people don't smoke?'

'What do you know of reefers?' Séverine laughed. 'Have you ever tried one?'

'Actually, no. But you see a lot of people doing it – making them, quite openly, and smoking them, I mean – in Marrakesh and Tangier and places like that. I often wondered what it would be like. It seems to make them happy anyway.

'It makes you feel good,' Séverine said. 'Time doesn't have any meaning any more; there's no hurry, no problems. Life's a big joke and you've all the time there is to giggle at it. But, no, that isn't what we plan to do: as you say, people could refuse. The idea is to make *absolutely* sure – one hundred percent, you know – that everyone joins the party. And has the same dose!'

The two girls were sitting on the balustrade surrounding the stone-flagged terrace below the château's rear elevation, enjoying the morning sun. A pitcher of chilled wine stood on an iron table beneath a striped awning which sheltered open French windows leading to the drawing-room. The oiled silk pouch had been delivered and was safely locked in the domaine office. Kirk and Jean-Jacques Ancarani were in the courtyard on the other side of the ancient building, discussing the relative merits of Delahayes and Alfa-Romeos.

'It must be a very special kind of party,' Margot said.

'*Very* special indeed,' Raymond Large's manager agreed. 'The host has, shall we say, special tastes. He wants to make sure they will be . . . appreciated . . . by all his guests. There might, you see, be some who were not quite – well, not quite *ready* for the kind of entertainment he will offer. We aim to help them over that little hurdle – without their knowledge!'

Shading her eyes against the glare, she stared out over the terraced vines stepped up the slope on the far side of the valley, past the honey-coloured stone of the outbuildings and the swell of wooded hills to the distant blue of the sea. Workers in blue overalls moved among the neatly planted rows and the tall tractor was puttering along a terrace down near the bridge.

'I don't mind telling you, since you asked,' Séverine said. 'After all, you played an important part in the supply line! But *I* must ask *you* on *no* account to say a word to *anyone*: you must be totally discreet . . .'

'Oh, I promise. Truly.'

'. . . because if the guests get wind of this, the whole thing will be killed stone dead. The point is that this should be a *surprise* party – in every way.'

'Cross my heart. Not a word.'

'Do you know what a *friande* is?' Séverine asked.

Margot shook her head. 'I don't think so.'

'It's a little cake, like a small oblong sponge, flavoured with almonds. You bake them in a slow oven, in those trays with cutout shapes. You know.'

'Yes, I think I've seen them in the *patisséries*,' Margot said, allowing her gaze to linger on the other young woman. Really, Séverine was *most* attractive: even in that blue working smock and white blouse with the rolled-up sleeves, even without make-up, she was . . . no, not pretty;

handsome almost. The erect carriage of the head, with its cap of fair hair, the wide, generous smile and the direct regard of those clear grey eyes combined to form an effect that communicated an instant impression of sincerity and warmth. Add to that a figure which, while not modishly slender, was nevertheless sensually alluring in its ease of movement and the ripeness of its contours . . . well, add those together, Margot thought, and you got Séverine. She must, the English girl imagined, be very successful with men. If she wanted them.

'It will be in the *friande* mixture, before I cook them, that the hashish will be incorporated,' Séverine was saying.

'I see what you mean by special *tastes*!' Margot said.

'Ah, but the whole point is, the almond flavour is strong enough to *mask* the unfamiliar taste of cannabis. As the anchovies and smoked salmon and garlic will be if I "doctor" the *canapés* I make.'

Margot was looking down below the balustrade. The gnarled trees in the olive grove beyond the flight of stone steps dated back to Roman times. 'Shall I be invited to your party?' she asked in a small voice.

'But my dear Margaret, what an idea! You're part of the family almost. Of *course* you are invited – provided you promise to eat at least one *friande*!'

She held up one hand, with the palm outward. 'I hereby give that undertaking. I swear it. Actually, the name is Margot.'

'My dear, I'm *so* sorry! How absolutely stupid of me. God knows why I always think of you as Margaret.' She laid a hand on Margot's arm. 'Do please forgive me.'

'There's nothing to forgive, Séverine. It's an easy mistake to make.'

'At least let me offer you lunch.' Séverine was over-contrite. 'There's nothing out of the way – just a rabbit with mustard sauce – but I'd be so happy if you and Kirk could join us. It would be a great—'

'I'd love to; I'd absolutely love to,' Margot interrupted. 'But I'm afraid I have to get back to Nice. I promised to see my brother at the Opera House.'

'What a shame. Another time then?' Séverine smiled. 'After the party.'

'That would be lovely,' Margot said.

Why, she wondered as the wind whipped her long hair back and Kirk hurled the Alfa around the hairpins leading down to the coast, had she said that?

The journey to Nice took less than half an hour. She was not in fact due to meet her brother until six o'clock. Was it that sudden, unexpected electric tingle she had felt when Séverine's hand rested on her arm that had stampeded her into that involuntary – almost panicky – rejection of the invitation?

On the fringe of the ancient, mediaeval city, whose steep, stepped streets and crowded houses date from the time when Nice was an Italian free port, owing allegiance to nothing and nobody but the dispersed kingdom of Piedmont and Sardinia, the Opera House was a lush example of nineteenth-century voluptuousness, resplendent with red plush and gilt and scrolled, ornamental ceilings. It lay near the casino gardens, not far from the short, blunt pier and half a block from the flower market.

Kirk Munroe steered the roadster carefully across the network of tramway lines webbing the Place Masséna and parked by the sea on the slope of the Quai des États-Unis. 'I've – er – got to see a fellow,' he told Margot. 'See you, let's say, on the terrace of Ruhl's Hotel at . . . oh, ten o'clock. All right?'

'I'll be there,' the girl said. She climbed out of the Alfa, waved, and set off for the stage door.

She left a message for her brother: she would see him after the matinée.

It was a hot and heavy day. The sun blazed from a

cloudless sky. The sea was a leaden blue, moving lazily shorewards, summoning enough energy only to flop over into small wavelets which crumbled into foam at the water's edge. Below the promenade railings the beach was crowded.

Margot walked west, away from the port, along the great curving front of the more modern part of the city, where balconied Edwardian apartment blocks jostled small red-roofed villas from an earlier era above the swarm of honking traffic jamming the Promenade des Anglais. She ate a solitary lunch at a glassed-in brasserie opposite the pier.

Toying with a *Salade Niçoise* and a small carafe of rosé wine, she started, not for the first time, to worry about this brother of hers. Although he was several years older than she was, Margot had recently felt a certain concern, an almost maternal solicitude, verging at times on anxiety, about the direction his life was taking. Or, rather, about its lack of direction.

Dale Fairleigh, she was the first to admit, was quite exceptionally goodlooking. He was tall, well-built, with curly fair hair and clear-cut, sensitive features. His voice was deep and agreeable. After winning a bursary, he had come down from Oxford with a reasonably good modern languages degree. He was fortunate to have landed a part in this continental version of Wilde's *The Importance of Being Earnest*, luckier still that the actor playing Algy had been taken ill and Dale had been offered the part. He had even received favourable reviews. An existence in fact without a blemish. And yet . . . and yet . . .

What *was* it that worried her about his life? A lack of solidity, perhaps? An absence of positive motivation? He picked up anything that came along, usually did it quite well . . . but she saw no signs of any central drive, no evidence of the will to succeed in life. And it wasn't just this lack of ambition either, for the condition extended into his private life. He was popular, he was quite amusing, people liked him as a rule, yet there had never been any indication whatever of an actual *relationship*. There were plenty of personable girls in Oxfordshire and Gloucestershire who had shown interest, one or two from well-to-do families who had made that interest very plain. But nothing had come of any of that. Nor did Dale seem attracted by any of the young women with whom he worked. He was not a pansy, though: Margot was very sure of that. Nevertheless, apart from one or two colleagues who were no more than drinking companions, Dale spent most of his non-professional life alone.

Margot sighed. Was her own life, come to think of it, any better? Never mind. That was different! She paid her bill and left the brasserie.

A few hundred yards away, below a section of the promenade planted with oleanders and tall palm trees, there was a less crowded beach bordered with striped bathing tents. She waited until there was a gap in the line of saloons and trams and open tourers crammed with shrieking girls, crossed the road and walked down the wooden steps to the beach.

Holidaymakers sunbathed on mattresses. Picnickers sweltered beneath parasols planted in the sand. Children screamed and splashed in the shallows, and further out, beyond the more serious swimmers, youths in kayak canoes showed off, windmilling their paddles as they skimmed beneath the pier.

You weren't supposed to bathe for at least an hour after a meal, Margot knew. There were risks of cramp, they said. The hell with it, she thought daringly. There was a bathing suit in the rush bag she carried. She was going in!

She hired a tent and went inside. The swimming suit was a little daring too. It wasn't one of the very latest, made of some elasticated material that clung to the body like a second skin: it was the same old cottony jersey, wrinkling when wet and sometimes sagging in the wrong places – a sober enough dark blue edged with white, fashioned with short legs, half-skirts back and front and wide shoulder-straps. The difference, and the daringness, lay in the fact that the suit was backless. Instead of revealing just the shoulders and the nape of the neck, it was cut away right down to the small of her back! She had bought it on a visit to Paris, from a shop in the Rue de Rivoli.

With some trepidation, she stripped, stepped into the legs, and drew the thin garment up over her body. She covered her breasts and thrust her arms through the straps. It was odd: in a room, alone or even with Kirk, she felt no shame, no inhibitions, when she was completely nude. Yet here, hidden inside a tent, the moment she sensed the warm air against her bare back, she felt as naked as she had ever been.

She bit her lip. Should she change her mind? There was nobody to notice, no one to mock if she decided after all not to bathe. But on second thoughts, no – what did she care what people thought? Why should she worry if a lot of holidaymakers on a foreign beach considered her fast? Squaring her bare shoulders, she unlaced the double tent flap and stepped out into the sun.

She stopped dead in her tracks. She was face to face with a man standing only a couple of yards from her tent.

He was no taller than she was, but he was sturdily built – a dark man with tanned, muscular arms, a bushy moustache and hairy legs. He was wearing a two-coloured bathing costume, the lower half plain brown, the top part with horizontal brown and white stripes. A mat of black hair curled around the edge of the scooped-out neck.

Margot stepped around him as he mumbled something she didn't catch – an apology perhaps, although he made no attempt to move out of her way. She hurried down to the water's edge.

She need not have worried, she saw at once, about her bathing suit: there were others like it on the beach, and some of the younger women were wearing the new halter-neck things – sun-tops, they were called – which revealed far more bare skin than she was showing. Confident again, she fastened the chin-strap of her rubber bathing cap as she threaded her way through the groups of sunbathers sprawled over the coarse sand.

The water was warm, almost tepid. She waded past paddling children and young boys splashing and frolicking with a beach ball, past the single line of wavelets creaming in. When the water was up to her waist, she submerged quickly and then swam a few yards out to sea with her labouring breaststroke.

She stopped suddenly, gasping, allowing her feet to drift down and touch the bottom. A bather had erupted, foaming, from the swell just in front of her. He must have been swimming underwater.

It was the man who had been standing in front of her tent.

He grinned, white teeth beneath the big moustache, shaking drops of water from his curly hair.

She turned away, striking out parallel with the shore. She recognized the man now. He had been sitting near her at the brasserie, measuring drops of iced water into a glass of absinthe a few tables away. He had kept staring at her, she remembered; he wouldn't take his eyes off her.

He was equally persistent now. He swam beside her, keeping pace with an old-fashioned sidestroke, the eyes – they were a particularly brilliant blue – unwavering. She went further out, towards a raft from which people were diving. The man was treading water a few yards away, laughing. Closer inshore, she floated on her back, staying close to a crowd of men and girls diving and ducking and splashing in the shallows. The laughing of these bathers,

the shrill cries of children, the shrieks of a fat lady w
husband was trying to teach her to swim, seemed sudde
very loud. The heat of the sun pricked through the thin stu
of her wet bathing costume where her breasts rose above the level of the water.

For a moment she thought she had got rid of the man with the piercing blue eyes, but then there was a submarine hand touching her thigh from below, and once again he surfaced beside her. 'Very salt here, the water,' he announced. 'But you do not have to stay on your back to float. She is so thick, this sea, that you can stay supported, even in a kneeling position, like a *hippocampe*, a sea-horse . . . See, I show you!'

'I am perfectly happy on my own, thank you,' Margot said coldly. She stood upright – the water welled up just below her breasts – and turned her back on him. She had plenty of experience of the Mediterranean male: when Gallic conceit was added to the insolent, presumptuous stare of the Latin, the combination could prove vexatious. But even for this part of the world, the fellow was exaggerating a little. Since he refused to allow her to enjoy her bathe, she would cut it short. She turned towards the shore.

At once a strong arm clamped itself around her shoulders, and another caught her behind the knees, lifting her half out of the water. 'What the devil do you think you're doing?' she cried angrily. 'Put me down at once!'

'There are stones here,' he said. 'Very uncomfortable. You could hurt the foot. I see you are not wearing bathing shoes. I take you to the sand, no?'

Margot compressed her lips. This was too much. There was no point, though in making a scene: it would only make things worse. Make her look silly, too. A timid little English virgin, terrified because she had been touched by a man!

She suffered herself to be carried back to the beach, the

arm beneath her thighs perilously close to those parts of her she preferred, for the moment, not to think about. When the man set her back on her feet, she strode rapidly up to her tent, wrenching off the rubber bathing cap and shaking loose her long blonde hair. He followed close behind, murmuring once more something she couldn't catch. The staccato delivery and heavily accented Provençal intonations sometimes defeated her. In any case, she wasn't interested in what he said. She went into the tent and let the flap fall behind her.

The wet bathing suit clung uncomfortably to her body. She smoothed some of the wrinkles out, flattening the material over her belly. The excess water, trickling between her buttocks and rilling down her thighs to escape from the short legs of the costume, swept past her labia like a caress. She was suddenly conscious that the sea water had enlarged her nipples and raised the puckered skin of the areolas surrounding them. She stripped the costume down to her waist and reached for the lacing which closed the flap.

It was thrust violently aside, and the man pushed his way into the tent.

Margot stared at him, speechless. She really hadn't thought he would go this far. Even by local standards, this was—

'You . . . are . . . very . . . beautiful,' he said slowly and distinctly. 'All afternoon I have been unable to take away my eyes from your body. You are English, no? *Une jolie petite Anglaise!* I wish to cover you with my kisses.'

She said nothing. What was she going to do? Call for help? The man hadn't actually *done* anything; he hadn't hurt or even offended her; all he had done was stay closer than she wanted, irritating her. It was a free country; legally she couldn't stop him. And even if it was totally unacceptable that he should force his way into her tent . . . well, at least he was being polite.

There was no point in losing her temper. The thing to was to be equally polite, avoid hurting his feelings, and g him out of there as rapidly, and with as little unpleasantness, as possible. She contrived a smile, pulling up the costume to cover her breasts. 'Monsieur is complimentary,' she began. 'I am flattered. But I am afraid I have to say that I do not wish—'

'Ah!' he cried in a strangled voice. 'What your beauty does to me! I cannot support it: my afternoon is ruined, my day, my life. Unless . . .'

He stopped speaking. Tears glistened in the blue eyes. It was very close in the tent. He was panting, the airless atmosphere heavy with the aniseed odour of the absinthe on his breath.

'Unless?' she prompted – and she never knew why she said it.

'Unless you take pity on me; unless you are kind; unless you permit me to love you the way you were made to be loved!' The voice was hoarse now. 'See what you have done to me!' he shouted . . . and with one swift movement he slid his arms from the straps and peeled his bathing suit down to his knees.

He stood there naked, compact, muscular, hairy, with his cock spearing out rigidly from the thick bush at the base of his belly.

Margot gasped. The effect could have been ridiculous; in fact it was both pathetic and impressive. She had noticed, walking back from the water – she couldn't help noticing – that he was very large . . . down there. The wet costume clung to a genital bulge quite out of the ordinary, outlining penis and testicles as clearly as if he had been in a nudist camp. But even that had given no clue to the eventual size of the erection she now saw. It was massive; there was no other word for it – a long, thick, dark-fleshed shaft, veined and quivering, with a blood-engorged knob swelling taut from the outer end.

'Please!' he said. 'Please!' before she could find any words. He took the weapon in one hand, arching his hips towards her. 'You want this, you need it, you know you do. Look!' – he waved the wand – 'See how it craves your flesh!'

She didn't know what to do. It was too silly to think of running away, impossible even now to consider shouting for help. Besides, in some curious way there was something almost dignified about this absurd little man, standing there like a schoolboy with that wet thing around his knees and his huge prick in his hand.

She hesitated, falling a prey to that lack of positive direction she reproached in her brother, which had led her so often to allow Kirk and others to do what they wanted, even though she herself got no pleasure from it. In any case – she shook her head – it was so much easier, so much less of a hassle, to say Yes. That way, it was all over much more quickly, and they didn't feel spurned.

The conceit, the arrogance and self-importance of this man, like all the others, was colossal. What kind of effrontery led him to believe – how dared he assume! – that just because he was *there*, she must automatically hunger for that great cock up inside her?

But what the hell. She shrugged. The cries of the children, the sun-bathers' chatter, the roar of a passing speedboat faded. 'You really want to? You really want to ... to make love to me?' she said.

'You can *see* I do!' He was almost incoherent with desire.

'Very well. If you really do. I don't mind.' She dropped the front of the bathing dress, sliding her fingers beneath the waist to push the garment down over her slender hips. But he snatched her hands away, seizing the damp material to drag the whole thing down to her ankles. 'So beautiful ... *Ma Belle! Ma Belle!*' he cried, burying his face in her naked belly.

The tent was proportioned like a canvas sentry-box with a pyramid roof. The floor was only four feet square. Even standing up they had been close together, so it was impossible to lie down or stretch out. He took her kneeling on the dry sand, forcing the thick staff into her cunt from behind.

Yet even under these ridiculous conditions, even when she had herself had no desire, had not even any interest other than to get the thing over with, Margot's body reacted of its own accord in a way her conscious mind denied. She was wet before she stepped out of the wrinkled costume.

Fortunately, she thought to herself as her hips shuddered under the impact of his heavy strokes and her pointed breasts buckled beneath his thick fingers: if she hadn't produced the necessary lubrication, he would never have wedged that great tool into her. She had never been impaled on anything so big.

Fortunately, too – since she felt at times as if she was being split apart – it didn't take long. As the man's grunts and groans rose up the scale, his heaving thrusts accelerated, became sporadic ... and then with a galvanic contraction of the loins he was squirting the hot spurts of his sated lust up into her with diminishing jerks.

When it was over, they sat companionably smoking cigarettes which she produced from a tortoise-shell case in her rush bag. His name, he told her, was Gaspard Romand. He was a native of Nice, by profession a *chauffeur de taxi*, a cab driver. This was his afternoon off.

'Do you always end up ... like this? In a tent? On your free afternoons?' Margot asked.

'The beach is not often favoured with one so beautiful,' he replied gallantly.

Talking of which ... In a few minutes, a very few minutes, he assured her, he would wish to express his admiration, his gratitude, again. And this time, if she were to lie on her back with her knees drawn up to touch those so delightful breasts, that enchanting *poitrine*, and if he were to place both hands beneath her *derrière* and draw her gently towards him, then surely . . .?

'All right,' said Margot. 'I don't mind.'

Seamus

'The trouble with you, boyo,' Seamus O'Reilly said to Dale Fairleigh, 'is that you don't dip the old wick enough. Shafting is good for the soul, they say – and I know from my own experience that sucking does wonders for the psyche! You want to put it about among the girls a bit more, instead of mooning around on your own in art galleries and suchlike.'

Dale looked uneasy. 'I get it as much as I want,' he said defensively. 'In any case, old bean, you're not a party to everything I do: I've met some pretty good talent in galleries. You find yourself standing next to some bird, studying the martyrdom of Saint Sebastian or a painting of bucolic revels by Breughel, and you've got a straight in, conversationally. What do you think the artist meant by this? Can they really be doing that? You should try it.'

Seamus grinned. 'It's easier to lay a hand on her arse and whisper, "Do you fuck, sweetheart?" Quicker too.'

'If that's the way you behave,' Dale said, 'you must get your face slapped a lot!'

His friend shrugged. 'Sure. But I get an awful lot of fucks.'

The two men were sitting at a table outside a sea-front café not far from the theatre. O'Reilly, who was playing Jack, the male lead in the Wilde play, had been responsible for Dale getting the Algy part when the other actor was taken ill. He had learned his craft in Dublin, both at the precious, avant-garde Gate Theatre and the stage-Irish

Abbey – known respectively, in the profession, as Sodom and Begorrah. Apart from an immaculate stage technique, he had brought away from his home country the outward image of a 'typical' Irishman, which he was at great pains to cultivate, and a fondness for dreadful puns and verbal clichés which nobody could stop him indulging. He was a big man – hefty was the word most often used to describe him – impressively tall, with dark, curly hair, a ruddy complexion and soulful brown eyes.

'Tonight,' he said to Dale, raising a finger to summon a waiter, 'after the show I'll be payin' a visit to a certain establishment where the fun, sure, is fast and furious and the divil take the loser. And provided you can di-vest yourself of your dear sister, I propose to haul you along with me.'

'What kind of establishment?' Dale was at once cautious.

The finger was laid alongside a large, rather red nose, 'That,' Seamus said, 'I'll be after lettin' you find out for yourself.'

'Well, I don't really know—' Dale began.

He broke off. A waiter with a long white apron was standing by the table. He flicked away non-existent crumbs with a napkin. *'M'sieu?'*

'Another carafe of the red,' Seamus said. 'And make sure, dammit, that the nectar within is filled up to the mark this time!'

'I thought it was the hindmost,' Dale said when the man had gone away.

'The what?'

'The hindmost. That the devil was supposed to take.'

'Ah, would you listen to this!' the Irishman cried. 'Here's a feller with the presumption, the bloody arrogance to instruct meself in the use of the sacred language! Have you no shame, man?'

Dale laughed. 'You still haven't told me what kind of . . . establishment.'

'Nor will I, young man, until you yourself set foot within.' Seamus snatched the carafe of wine from a tray before the waiter could place it on the table, and splashed two glasses full. 'And talkin' of establishments, what's with this invitation to a weekend party at some damned vineyard up in the hills, that came with the post this mornin'? They told me you would be there too. At Courmettes or somesuch. What kind of a place is that?'

'The Château des Courmettes,' Dale said. 'It's very old; the chap who owns it is stinking rich. Our invitations came through my dear sister, as you call her, though the person really asking us is Séverine Rouffach, who runs the vineyard. I think you met her: she came backstage last week with Kirk Munroe and some other boating types.'

'I did indeed. I remember it well. And in my considered opinion there's nothing hindmost about *that* lady!'

'Apparently the party's going to be quite something,' Dale said.

Seamus raised his glass. He drank. 'Ah, well,' he said, wiping his lips with the back of a large hand, 'sure I always did fancy meself as château material!'

The 'establishment' was between the sea-front and the Boulevard Victor Hugo, in an Edwardian quarter with streets named after famous composers. It was a five-storey mansion halfway along the Rue Rossini, an impressive building with a dressed limestone façade and green shutters opening on to elaborate wrought-iron balconies. Protesting still, Dale had been browbeaten into going there with Seamus O'Reilly: since he had been obliged to deliver Margot to her boss at Ruhl's Hotel before ten o'clock, he had no excuse for refusing his friend's invitation. In any case, Seamus was a hard man to turn down.

The polished mahogany double doors were opened by an impassive manservant. 'Madame Arlette is expecting us,' O'Reilly said. 'I did telephone earlier.'

'Just so, sir. If you gentlemen would step this way . . .'

'Very good English,' Dale murmured as they followed the man along a thickly carpeted hallway and up a wide, shallow staircase. 'Unexpected this far south.'

Seamus grinned. 'Sure, the feller's as English as I am! A trifle more, if the truth be told. He was born in Camberwell, but. He learned the lackey's trade at one of ould Kate Meyrick's clubs in London.'

'Is this place a club?' Dale asked, glancing at the heavily carved wood panelling which covered the walls of the first floor landing.

'Not exactly,' Seamus said.

The manservant opened tall double doors with brass lion's-head handles, ushering them into a spacious, high-ceilinged room with the announcement: 'Mistah O'Reilly and friend, Madam.'

There were perhaps a dozen people gathered around a bar at the far end of the big roam, and several couples installed in leather easy chairs or on florid Victorian sofas. A lazy, subdued hum of conversation was punctuated as they came in by a peal of female laughter.

A tall, bosomy woman of about fifty detached herself from the group at the bar and sailed towards them. 'Seamus, you old rogue,' she cried, 'what's come over you? It's three whole days since you've been to see me!'

'Absence, dear Arlette, makes the heart – and other parts more private – grow fonder,' said Seamus. 'Meet my friend and fellow Thespian, Dale Fairleigh.'

'But of course,' the woman said, shaking Dale's hand. 'I've seen the play. I thought you were awfully good.'

'You are very kind,' he said awkwardly. She had a deep, pleasantly modulated voice. Her platinum-coloured hair was cut very close to the skull.

'Before you tell me your news,' she said to Seamus, 'the important thing is to supply you with a drink. At least then you'll keep *one* of your hands to yourself! I think champagne is called for.'

'Ah, 'tis the stuff that's *un*called-for that interests me!' Seamus said with a wink. 'Hands – or one hand if you insist – across the C.' He glanced meaningly at her padded hips. Her generous, probably corseted, body was swathed in a low-cut scarlet silk dress reaching halfway down her calves. Flying panels of the same material floated from the waist to minimise the width of those hips. The solitaire diamond glittering at her throat was attached to a scarlet velvet neckband which effectively hid the not-so-youthful flesh underneath her jaw. She wore no rings, but a diamond-studded cocktail watch graced her left wrist.

'Seamus, you are impossible!' she laughed. She turned to call out an order to the white-jacketed barman.

Dale, who was sometimes embarrassed by his friend's heavily underlined innuendos, had been looking around the room. Most of the guests at the bar were men, some of them in evening dress. The three women amongst them were all young and slender. The only other thing they had in common was the proportion of breast revealed by their expensive frocks. One was a redhead, another a blonde with hair tightly drawn back into a chignon on the nape of her neck. The third girl was a nubile, dusky beauty with silky black hair cascading down her back and cut off in a straight line at the level of her waist. She wore a white gardenia behind one ear.

The couples seated around the big lounge were equally diverse. An elderly man with a white moustache was deep in conversation with a fat woman whose bulbous breasts threatened to escape from a strapless woollen top. A thin, completely bald character in white tie and tails sat with a precociously developed child on his knee who looked no more than sixteen. Before Dale could take in the rest, Arlette was back with glasses of champagne on a tray. She wore high-heeled gold shoes; the seams of her stockings were very dark. 'Pity you weren't in a bit earlier,' she said to Seamus. 'A friend of yours spent the evening with us.'

'So long as it wasn't a friend in need,' Seamus said.

'Well, whatever it was he needed, he got it,' Arlette said. 'He didn't leave until just before ten. You missed him by less than half an hour.'

'A miss is as good as a mile, sure. So who was this joyful spender?'

'Sir Kirkpatrick Munroe.'

'Ah, then we know why he left so precipitately. He had a date with the charming sister of your man here. But talking of misses . . . is Bella in tonight?'

Arlette glanced down at the diamonds sparkling on her wrist. 'She should be down soon. A quarter of an hour at the most. So drink up: you have just time for another bottle!'

For a while the conversation became general. Then Arlette excused herself and returned to the group at the bar. Seamus and Dale carried their glasses over to a vacant coffee table and sat down. Heavy velvet curtains at one side of the bar were suddenly swept aside and a tall, lean brunette with an Eton crop and thin features strode into the room. She was wearing laced, black leather ankle boots and black fishnet stockings below tightly fitting black knickers and a silver sequin top hugging her from wrist to neck.

'What ho!' Dale exclaimed. 'Do you mean to say your friend Arlette provides a cabaret as well?'

Seamus stared at him. 'Look, boyo,' he said, 'I do not for one minnit believe that you are, that you could possibly be, as naive as you make out.'

'This isn't a nightclub then?' Dale asked with a straight face.

'It's a knocking shop, for God's sake! A whorehouse, a brothel, the bloody stews! Not like the famous ones in Paris, mind. The ould Chabanais or the one in the Rue du

Monthyon. Those places were designed for bloody archdukes; decked out, by God, like Nebuchadnezzar's palace. But it's fair enough: the rooms are comfortable, Arlette's an honest woman, and her girls give good value. In any case, it's the best this city has to offer.'

'It's a licensed brothel, I suppose?' Dale said.

'Of course it's bloody licensed! Don't be more of an eejit than you are, man. Would Seamus O'Reilly demean himself by takin' a friend to an unlicensed bawdy house now?'

'I thought,' Dale said mildly, 'that there was a movement in government circles in Paris to have them officially banned.'

'So there is, so there is. Bad for the country's image: too much of the Ooh-la-la and naughty Paree. They'll not close them down, but. They'll simply go underground if they're made illegal – and open the doors to the criminal fraternity. Close them too, I shouldn't wonder, to many an honest punter who will no longer feel his wallet's safe from thievin' hands and his tool safe from the clap.'

Seamus drained his glass of champagne and set it back on the table. 'It hasn't come to that yet,' he said. 'But as you see' – sweeping an arm around the decorous lounge – 'what's on offer for the man with money to spend is a sight more discreet than it was, say, twenty years ago.'

'Talking of money, I thought you were the cove who always boasted he'd never, ever pay for it. It was so easy, you said, to get a free fuck—'

'Sure that's pub talk, that is,' Seamus interrupted genially. 'To bolster the O'Reilly public persona among the drinkin' classes. Not on any account to be taken seriously. For I'll tell you, boyo, there are certain things to be found in a professional house that a man would be hell's own lucky to discover in a . . .'

He broke off, staring in the direction of the bar. 'Here's one of them now,' he said in a low voice.

The velvet curtains had parted again. The young woman who came into the room was not especially tall, although she gave an impression of willowy height. She was wearing a floor-length, backless evening gown in midnight-blue moiré taffeta. And although the dress had long, loose sleeves and was not cut low in front, it was evident at once that her figure was perfect – svelte over the hips, trim at the waist and shapely at breast level. The marcelled waves of her dark hair shone in the subdued light. The only exaggerated thing about her was her carmined mouth, which was wide and full and generous.

Seamus was on his feet. 'That's Bella Cohen,' he said. 'And now, my boy, you'll have to be after excusin' me a while, for Bella and I have certain business matters to discuss that'll not wait a single minnit.' He laid a hand on the young man's shoulder. 'Arlette will look after you,' he said. 'And you don't have to feel obliged to ask for a girl, or take one upstairs if she should come over to you. Feel quite free just to sit and drink if you wish.'

He walked across to the newcomer, took her hand, and bowed over it. She smiled and at once started to talk in an animated fashion.

Several couples – the redhead and a uniformed army officer from the bar, the bald man and his child – had already left through the double doors. Soon they were followed, heads together and hand in hand, by Seamus and Bella Cohen.

The room was large and comfortably furnished, warmly and discreetly lit by lamps with pink silk Tiffany shades. The brass bed was wide. A white bearskin rug covered the deep-pile carpet in front of a hearth in which a gas fire burned. Seamus walked across to a bow-legged marquetry table and twirled a champagne bottle waiting there in a silver ice bucket.

'Dear Bella,' he said, 'if there's one thing true in this life, 'tis that you get more beautiful each time I see you.'

She flashed him her brilliant smile. 'I'm not going to say, "Flattery will get you nowhere, sir!" – because you know very well where it will get you. It's what you're paying for, after all!'

'That's my girl!' Seamus enthused, twisting out the cork and pouring the wine into two *flutes*. 'That's one of the things – just one – that I love about you: a certain kind of . . . well, call it honesty. A refusal to pretend, sure.'

'If you'll unfasten this dress – at the back; just that short bit below the waist,' Bella said, 'perhaps you'd care to see some of the other things?'

'The O'Reillys were always a race of explorers,' he said, handing her a glass and moving swiftly behind her.

She sipped champagne as he manoeuvred press-studs, then put down the glass and peeled the blue dress down over her hips so that it dropped to the floor and pooled around her slender ankles. She stepped out of it and stood facing him, a provocative smile twisting her full lips.

She wore high-heeled black patent pumps, black silk stockings held up by a dark blue suspender belt, blue lace-edged French knickers and a lacy blue camisole top. Her creamy skin glowed parchment-white against the dark materials.

'Would you look at that!' Seamus breathed, turning her towards a huge gilt-framed mirror on the wall opposite the bed. 'A thing of beauty . . . a joy indeed!'

'But not forever,' Bella said. 'The law requires us to close at three.'

He stood again behind her. She wore no brassière; the short camisole top, thrust out by her firm breasts, fell sheer to a position just below her diaphragm. Sliding his arms around her waist, he moved both hands up the smooth, resilient slope of her rib-cage, up beneath the flimsy undergarment until he could cup the warm, soft swell of those breasts in his palms.

She murmured something he couldn't hear, tilting her dark head back so that it lay against his shoulder, very faintly gyrating her hips so that the fleshy contours of her bottom ground into the rigid bulge she could feel at his loins.

She was breathing a little fast; he could feel her heart beating against his left hand as he fondled her nipples with forefingers and thumbs, kneading them into erection. 'That's nice,' she said. 'That's *gooood*! But what you really want to play with, I know, is *ma petite chatte*, my little lady cat.'

'And pussies are made to be stroked,' said Seamus. 'Ladies too, if they are honest.' He slid his right hand down past her waist, across the taut curve of her belly, and under the waistband of the knickers. His stretched-out fingers trailed through springy hair, touched folds of tender skin, sank into warmth . . . and sudden wetness.

Bella uttered a small sound. A nerve in her stomach fluttered. In the glass, Seamus saw the knuckles of his hand pushing out the blue silk of her knickers as he probed and caressed her cunt.

After a while, backing harder against the hardness at his crotch, she said: '*Chérie*, I want us to be lying down. I am going to leave you for two minutes. When I come back, I want you to be without clothes on that bed.' She disengaged herself and disappeared into a curtained cubicle on the far side of the room. He heard water running.

He was lying naked on his back when she returned, his large penis reared like a flagstaff above the dark bush thatching his loins. Bella was wearing nothing now but the black stockings, rolled down to the knee, without the suspender belt.

Seamus thought – as he had thought every single time he had seen her like this – that her body was as near perfect as a woman's body could be. Although the actual shape, the curves and hollows and planes and contours, was compact and trim, the impact as a whole was as voluptuous and nubile as the fleshiest of last-century beauties. Above slender, exquisitely tapered legs, cushioned hips melted gracefully into a waist whose sculptured, pliant elegance matched with breathtaking art the swelling splendour of the breasts above. Her hands and arms could have been designed by Leonardo. The dark triangle of hair above her thighs promised infinite bliss.

His breath expired with an ecstatic groan as she knelt at the foot of the bed, parted his legs with tender hands, and leaned over to take him in her mouth. Every quivering nerve in his body flew down to centre on the hot throb of lust tingling at his loins the moment those generous lips closed over the tip of his cock. 'There's some feller, a writer, name of Shakespeare, an Englishman they say,' Seamus whispered, 'with a certain talent for words. There's a line in one of his plays – *The Tempest*, it could be – where some character says: "Her lips suck forth my soul". Did you, me darlin', ever work your charms in Stratford-on-Avon?'

Three times Bella brought him within a hairsbreadth of the point of no return, expertly quenching the flame on each occasion. Then she withdrew her head, letting the stiff, gleaming cock thwack back on to his muscled belly, and rolled over on to her back. Lasciviously, she spread her legs. 'Time now,' she murmured, 'for the other half to – shall I say? – pull his weight!'

Seamus levered himself up. His body was thick and meaty but nowhere fat. Dark hair that was surprisingly silky matted his chest, the middle of his belly and the top surface of his forearms. With surprising gentleness, he sank down between her thighs, placed tender hands beneath her hips and drew – almost caressed – her towards him. He slid into her with a practised ease, the thick staff parting warm, wet folds of flesh to be swallowed in the scalding clasp of her vagina.

Bella hooked her legs over the backs of his thighs; her arms wrapped themselves around his back. Seamus lowered himself along her body, his weight partly supported on spread elbows, cupped hands cradling the swell of those perfect breasts as they were crushed down beneath his chest. Very slowly at first, and then with increasing speed and intensity, they started to fuck: the cock plunging in and the cunt, propelled by arching hips, raised hungrily to meet it . . . the cock withdrawing and the cunt, reluctant to relinquish it, straining still further up . . . and then sinking gratefully back, buttocks ground into the mattress, flowering open to receive the succeeding downstroke.

There was a certain elegance about that fuck, the intimately reciprocating fusion of two attuned and experienced partners, each perfectly anticipating and reacting to the movement of the other in a relentless emotional advance mounting inexorably to the flashpoint of physical climax. If a graph had been drawn, plotting elapsed time against gathering excitement, the line would have been arrow-straight, climbing at an angle of precisely forty-five degrees.

They came exquisitely together, then each floated away into their separate heavens.

It seemed a long time later that Seamus rolled off her and reached for the champagne bottle. 'Oh, Bella, my Bella,' he murmured, 'what a party that was!'

She whispered some affectionate reply, rubbing her face against his bare shoulder like a cat. 'And talking of parties,' she said a little later, 'are you by any chance invited to some grand do next weekend, at a vineyard château up in the hills behind the city?'

'I am that,' Seamus said. 'With my young friend downstairs. Don't tell me, darlin', that the affair will be brightened by your lovely presence!'

Bella nodded. 'The party's being thrown by a man called Raymond Large, an old friend, a longstanding client, of Arlette's.'

'Longstanding's a fair description of *any* client of Arlette's,' Seamus chuckled.

'You never give up, do you? . . . Anyway, yes, I'll be there. Raymond has asked me, at a very generous fee, to . . . what shall I say? To help with the evenings' entertainment, if you like.'

'If you're going to be there, I shall like it fine,' Seamus said enthusiastically. 'But there's a funny thing now: our invitations came in the post this mornin'. But damn me if ould Séverine, who runs the place, didn't phone me just before curtain-up tonight with another proposition. And you know what? She wants us, young Dale and me, to help with the entertainment too!'

Bella laughed. 'The same line of . . . entertainment . . . as mine, Seamus?'

'I doubt not.' He upended the bottle over their two glasses. 'Didn't she ask us to come up with a skit on the play, now. A skit that's to be as spicy, would you believe it, as we can make it! Spicy was the word she used.'

'Knowing Raymond,' said Bella, 'and with you and me on the production side, we can be sure that, on this one weekend anyway, spice will certainly be the variety of life!'

'Young woman,' Seamus said severely, 'that approach to words is copyright.'

Now that the champagne was finished, it was time for him to indulge the other, more boisterous, aspects of his personality. Within a few minutes, the transformation had taken place. Now the Seamus familiar to drinkers all over Europe was in the saddle. 'Come on, me ould darlin',' he cried, slapping the naked girl playfully on the bottom, 'they tell us a mistress is "something between a mister and a mattress" – well, we'll prove them wrong, won't we, you and me? We'll show 'em she's a sight more versatile than that! Variety, did you say?' – he pulled her up off the bed – 'Well, how about the ould bearskin for a start!'

Prick stiff and eyes gleaming, he pushed her down on the white rug.

Kneeling, he took her on her hands and knees, parting the lush cheeks of her bottom to penetrate the hairy furrow between her legs from behind, shafting his rigid penis between the glistening pink lips of her cunt as his hips thudded unceasingly against her.

He laid her on her back in an armchair, knees shamelessly drawn up to reveal the wide labia gaping amongst her pubic hair, and dropped down to suck the wet lips lasciviously up into his own mouth, spearing with his tongue the erectile, rubbery bud of her clitoris.

Laughing, he sat on the bidet in the cubicle, with Bella impaled on his throbbing cock, bounced lewdly up and down on his knees with his strong hands around her waist.

He stood her against a wall, fucking up into her with flexed knees as he lowered his head to take into his mouth the nipple of a breast upthrust by Bella's willing hand.

He lay on his back on the floor, face smothered by her loins as she thrust her hot cunt hard down on his probing tongue and his cock was swallowed again in her mouth.

He fucked her standing up, with her arms around his neck and her legs twined around his waist.

And when at last Bella exhaustedly called it a day, after they had twice – or was it three times? – come again, he still had a sexual arrow left in his quiver, even if it was only a verbal one.

'If it's three o'clock and the shutters must come down,' said he, 'then, sure, I'll bless the beauty of this encounter with a well-chosen *valete*, a spot of poesy from me own home town.'

'Your home town? You mean Dublin?'

'Not at all. For this evening at least it's Limerick – though divil a bit that place has to do with the species of art I propose.' He struck an attitude and declaimed:

'That's enough!' cried Lady Maud Hoare.
'I really can't stand any more.
'You're sweating like hell,
'There's the deuce of a smell,
And look at the time – half past four!'

He took her face between his two hands, murmured 'Dear Bella!', kissed her very gently on the lips, and went to look for his clothes.

In the lounge on the floor below, the barman was lowering shutters over the bar counter. Only two guests remained in the big room, which was now heavy with cigarette and cigar smoke. A man in a black tie and a white tuxedo sat talking conspiratorially with the dusky girl and the blonde with the chignon; Dale Fairleigh, stifling a yawn, nursed a final balloon of brandy as he listened to Arlette. Several strands of the blonde's tightly drawn back hair had escaped from the bun on the nape of her neck and straggled over one of her eyes.

Dale, who had politely refused the blonde, the redhead and several other girls during Seamus's protracted absence, had remained a fascinated observer of the 'traffic' in Arlette's establishment. Judging from the entrances and exits, the comings and goings of clients, there seemed to be at least a dozen young women working there. And the amount of time each spent with a client when chosen – depending doubtless on the man's demands and the sum he was prepared to pay – varied considerably. The redhead and the girl in fishnet stockings, for instance, had each taken three different clients to the rooms upstairs since Dale arrived; the fat woman and her elderly cavalier, on the other hand, had vanished early and were, like Seamus himself, yet to return.

When the Irishman, looking pink and contented, did at last make his entrance, Dale, more than a little tipsy by now, appeared to be confiding in his hostess. His face, flushed a deeper pink than his friend's, wore a faintly shamefaced expression as he whispered his confession.

'But, my dear boy,' Arlette exclaimed, 'why ever didn't you say so? We have a special room in the basement, with the most comprehensive selection of equipment south of Paris. Ghislaine' – she glanced across at the blonde – 'and Bella too are absolute experts. You could have had the time of your life, if only you'd said . . .'

Dill and Doll

Dilwyn Jones and his wife Dorothy, known to her friends as Doll, lived near the casino in Monte Carlo. Dill was a journalist, enjoying an agreeable freelance existence supplying gossip items on the rich, the famous and the infamous along the golden stretch of the Côte d'Azur to editors in London, New York and Berlin.

Since the rich, the famous and the infamous all liked to see their names in fashionable newspapers and magazines – and indeed the names of their friends if the story was discreditable enough – the names of Dill and Doll featured on the guest lists of many of the coast's richest and most important residents.

But it wasn't only because of the hectic social life lived by these particular Joneses that their own friends found them difficult keep up with: only those with an abnormally high energy quota – and an exceptionally broad mind – could hope to raise themselves to the somewhat specialized Dill-Doll level.

For the Joneses were fanatics, proselytizers, crusaders for a Cause. They were enthusiastic converts to what the French term the *partouze*, and the Anglo-Saxons, less poetically, group sex or wife-swapping. And they tried, with missionary zeal, to row everyone they knew into their particular sexual orbit.

On the morning that Séverine Rouffach's invitation to the party at the Château de Courmettes arrived, they were, as usual, inhabiting separate beds. Separate dwellings too, on this occasion, for the gathering the night before had terminated in a way that Dill preferred and his wife liked less. Instead of the more intimate pattern she warmed to, when two or more couples were able to make a choice of partner on a personal level, this really had been a random group affair, with the men dropping their car keys into a bowl and each woman having, as it were, a lucky dip – and then taking the owners of the set she picked home with her.

'But this isn't really a *group* thing at all,' Doll had complained. 'I mean once the couples are paired off, and the girls have taken their prizes home . . . well, frankly, apart from the fact that it's a different cock, you might as well be in bed with hubby. If we make a *choice*, after all, and all the couples are in the same house, at least there's a chance of a change if it doesn't work out; one's basically "on approval", you might say. Whereas with the car keys, once the cards are drawn, that's it.'

Dill had nevertheless overruled her. The gathering was in their house, and the host had the casting vote. Those *were* the rules.

In the event, he had in fact come off much the worst. Doll had the luck to draw a middle-aged Italian gardener, who had only come into the party by mistake, delivering a consignment of geraniums, and had been totally enchanted to find himself in bed with a naked woman he treated like a piece of rare pottery. Throughout the night, he continued to address her respectfully as Signora Jones.

Dill's keys, on the other hand, were picked up by a German hermaphrodite, a large, rather formidable transsexual with splendid breasts but an alarming cock, who insisted on driving back to her/his apartment in his/her enormous Mercedes-Benz racer with chromed outside exhausts – and then proceeded to instruct the prize in certain byways of sex even he had never penetrated.

He was still a trifle shattered when he returned home to find his wife having coffee and *croissants* with the gardener, who shook his hand warmly before he left.

'Seems a nice enough fellow,' he said when he had recounted the saga of his own disastrous night. 'A gardener, you said? I hope he . . . plowed a good furrow!'

'He was sweet,' Doll said. 'I had a lovely time.'

'Great. Does he – er – does he have a wife?'

'You don't know Italians,' Doll laughed. 'It's absolutely fine for *him* to have a ball. But if you even *mentioned* his wife, darling, he'd knock you straight through that window!'

'Too bad. So what's this one then?' He picked Séverine's invitation from several which had arrived by that morning's post. 'From the Château indeed! What's old Raymond up to now?'

'You'll see if you read it,' Doll said. 'It might be our kind of thing at that. You know Ray's a frightful *voyeur* – so at least there should be something laid on that would be interesting to *see*.'

'What I'd like to see,' observed her husband, 'is that Séverine lying on her back with her legs and arms open. I've always been sad that we never persuaded her to see things our way.'

'Everything comes to those who wait. But I'm next in the queue, mind!'

'I suppose, being Raymond, there'll be nothing in it for any of the columns,' Dill said. 'Discretion being the better part of *voyeur*, what!'

'Absolutely not. Read Séverine's handwritten PS. This is one pleasure we simply do not mix with business.'

'All right, all right. Point taken. Honour among thieves.' Dill poured himself a cup of coffee. He was a slight man with thinning hair and mild grey eyes, popular in his set because nature had blessed him with the genitals of a giant. Doll had once been a dancer at the Moulin Rouge; she was much in demand because of her ability to enjoy sex in the most extraordinary variety of acrobatic positions. Lean and muscular, she was nevertheless equipped with small, pneumatic but well-formed breasts and very shapely calves and ankles.

'There's another one here that might interest you,' she said, picking up an envelope and drawing out a gilt-edged invitation card. 'A poolside party at the Van den Bergh place on Cap Ferrat.'

'Oh, I don't know,' Dill said. 'Surely we've done the old Countess to death by now? I mean the old gossipmongers are up to here with snide stories and veiled innuendos about girls-who-prefer-girls in the fast set.'

'Lorraine Sheldon will be there.'

Dill whistled. 'Miss Hollywood 1933! I say! You're dead right, old thing: that does make a difference. If the biggest, best and brightest – not to say the bustiest – star thrown up by the talkies is going to be there . . . well, there's sure to be a retinue of Texas oilmen, Greek shipping magnates and newspaper proprietors in attendance. We might do ourselves a bit of good there, one way or another.'

'Very well. I'll ring the Countess and say we'll go. Oh, and there is one other thing.' Doll poured more coffee and pushed the percolator across to her husband. 'Madam Arlette phoned me early this morning: she may have something you could use for *L-L*.'

L-L was an English magazine called *London Life*. Despite the title, it was no chronicle of high life among the socialites of the capital, but a disguised shop-window for the parading of what the Vice Squad called 'certain tastes'. It was in fact a publication designed to attract fetishists, deviants and devotees of what the French termed 'the English Vice' – flagellation, bondage and the domination of men by women.

Because of the puritanical and censorious eye of the law in England, no articles extolling the virtues of these vices could openly be published. The magazine would immediately have been closed down and the editor prosecuted.

The problem was circumvented by that amalgam of hypocrisy and compromise typical of jurisprudence in Britain: *London Life* would print a description of a situation or an experience, usually via reader correspondence – genuine or office fabricated – and then comment editorially, with wide-eyed mock innocence or simulated horror – on how extraordinary the story was. In a recent issue, for example, a letter from a Brighton reader had mentioned the curious feelings experienced by the writer when (for reasons unexplained) he had got into a bath full of water with all his clothes on.

'How very odd,' the editorial said solemnly. 'In an attempt to discover what such feelings might be, and why, we ourselves filled a bath with water and stepped into it fully dressed . . .' and there followed a long and detailed description, spiced with astonishment, of this mild deviation.

'What does Arlette have this time?' Dill asked his wife.

'The young actor who took over the second rôle at the Opera House,' Doll told him. 'Dale Somebody. Apparently he's hooked on the lot – rubber, bondage, a touch of the lash.'

'Well, that's certainly *L-L* material. But what does she—?'

'It seems,' she interrupted, 'that he's dying to talk about it. You know: the confessional syndrome. Until he confided in her, he thought it was practically a solitary show; now she's put him right about the big, wide world, he wants to share. I think you should help him . . . and help yourself.'

'Yes, but I can hardly quote Arlette. We always promised her—'

'You don't even mention her name, you goose. You mustn't know anything about him, and certainly not his tastes in sex. Otherwise he'd probably clam up at once. No, you have to contrive it that the stuff comes from him.'

Dill nodded. 'Yes. I begin to see it. Maybe a local-boy-makes-good, first person interview. The understudy whose dream came true. It's an ill wind, and all that. I could even sell that, probably, on its own merits.'

'And while you're plying him with questions, you lead the conversation around . . . you manipulate it . . . you drop the merest hint maybe that you yourself could have similar interests . . . you seed in an occasional key word: rubber, leather, chains, whipping . . . and once you've got *him* asking *you* questions, you're home and dry.'

'Wizard! I'll see if I can fix an interview this afternoon. Do we have anything else on today?'

'Nothing in the work line,' Doll said. 'Just the Clockwork Game with the Davids tonight.'

The Clockwork Game, which involved three or four couples, had been invented by Harry David, an investment consultant who lived in Cannes, and his fleshy and energetic wife Joan. It was played for money and it involved as many 'sessions' or 'periods' as there were couples. Lots were drawn to determine who paired with whom, and husbands who drew their own wives had to draw again. Each man then put a thousand francs into the kitty, and a kitchen alarm clock was set for an arbitary period – fifteen minutes, twenty, half an hour, according to the players' wishes.

Once the clock was wound up, the players stripped – or not, as they wished – and started to fuck. The first man to make his partner come took the kitty. If nobody had succeeded by the time the alarm sounded, the money remained in the kitty. The couples changed partners then, a similar amount of cash was deposited, the clock was re-set, and the game started again – winner to take the double kitty if there was one. It was a game, Doll always said, that combined not only the delights of physical exploration and the thrill of gambling: it was also both sexually democratic and instructive. Because for once the woman's pleasure was put first . . . and so far as the men were concerned, they would jolly well have to learn not to spend prematurely, or risk losing their money!

'You did say nothing in the work line,' Dill Jones said to his wife. 'But if I draw that Joan David in the first session, I'll have to work so bloody hard that I won't be any use to the rest of you in the following rounds!'

'Perhaps we should regard you then as a *seeded* player,' Doll said.

He put out his tongue at her and reached for the telephone. He unhooked the receiver and jiggled the rest up and down. 'Mademoiselle?' he said when finally a response quacked in his ear. 'Mademoiselle – I should like to put a call through to the stage door of the Opera House, please.'

Lorraine

Pink flamingoes waded in the lily pond at the far end of the terraced gardens below the tennis courts. Lower down still, a powerful six-berth motor cruiser rode at anchor in a small private harbour with a curving breakwater. The Italian destroyer off Villefranche, shimmering in the sun on the western side of the bay, was on a courtesy visit from Genoa.

Geraldo Porrelli, his weatherbeaten features shaded by a wide straw hat, emerged from the greenhouses pushing a barrow laden with potted plants. It was hot enough beneath the cloudless sky outside – the straps of his blue dungarees cut painfully into his bare shoulders – but the atmosphere under the glass, humid and airless, pungent with the sickly scent of tropical blooms, had been insupportable. He trundled the barrow past weedless flower beds flaming with scarlet salvias, blue with vivid masses of agatea, and moved slowly up a gravelled path bordering a slope of lawn. The house, blinding white below its shallow, pantiled roofs, lay in two huge arcs around a stone-flagged patio with a fountain. Porrelli crossed the sun terrace and unloaded his barrow by a freshly turned bed beyond the swimming-pool.

Most of the Countess's guests were indoors, taking a siesta, but the latest arrival, the actress person from Hollywood, lay on a padded *chaise longue* under a striped poolside umbrella, sipping whisky and soda from a tall, frosted glass. Perhaps in California they were accustomed to this kind of heat.

Thumbing his begonias and calceolarias into the carefully prepared earth, Porrelli stole a glance at her from beneath the brim of his hat. He never went to the cinema, but he was familiar with the face – and especially the shameless body – from lurid posters and the covers of magazines displayed on the bookstalls in Villefranche and Beaulieu.

Lorraine Sheldon had made a name for herself at the age of eighteen by winning a solo rumba competition in Barcelona, the birthplace of that difficult dance. Admittedly she was there as the 'secretary' of a rich old man who made his fortune from the importation of cheap Spanish shirts, but the fact that the daughter of a pants-presser from Brooklyn could beat the Latins at their own game, in their own country, was sufficient in the silly season to rate her a spread in the *New York Daily Mirror* and a quarter-page photo in the *News*. Hollywood followed, and the importer was paid off.

More than any innate histrionic talent the arrangements of flesh which had helped win her the rumba competition were responsible for the success of the five films she had made. Now she was a genuine star. A soft, almost cooing voice, a wide-eyed, little-girl expression, and a nubile, voluptuous body that shouted sex from its every heavy curve had combined to make her the dream lover of countless young men who lusted after her from every corner of the earth.

And well they might, Porrelli thought, stealing a second look. Lorraine was tall, with very long legs, billowy hips and exceedingly large, apparently firm breasts above a small, soft waist. Her pale blonde hair, cut in a level bang across the forehead, hung around her head like a golden bell.

She could have looked blowsy, overripe, almost absurdly sensual. But lying on the dark blue *chaise longue*, the smooth tanned flesh constricted by a lemon-yellow elastcated bathing suit that pressed the big breasts together and composed a fathomless cleft between them, she looked every inch the Hollywood publicity machine's ideal: the woman every man wanted in his bed.

Especially every Italian man, the gardener thought. Lorraine Sheldon was very big in his home country, where the men liked their women rounded. She was like one of the exotic calceolaria blooms, puffed out in reds and yellows and spots and stripes, shaped like one of the little purses women took to dances. He dragged his eyes back to his flower bed. There was a gap. He would need a few more calceolarias to complete the pattern. He picked up the shafts of the barrow and headed back towards the greenhouses. Lorraine was replacing the whisky bottle in an ice bucket on a white wooden trolley.

Beneath the glass roof, the heat was more stifling than ever. Porrelli felt the sweat starting out all over him as he selected pots from the slatted shelves banked on each side of the central alley. Warm mist hazed the air over a long wooden bench at the far end, where an automatic sprinkler had started to pump a fine spray over a mass of young geraniums.

Choosing a final plant, Porrelli turned back to the barrow. His mouth fell open and he uttered a small cry of astonishment. The pot dropped from his hands and smashed on the tile floor, covering his sandalled feet with moist earth.

Lorraine Sheldon stood by the shelves a yard away, and she was completely naked.

The Italian gaped. The big breasts, thick-nippled . . . a bulge of belly . . . a thatch of wiry hair, unexpectedly dark, between the thighs . . . His heart suddenly felt very large within his own chest. 'Signora!' he stammered.

She had a very wide mouth, with rather full lips. She smiled. 'Don't look so shattered!' she said. 'You've been ogling the visible parts of me for the last half hour. You work hard. Why shouldn't you see the *ganz*, the whole shoot, if it interests you?'

Porrelli swallowed. She held the yellow bathing costume in one hand. Desperately he tore his eyes away from her pervasive nudity, from the droplets of sweat dewing her cheekbones, the tiny rivulet glistening between those breasts. Beyond the open glass doors, past the palms and the tall dark sentinels of cypress trees, the destroyer, dressed overall, was carving a white wake into the aching blue of the bay. 'Signora,' he mumbled again, 'I am an employee here. If Madame the Countess should ever . . . I beg of you . . .'

'Bullshit!' Lorraine said coarsely. 'If the Countess wasn't queer, she'd have had you in her bed a month ago. Surely you must know that, a goodlooking, *mature* man like you?' She had moved closer to him. He backed up against the shelves of calceolarias. It had been cold in the spring and early summer: they were blooming late this year. He gasped as she reached out both hands and pulled the overall straps down from his bare brown shoulders. 'In any case,' she said softly, 'it's Signorina. I never found a guy interesting enough to marry yet. But I sure as hell get my kicks out of a little sampling!'

'Signorina . . .'

She was very close now, as tall as he was, the wide eyes boring into him, her whisky breath hot on his face. Smiling still, she yanked down the dungarees as far as his waist. Leaning forward, she allowed the tips of her breasts to swing against the hair matting his chest. 'Well . . . ?' she said lazily.

Porrelli gulped. What was he to do? Push her off? He dared not; if he were to lay a finger on this fabled creature, and she chose to complain . . . it didn't even bear thinking about. On the other hand . . .

He jumped. She had dragged the overalls down over his

hips He couldn't help it: with the proximity of all that gorgeous flesh, the musky woman scent underlying the aromatic pungency of the geraniums, his maleness subdued his fears and his cock jerked to immediate rigidity, thrusting out the white undergarment, which was the only other thing he wore, like a released spring.

'Ah!' Lorraine breathed. 'I thought so; I was sure of it!' She peeled the slip slowly down, so that the stiff shaft throbbed into view. 'Now that I could use! So bring it right over here, where there's more space.' She grinned. 'And that's an order!'

She seized the thick staff with its empurpled head and dragged Porrelli to the far end of the glasshouse. He stumbled after her, panting, holding up the dungarees with one hand, his eyes feasting on the swaying, fleshy globes of her buttocks as his penis pulsed in the hot clasp of her hand.

Geraldo Porrelli could have been forty years old; he could have been as much as fifty. He was not the class of person who sunbathed, so it was only his face, arms, shoulders and the upper part of his chest which were the deep mahogany tan of the outdoor worker. But the rest of him, beneath the light furring of body hair, was a pleasantly neutral colour, the skin of a healthy, hardworking man. He was neatly built, with very strong arms and legs, the body quite thick, but all muscle and planes of hard, well-disciplined flesh, with not an ounce of surplus fat anywhere. His cock, sprouting from a thick forest of pubic hair at the base of his belly, was neither particularly large nor especially long: it was of exactly the right size and thickness to harmonize with the rest of his compact, masculine body.

Lorraine looked at it, and at the body, with undisguised approval. She had been obliged to minister to enough white, flabby, poorly maintained examples in the furtherance of her career to appreciate a good one when she saw it.

Porrelli never remembered tearing off his plundered clothes. Was he still wearing his sandals, or had they gone too? All he recalled was that first explosive physical shock as his bursting, quivering rod was swallowed in the warm, wet, clasping tunnel of Lorraine's heaving belly.

He slid in, easily, effortlessly, as if the great mouth of her hungry sex was sucking him greedily to the dark centre of her being, her arms open to him, clamping him to the cushioned softness of breasts and belly while she murmured in a crooning undertone: 'My lover, my sweet . . . my honey man . . . now give it to me now! I want all of it, all! . . . Push it into me – *Yes!* – let me have that strong thing inside; fuck me, darling, and give me all of it NOW!'

Porrelli was in a dream world. He had surrendered his morality, his code of conduct, his fear for his job and his whole conscious ethos to the imperatives of the nerve-ends screaming for relief in his loins.

He shafted her with powerful thrusts, meeting the upsurge of her hips with a force that was somehow curiously tender. 'Signorina!' he whispered into her open mouth, against the tongue writhing within it. 'Signorina – such a *beautiful* lady!'

In the humid, airless atmosphere of the pungent hothouse, their straining bodies were soon slippery with sweat; their bellies slapped and squelched; moisture ran from their hair down into their eyes; Lorraine's great breasts slid like fish, squashed beneath his hairy chest and the heart hammering inside it.

Like so many millions of ordinary men the world over, Geraldo Porrelli had wondered sometimes about the fabled creatures glimpsed from time to time in newspaper pictures, on the covers of magazines, in the newsreels. Suzanne Lenglen, the tennis queen, Josephine Baker, Clara Bow, Mistinguette, the young Princess Astrid – what were they *really* like? What did they talk about? How would they look – a censored thought – with no clothes on? And now here he was, a simple gardener employed by the Countess van den Bergh, actually *making love* to one of the most famous of all, a woman whose pictures covered the bedroom walls of Giuseppe, his teenage son!

They were twined together like greased wrestlers when they came.

'Oh, *man*!' breathed the Hollywood star when the shared convulsions had dwindled to an occasional muscular tremble. 'How *refreshing* a thing can be . . . !'

Porrelli was attempting to disengage himself (he *hadn't* torn off all his clothes: the dungarees and slip were still tangled around his ankles!). He was on his knees, still between the spread legs of Lorraine Sheldon, when he heard the voice, quite close and above the pile of sacks on which they had been lying.

'Bravo, Porrelli! A royal service for a movie queen!'

He raised his eyes. Green lacquered toenails emerging from silver sandals, the wide legs of jade green beach pyjamas . . . and, further up, a loosely tied smock of the same colour, a neck with a heavy silver crucifix, aquiline features half hidden behind very dark sunglasses.

The Countess Dagmar van den Bergh. His employer.

Porrelli was struck dumb. Mouthing incoherent excuses, he scrambled to his feet, hauling the overalls up shaking legs to hide his nakedness. His craggy face had flushed a dark red.

'It's all right, it's all right,' the Countess soothed. 'You don't have to worry, Porrelli. We like our guests to be . . . shall we say comfortable? Besides, it was a splendid sight!'

Dagmar van den Bergh was almost sixty, but she still had a trim, curvaceous figure and her chestnut hair, worn unfashionably long, was only tinged with grey. A notorious member of the *Amazones*, the lesbian cult popular with Parisian socialites at the turn of the century, she had soon parted from the Belgian Count who married her, devoting her charged life – with the help of the huge sum he had settled on her – to the seduction of the young, sometimes of both sexes. It was only recently that she had sold her mansion in the Avenue Kléber to Raymond Large and moved permanently to the Coast.

Lorraine Sheldon, still unconcernedly nude, had raised the top part of her frame, supporting herself on her elbows. The swells and hollows of her body were still glistening. She grinned up at her hostess. 'You waste this guy's energy giving him gardening chores, you're *crazy*!' she said.

Dagmar smiled. She was standing – had been standing for how long? – at one end of the geranium bench, just inside a doorway leading to the garages. 'There's a friend of mine, Doll Jones, who I think would agree with you,' she told the star. 'I just got a phone call and it seems' – she turned to Porrelli – 'that you were able to offer her solace and – er – comfort during her enforced loneliness last night?'

The gardener hung his head. Clearly, it *was* going to be all right. '*Si, Signora*,' he mumbled. 'It is sometimes necessary to be polite . . . one likes to do what one can. In this case, I could not help it. There were guests who—'

'You don't have to make excuses to me for your private life,' the Countess reproved. 'In any case, as the man said – *never* explain.'

She looked towards the open glass doors. On the sun-drenched lawn, a peacock, its iridescent tail fanned out, strutted past a stone wall covered with purple bougainvillea. 'Oh, and by the way,' she said, 'there seems to be a gap in the flower bed on the other side of the pool. I think maybe you should take a few more calceolarias down there . . .'

Dale

'What you tell me,' Dilwyn Jones had said to Dale, 'is absolutely fascinating. And I'm sure you are right: there must be a hell of a lot of people sharing these . . . tastes . . . who'd be only too glad to know they weren't alone, in the grip of some mania nobody else had ever experienced! I have tastes myself, though in a somewhat different direction' – he permitted himself a secret smile – 'which a lot of people would disagree with. The magazine I'm thinking of would be delighted to print anything you cared to tell them.'

'Yes, that's all very well,' Dale said, 'but how can I . . . I mean, frankly, how do I know I can trust you? How do I know . . . how can I be absolutely, one hundred percent *certain* . . . that my anonymity will be respected, that you won't quote me by name when you write—?'

'Very simply,' Dill said. 'Because I won't write it. It won't be a piece submitted by me at all. It'll be much better, and ring much truer, if you do it yourself. Put in the form of a letter – the editor prefers that anyway – it will be no more than a document I happen to pass on. My name won't appear on it and neither will yours. And you can put in – and leave out – what you like.'

Dale had been dubious at first. It had taken a heavy lunch at La Poularde and several brandies afterwards, plus a quantity of loaded phrases artfully seeded through the conversation by his host, before the young actor had found the courage to confess, for the second time in two days, what he had considered to be his shameful secret. 'But I'm not a writer,' he had finally complained. 'I wouldn't know where – or how – to start.'

'Just write it down as if you were telling it to a friend,' Dill said patiently. 'Put it the way you put it to me. Don't mess around with explanations; just stick to the facts, then it will read fine.'

'Talking of friends,' Dale said a little uneasily, 'there's one chum – my partner Seamus O'Reilly – who must never, ever hear a word of this. I'd rather die than have him know that I like to be—'

'He won't hear from me,' Dill promised. 'Cross my heart.'

Since there was no matinée that day, Dale bought a block of writing paper as soon as he left the journalist and went straight back to his hotel. Once he got over the first few lines, the words flowed freely; the particular demon driving his physical desires was strong enough to spill over into continuous literary composition. He wrote until half an hour before curtain-up, and then – refusing a final drink with Seamus – feverishly far into the night. His pen flew over sheet after sheet of the ruled paper. The completed, closely handwritten manuscript read:

It started one night as I was walking home along Piccadilly. There were two girls standing in a doorway on the corner of Bolton Street. They wore shiny black mackintoshes, although the summer evening was warm and cloudless. On the legs of the taller one, cuban-heeled boots laced halfway to the knee.

My pulses quickened. I slid them a sideways glance as I approached. The tall girl smiled, offering me the time-honoured invitation: 'Like to come home with me, darling?' Then she added: 'Give you a bad time?'

I paused in mid-stride. Normally the girls promised a

good time. And there were plenty of girls. Once, just for the hell of it, I kept count of the number of times I was accosted on an evening promenade along the one-mile stretch between Piccadilly Circus and Hyde Park Corner. One hundred and eleven – not counting the older harpies beckoning from dark doorways a little way up Bond Street, Albemarle Street, Clarges Street and the alleys nearer the Circus. Sometimes I stopped and spoke to the women who made an overt advance. I was rarely tempted to go with them; I couldn't afford it anyway. But whores have always fascinated me, and they were usually ready to exchange a few words or a joke, perhaps even accept a cigarette, even from someone who was not a possible client. I suppose it was a change for them to be treated as ordinary human beings rather than passed by as if they were a bad smell or contemptuously dismissed once their bodies had been used. In any case (I told myself), it was only polite to speak when you were spoken to. I got to know some of the regulars quite well.

This time, although I had not seen the girl before and her opening gambit was different, I made my customary reply: 'I'd love to, but I'm afraid it would be too expensive for me.'

'Two pounds,' the girl said, 'for a short time. Three if you want to stay a while.'

For once I was tempted. I don't know why, but there was something I found particularly attractive, compelling if you like, about this girl. When I looked more closely, the street lighting revealed that she was in fact about forty years old, a slender woman with a prominent nose and piercing brown eyes. Her mouth when she smiled shaped itself into a challenging twist that I found enticing. 'I don't think I could afford to stay,' I said weakly.

She saw at once that I was as good as hooked. 'I'd have to punish you if you didn't,' she said with a level stare. 'Tie you up, maybe, and smack your bottom.' Her companion, who was shorter, plumper, and younger, had moved tactfully away.

'That might be . . . rather nice.' The words came out shakily. They seemed to escape from my mouth of their own volition, before I was even aware that I intended to say them.

'Well, why not?' The smile grew more challenging still – and then, seeing that my hesitation implied indeed that I was already lost, she took my arm. Her friend was talking to an elderly man in a bowler hat.

'Come on,' my girl urged. 'You can spare a couple of quid.' She raised a hand to call a cruising taxi.

I sat next to her in the cab, trembling with a mixture of dread and intense excitement. She leaned back close to me, her thigh pressed against mine, one booted foot touching my ankle. Each time she moved, or the cab swung around a corner, the black raincoat made a stiff, rubbery rustle that made me catch my breath.

I was just twenty-one. It wasn't the first time I'd been home with a prostitute, but it was the first time another human being had openly alluded to what until then I had considered to be my sole and shameful secret: the desire to be tied up, to be abused, to be in someone else's power.

Since I was twelve years old I had been obscurely stimulated by the words, occurring so often in boys' adventure stories, 'bound and gagged'. Photographs in geographic magazines of 'natives' wearing tight loincloths that outlined their genitals produced the same reaction in my immature cock as that strange feeling I experienced when soaping it in the bath. Accounts of imprisonment and torture I found compulsive reading.

By the time I was in my late teens I knew of course what masochism was (there were plenty of school stories circulating, like the one where the masochist says 'Beat me!' – and the sadist says 'No!'). I knew about fetishists; they were the ones who had a 'thing' about hair, or high-heeled shoes, or ladies' knickers. But it had never occurred to me that both terms could have been applied to myself.

For although since puberty I had masturbated to bondage fantasies stimulated by those boys' stories, although I had fashioned ineffective gags from triangled handkerchiefs and manacles from leather belts twisted into a loop, I had never related such fantasies to any kind of fetishism – to the exteriorisation of the desire for domination in the form of whips, boots, restrictive garments and suchlike. And I had never associated them with leather or rubber.

It was the woman sitting beside me in the taxi on that summer night in 1928 who made the connection for me.

Her name was Sonia and she lived, to my surprise, in Chelsea, only a few streets away from my own rooms.

Her flat was small: a sitting room furnished with a desk, a table and a narrow divan; a bathroom, a kitchenette, and an alcove filled by a double bed. A flight of china ducks arrowed across one wall, but the usual tart's working apartment décor – kewpie doll on the bed, pink-shaded lighting, nude paintings and rainbow-coloured cocktail glasses – was absent. This was because Sonia rarely 'went out': she worked mainly through the telephone, either with regular clients or via carefully worded announcements displayed on notice boards in certain Soho newsagents' windows. She had thus no ponce or 'protector', no payoffs to make, no bribes to hand over. She could work where she lived.

Her s-m 'gear' at that time was contained in a single suitcase stowed beneath the divan. It comprised a collection of straps and buckles, rubber gloves, aprons and bathing caps, a gas mask from the Great War, several lengths of rope and chain, a pair of mackintosh fisherman's waders and a number of raincoats – all of them made from

Wigan or Indiana, the same highly polished, black rubberized material that fashioned the garment she was wearing. Compared to more specialized equipment I was to see later, most of it made by very expensive bootmakers or corsetières in Soho for the mistresses of rich deviants, this stuff was rudimentary. But right then the sight of those ropes and that shimmering rubberware – and the knowledge of what it was used for – had me stiff and erect in seconds.

The most banal household objects – a rubber suction plunger, a fat candle, a roll of adhesive tape – became invested with instant-rise significance once they had been associated, in one way or another, with physical dominance.

So far as the rubber was concerned, I had no idea then why it appealed so much. When I was five or six, each time it rained I was dressed in black rubber Wellingtons, a fisherman's sou'wester, and a small, shiny mackintosh like those in the suitcase. They were kept in an oak chest in the hall of my parents' house, and I can still recall the rich, close, oily odour of that rubber wafting out each time the lid of the chest was raised. Yet the feeling I associated with that smell as a child was not pleasure but an obscure kind of apprehension.

Was this because of a dimly remembered incident that happened one day as I was walking home from nursery school? It seems that ever since my fourth birthday I had been fearlessly aggressive, challenging boys twice my age to fight, and frequently winning despite my slender build. On the day of the incident I was ambushed by a group of schoolfellows who jumped me from behind a hedge, tore the black mackintosh from my back and threw it over my head, bearing me to the ground. The rubberized material was wound tight around my face. I cried out, unable to breathe. In a moment, friends rescued me, putting the attackers to flight. But from that day I lost all my own attacking spirit, remaining timid and a little fearful, avoiding fights whenever possible, throughout primary and secondary school, right up until my second year at university when, in the back of a parked Graham-Paige saloon, I succumbed to the powerful advances of a coroner's daughter two years older than me, who was a stirring advocate of women's rights at Union debates.

Indeed, ever since that scrambled seduction I have preferred the female to take the lead on the not-too-frequent occasions when bed seemed the better option. And the women appealing to me most have always been the maternal type, broad-hipped, fleshy, big-breasted. Sexually, breasts turn me on more than any other part of the female anatomy, and I guess that reveals a desire to regress subconsciously to the state of an infant, suckled by the archetypal earth-mother. Psychologists maintain, too, that masochism in men is a back-to-the-womb reaction, a refuge from the decision-taking and responsibilities involved in adult life.

This may be true, but it doesn't explain my fetishist cravings, especially for rubber. For none of the Freudian basics usually associated with deviation apply to me: no nanny tickled the more sensitive parts of my naked pink body with the toe of a boot when I was in the cradle; no mackintosh draw-sheets covered my bed when my mother kissed me goodnight, nor did she wear a rubber apron when she bathed me. I had no homosexual adventures at school and neither I nor the teachers administering the few beatings I received appeared to derive any pleasure, overt or covert, from the experience.

Whatever the reasons, I stopped looking for them after I had been home with Sonia a few times: I just lay back and enjoyed watching my fantasy made real. I was happy enough now to accept the fact that *I was a masochist* . . . that I was not alone, that there were others who understood.

I cannot remember the details of that first encounter. If it was anything like the dozens that succeeded it, Sonia would have made me strip naked and put on one of the rubber raincoats, reversed so that the cold, polished outer surface was next to my skin. A second mackintosh would then be buttoned, right side out, over the first, I would be bound hand and foot and strapped to the divan, and finally my erect penis and testicles would be dragged out through a gap between two of the buttons. Still wearing her tightly belted black coat, Sonia would then light a cigarette and sit regarding me through slitted eyes while she debated with herself what 'treatment' she would inflict on the exposed genitals.

I cannot remember the details, but I can remember as though it was yesterday the thrill mingled with dread that swept through me at the touch and smell of that rubber, recapturing with a new, pounding excitement the buried fears of what had in fact been a childhood trauma. What was she going to do? Would it hurt? Would I cry out or would I be gagged? How long would she keep me there? *Was she really cruel?*

I remember too that after the experience I looked at the girls on the street with new eyes. I had of course realized that the black-mack-and-boots uniform I had seen often enough was a badge, a signal. But I had thought of it as no more than a 'For Hire' sign, like the bunch of keys carried by some girls, or the poodles – always poodles – walked by others; a way of confirming to punters that, yes, this lady was 'on the game'. Oddly enough, despite my secret cravings, I had never made the connection between the gear and the domination it so clearly symbolized.

Once the penny had dropped, I was therefore eager to find out how many of the girls on display pandered to the desires of men like me. The number who did astonished me.

Not all of them, of course, were satisfactory. Many of the women who professed to practise domination in fact merely used the fetishist attire as a kind of stage 'property', a carrot to urge on the donkey. They worked on the principle that a couple of cuts with a riding crop and a quick toss-off with rubber gloves justified the extra charge and was good enough for a casual client – and the hell with it if he never came back for more.

This is useless from every point of view, and not just the value-for-money one. Because for the masochist a slave-mistress relationship becomes invalid if the mistress has no feeling for her rôle. And this was why I was so fortunate to have met Sonia – as I realized once I had been tricked by one or two of the phonies.

Sonia was a true enthusiast: there was no question of her adopting a sado stance because it paid better; she had become a 'business girl' precisely because it gave her the opportunity to indulge her own fads and fancies at the same time as she earned a living. Sonia was a rubber fanatic, with bondage and flagellation a bonus on the side.

Another natural was Joanna Wilson, a black girl from Cardiff – but with her the beating was the attraction.

Joanna's parents were Jamaican, but there must have been Indian blood in the family because she had fine aquiline features and a chiselled mouth. I found her very attractive – and I had in fact been home with her once or twice, not altogether successfully, when I ventured, late one night in Piccadilly, to ask hesitantly if she would consent 'to tie me up'.

She laughed. 'But of course, sweetie! That's my thing, givin' my friends a good whippin'. It's only because I rather like you that I've agreed to do the straight sex bit with you until now.'

Joanna had elevated the flagellant's art to a point that was near poetic. So far as she was concerned, the bondage was no more than a means to secure her victim in a suitable position for the chastisement. There were no boots, corsets, punishment masks or rubber garments in her Beaufort Gardens flat; just the leather wrist and ankle cuffs and the lengths of rope that attached them to the four corners of the bed.

Spreadeagled naked and face down on that bed, I would turn my head to see Joanna select a cane from a row hanging on hooks beneath the window. She stripped, dusky breasts bared, to the waist. Then, positioning herself carefully, she touched me with the tip of the instrument to gauge her distance, and the beating began . . . slowly, playfully, almost caressingly at first, and then, as the blood was brought to the surface and the skin reddened, with increasing force.

Beating was not really my thing. At least not yet. I loved to be helpless, in the power of a woman, subjugated to her desires, her wishes. Sonia had taught me that. But the excitement was still mainly mental; I was still afraid to be hurt. There was also the possible embarrassment of having to explain away distinctive marks on my flesh.

Too late to think of that now.

The blows stung, scorched, seared, and felt finally as though they were splitting me apart. In a mirror tilted above the bed I could see the angry weals, some already blackening, raised on my defenceless buttocks.

The cane was lifted high, whistling down to thwack across the bruises unbearably . . . slower now as the impact of each stroke was allowed to make its point . . . accelerating so that the instinctive muscular flinch away from the implement itself became part of the rhythm and at last, a certain threshold of pain being passed, the bottom appeared to be rising up of its own accord to meet each blow in a harmony that united beater and beaten in a strange conspiracy of action and reaction, equal – but definitely opposite!

I gasped, crying out as I raised my head to look imploringly at my mistress. This was already becoming too much. She jammed a sponge into my mouth to muffle the cries.

The cane rose and fell with increasing fury. Joanna was transported, eyes flashing, nostrils flared, the breasts with their empurpled nipples heaving frantically.

Faster and faster the stinging blows came now. I could hear her breath hissing between clenched teeth as the cane cracked across my tortured buttocks with agonizing force. And then at last she climaxed with a shuddering groan, sank trembling to her knees, and reached beneath me to seize my penis and jerk me roughly to orgasm.

Sonia beat very rarely. Her wicked imagination ran more to the complexities of bondage, so that one was strapped in improbable positions on the divan, roped into a chair or bent double over an upturned occasional table, invariably smothered in a variety of rubberwear, while she worked out which of her many gadgets she was going to use.

She had found a seamstress who could make up the thinner of the polished Indiana material into a dress, a skirt and top, a laced helmet with a built-in gag, or a device that was half sleeping-bag, half strait-jacket. She herself very rarely undressed. She never touched her slaves with her bare hands: surgical gloves were worn for the 'tortures'; orgasms were almost invariably induced by means of an electric vibrator. Her own release (for, along with Joanna, she was one of the few whores who allowed herself to come with her clients) could be sparked off purely visually – by the sight of a man in heavy bondage, or by the simple smell and feel of rubber, any rubber.

Once she fashioned an excruciating harness that drew back the head and coupled it to manacled hands forced tightly up between the shoulderblades. The web of strapping forming this barely supportable piece of equipment fanned out from a gag bit which was in fact the solid rubber portion of a bicycle pedal.

Sonia knew just which path to tread along that knife-edge that separates 'I would rather not' from 'Stop, I can't stand it'. A masochist, after all, is ill-served if he is lying comfortably in bondage, receiving treatment exactly as he has asked for it. Although he may be physically restrained, such a man – saying in effect, 'Tie me this way; dress me that way; treat me thus' – such a man is really in the driving seat, giving the orders. So who, then, is the master, who the slave? Which is the masochist, which the sadist?

Sonia knew better than anyone I ever met that a dominatrice must always go just that little distance further than her slave desires. Otherwise where is the thrill, the humiliation, the delight – even if it only comes in retrospect – in subjugation? On the other hand, she must at all costs avoid the excess, the exaggeration, the 'turnoff' that will break the slave's fantasy and make him frightened, panicky or even disgusted.

(I was once, as a great favour, introduced to a famous dominatrice who was the kept woman of a royal duke. Dazzled by her display of expensive equipment, I had begun to explain what kind of domination I was keen on when she cut me short. 'I am not interested in what you like,' she said curtly. 'It's what *I* like that matters!')

The third mistress I got to know well – and she was a borderline case if ever there was one – was a Cuban woman named Carmen Ruiz. I met her almost by chance – a discreet advertisement in one of those Soho newsagents announcing that 'a lady psychiatrist engaged on post-graduate research into sexual deviations seeks specialized literature on this subject, also personal recollections, published and unpublished'. Any documents confided to the lady, the notice added, would be treated in the strictest confidence and returned to the owner.

A sophisticated come-on from a prostitute? I wondered. In which case the key words would be 'specialized' (meaning kinky), 'post-graduate' (implying adult or pornographic) and 'strictest' (domination or punishment). Or could the ad conceivably be genuine?

Interesting, in either case.

The hoarse voice that answered when I rang the number quoted gave nothing away. It sounded autocratic; on the other hand a literary flavour and the use of psychiatric jargon sounded genuine. I made an appointment and went to see her one afternoon.

The apartment was on the attic floor of a block in Savile Row, above an exclusive tailor's premises. I saw a grey-haired woman of about sixty, with features like those of a Red Indian carved from teak. She was flat-chested, dressed in a skirt and a white silk shirt. The room was normal, a little dusty, clearly lived-in.

I had a few copies of the American Irving Klaw's fetishist magazine, *Bizarre*, a couple of rubber and spanking publications from Paris, and some typewritten sheets describing a torture session that I wished to dispose of. There were also two circulars I had received after I had answered other Soho small-ads. One offered dominant society débutantes who had been Presented at the Palace, guaranteed under twenty-one, above an art gallery, at fifty pounds a throw. The other was from a woman running a Surrey contact agency. Among other delights, it promised that 'a Spanish Inquisition Chamber can be arranged, complete with two Continental interrogators'. The circular added: 'This is expensive but very severe.' Neither had interested me.

Carmen Ruiz examined the material, expressed interest, and talked intelligently, articulately, about aspects of sexual deviation I had never heard of. I was just about persuaded that she was a genuine researcher when, through a door I realize now must have been left half open deliberately, I saw the thigh boots, a black leather corset, a martinet lying across a pair of handcuffs.

My throat was suddenly dry. 'Do you . . . do you – er – use those things in there?' I asked huskily.

She followed the direction of my gaze. They were strewn

over the foot of a bed. 'Of course,' she said.

'Why didn't you say so before?'

'I cannot suggest; you have to ask,' Carmen told me. 'With ads it is always a gamble: you could have been a member of the Vice Squad checking up.'

After she had questioned me about the little s-m experience I had had, and a few formalities had been completed, she said tersely: 'Very well. Take your clothes off; now I will show you what it is like to be a *real* slave . . .'

The equipment she laced me into was like nothing I had ever seen before. It had been made, she told me later, for a wealthy landowner, a member of the House of Lords who spent a whole weekend as her prisoner once a month. It was a set of four pieces, each made from the stiff, unyielding canvas used for real prison and mental asylum strait-jackets. First there was an 'erection-inhibitor', a kind of loincloth incorporating a penis corset lined with sharp spines, which bent the organ down and between the legs, and could be laced as tight as a second skin. Next came the corset proper, sheathing the body from armpit to knee, with shaped steel and whalebone inserts which enabled the garment to be drawn in far enough to reduce the wearer's waist to eighteen inches. The strait-jacket that fitted over this was not of the normal type with sewn-up sleeve extensions that could be wound around the torso and knotted behind. The arms were thrust down into deep pockets *inside* the jacket, which was then hitched up on to the shoulders and laced front as well as back.

The laces, many yards long, were threaded through more than one hundred eyelet holes on each side, and could be pulled so tight that finally the tough, dull canvas actually shone with highlights as if it had been polished. Covering the prisoner from the stiff collar to just below the corset at knee level, the jacket effectively pinioned the thighs as well as preventing any possible bending movement from the waist.

The punishment mask that completed the bondage set laced from crown to medulla and was further constricted by three straps of the same material which buckled beneath the chin, at the nape, and on top of the head.

The effect of the combination was extraordinary. The body was confined with such force that it was impossible not only to bend forward but also to twist or move in any direction at all. Yet, despite Carmen's savagely severe lacing, the artistry of the bootmaker who had fashioned the set was such that the circulation was nowhere impaired and no bone or nerve was unbearably compressed.

Beneath the corset I wore red leather thigh boots with spike heels so high that only the tips of the toes touched the floor and it was impossible to stand still: it was necessary to keep the feet constantly moving to maintain one's balance.

At one point during the bondage ceremony, rather hesitantly, I had suggested a gag. 'You won't need one with this helmet, once I've finished with you,' the woman said curtly.

She was right. A springy hoop of steel held the nose hole open, but the rest of the eyeless, mouthless sac was laced so tightly, smoothed back over the skull and re-laced, and then smoothed and laced yet again, that not only was the jaw clenched shut but it was actually impossible to move the lips. A muffled humming, halfway to a groan, was the only noise that could escape.

After this, a single strap around the ankles was enough to render me completely immobile.

But Carmen was not content with this. She bound me to a ladder, a steel and wood contraption on a counterweight, which she pulled down from a fire escape hatch in the ceiling of her hall.

Then she left the flat and locked the door. I heard her feet on the stairs.

I lay in the dark, listening to the distant sounds of traffic. I had never been so helpless, ever. The total humiliation of my position, unable to move a limb or a muscle, unable to see or to cry out, irretrievably in the power of this woman I didn't even know, excited me frantically at first. My cock started to stiffen. The spikes lining the inside of the inhibitor dug painfully into the tender flesh. This excited me more. The penis swelled further. The pain increased and the sharp points now felt as though they were piercing my testicles. I was breathing very fast, the chest squeezed by the corset. Almost . . . not quite . . . I felt the mounting tension that signalled an orgasm.

And then suddenly I was frightened. If I came, I would want out, and there was nobody to let me out.

Nobody. I was alone in the apartment.

That was when the near-panic started. What was the last thing I had heard Carmen say? 'Well, you can stay there,' she had grated, 'until I decide what to do with you.'

Where had she gone? Suppose she was sadist enough to have gone to a movie? To visit friends in another part of the city? Suppose she was knocked down by a bus, crossing the road? *Suppose there was a fire in the building?*

I would be done for, finished, dead. Nobody knew I was here: my skeleton would be found inside this damnable strait-jacket weeks, months ahead. For there was no way I could escape this bondage, no way I could reach a lace, a buckle, a knot: my hands were buried deep in the pockets lashed to my sides. I couldn't even cry for help (I tried an experimental yell, managed no more than the same humming groan). In any case there was nobody to hear: the tailor was on holiday, the other floors were all office suites, the staff would have gone home.

I knew nothing of my new mistress. I had noticed a continual sniffing of one nostril, almost a tic, when we talked. Was she a drug addict, somebody hooked on coke? Suppose she had actually forgotten I was here . . . ?

The very extent of my helplessness excited me again. I moaned as the points dug into my genitals.

I had no idea how long I lay immovably there, alternately experiencing fright and delight. I hadn't the faintest notion what time it was: it had taken well over an hour just to get me into this bondage; now I was in a dream world; it would already be dark outside; the last bus would have gone . . .

And then suddenly, with no warning, out of the void a sharp crack that sounded as loud as an explosion . . . the smack of an open palm across the face mask . . . then the juddering tingle of a vibrator jammed against my bound loins rocketed me to ecstasy . . .

Carmen had fooled me. She had never left the flat at all; she had stolen back from the stairway after that pantomime with the locked door, and had been silently watching me all the time!

I saw her again, of course, although I was always a little fearful of what she might do, how far she might go. She *was* on cocaine, and so she tended of course to be unpredictable. But it was this very uncertainty, the extension of the thrill-dread syndrome to its maximum, which kept me such a willing slave to her caprices. Once, late one night, she even encased me in rubber, helmeted and gagged, strapped me into a parachute harness, and suspended me for an hour outside her kitchen window, hanging over a five-storey drop to the bottom of an air-shaft at the back of the building.

Such excesses were the exception rather than the rule, but they certainly contributed to the suspense – in every sense of the word! – which was one of the strongest ties binding me to her. I didn't even find her attractive, you see. But in its way this itself could be interpreted as a logical complement to the dichotomy characterizing my relationship with Carmen.

Some people – I am one of them – find the mere fact that the partner is a sex professional a turn-on. But the reaction in truth belongs to the s-m character: having sex with someone who is by definition promiscuous emphasises the sense of being used oneself, of being regarded impersonally, as an object. And taken to its theoretical conclusion this should result in the choice of a partner actively *un*attractive, whom the masochist is *un*willing to service – in other words the *imposition* of sexual relations, equivalent to the famous rape complex in women.

Certainly the slave-mistress concept was underlined on the infrequent occasions involving actual physical contact with Carmen – when she whipped off her skirt and forced me to suck her, or stripped naked and straddled me as I sat roped into a chair, bouncing herself to orgasm on my impaling cock. But whether this was a major contributory factor or nothing more than a spicing of variety I wouldn't know.

What I do know is that Carmen, along with Sonia and Joanna, has became an essential component of that secret 'second life' in which I now find myself subject to a veritable 'body rage' thrusting me towards ever more extreme experiments in the fields of fetishism and bondage.

Which is why (*Dale wrote in a final flourish, with a mental bow in the direction of Seamus O'Reilly*) I cannot find it in me to work up enough interest in girls picked up in pubs or at parties, when the end product will at best be an unproductive wrestle between the sheets, and at worst a replay of that scene in the Graham-Paige, on the back seat of a more modern motor car!

Tony

Wisps of cloud, teased out by the slipstream of the four 490-hp Bristol Jupiter engines, streaked past the passenger windows as the giant Handley-Page Hannibal airliner circled the aerodrome at Le Bourget, on the northern outskirts of Paris, and prepared to land.

It was less than two hours since the machine, with its 115-mph cruising speed, had taken off from the Imperial Airways headquarters at Croydon. During that time, the steward and stewardess had served the twenty-four passengers with a four-course luncheon, prepared in a kitchen separating the two passenger compartments.

In the rear compartment, Tony Hill sipped his coffee and nursed a balloon of brandy as he stared down through the double glass porthole at the French capital swinging slowly around beneath them. It was easy enough, between the filaments of cloud, to pick out familiar landmarks – the Eiffel Tower, of course; sunshine gilding the white dome of the Sacré Coeur; the lazy double curve of the Seine, with Notre-Dame on its island.

Hill was an aero-engineer. He worked for the Vickers company, which supplied components for the Imperial Airways fleet, and he was interested in every detail of the plane he was flying in. He was a short, spare man, about thirty-five years old, with thin, dark hair, very pale blue eyes and a pink, closely shaven face which nevertheless retained a faint shadow around the chin.

The huge machine lurched suddenly, encountering a patch of turbulence and dropping fifty or sixty feet in an air pocket. One or two passengers exclaimed aloud; a woman's shrill laugh pierced the roar of the engines; a glass rolled off a table and smashed. In front of Hill, a tumbler of mineral water toppled over and splashed the wide grey 'Oxford bags' he wore below his blue blazer with its RAC badge.

At once the stewardess was by his side, apologizing, dabbing the soaked knee of his trousers with a clean white cloth. She was a pretty girl, very trim in the dark uniform, with deep red lips and marcelled hair. 'Quite all right,' Hill said. 'Only water, dammit. Not as though I'd wasted the booze! . . . Thank you, thank you.'

'In any case,' the stewardess said, 'we'll be touching down in less than two minutes.'

Trees and hedges and buildings flashed past beneath the wings. A white road beetled with motor traffic spun away. The racket of the four-bladed propellers deepened as the single-storey terminal and the short green grass of the airfield raced towards them.

The airliner grounded, bounced, bounced again, and rolled to a stop by the wind-sock at the far end of the field. Turning, it taxied slowly back to the tarmac apron in front of the terminal. The engines, throttled right back, wheezed into silence.

Tony Hill carried only one small hide valise on a shoulder strap. He was careful to be the last passenger to leave the plane. The steward was busy in the galley. His colleague was on the way to the terminal with the ship's papers. Hill stopped at the foot of the exit stepladder to talk to the Captain and Chief Officer as they climbed down from the cockpit. 'Good flight,' he approved, staring up at the enormous biplane. Two of the engines were slung beneath the 130-ft top wing, high above the fuselage and twenty-seven feet from the ground; the other pair were slotted into the lower wing on either side of the cabin. 'Pretty smooth too, remarkably steady in these weather conditions.'

'Sorry about that last spot of turbulence,' the Captain said.

'Hardly your fault, old man, when the crate weighs nearly fourteen tons!'

The Captain's brows raised. 'You're very well informed.'

'I'm with Vickers.' Hill gazed along the aircraft's slender tail, past the registration letters G-AAXF to the triple rudders. 'You've got one or two of our bits in there, one place and another,' he grinned. Nodding to the two officers, he hurried after the stewardess.

He caught up with her on the apron. 'You've looked after me very well,' he said. 'I reckon the least I can do is offer to buy you a drink. In the lounge after I've shown the jolly old passport to the gaolers?'

She smiled. 'That's very kind of you, sir. I'm not sure, though, that I should be—'

'Splendid. Five minutes, then?'

They sat on high stools at the bar. The girl had beautiful legs, set off by the black silk stockings with their dark seams. She accepted a Dubonnet; Hill stayed with his brandy.

Her name was Zita Page. She came from Bournemouth, where her father was a doctor. She had only been working for Imperial Airways for two months.

Hill kept the conversation general, confined to subjects actually within range visually: the behaviour of drinkers at nearby tables, the enlargement of the terminal buildings, which could be seen through the wide windows, the probable professions of the ten passengers about to take off for London in a three-engined Wibault monoplane of the French Air Union company. There was material, too, for a certain amount of shop talk. The fact that a Dewoitine D-332 ten-seater passenger plane parked in front of one of the hangars was capable of 200mph. The grace of a Savoia-Marchetti high-wing monoplane which had just landed eight travellers from Rome; the ugliness of a chunky Breguet freighter being loaded outside the windows with mail for Marseille. Zita, too, had contributions to make here. 'The Percival Gull,' she said, 'the little blue monoplane with spats and a white line . . . G-AGFY, the one the mechanics are wheeling out over there . . . that's the one Sir Charles Kingsford-Smith used when he set up the new England-Australia record earlier this year.'

Hill was not sure at first whether he was storing the girl up simply for future reference. But once she had revealed that she had a stopover, and would not be flying back to Croydon until the following day, he steered the conversation subtly in a more personal direction.

He himself was at a loose end until the next morning, when he was due to catch the Blue Train going south. An industrialist, a non-executive Vickers director he had once been on a pub crawl with in London, had asked him to a house party somewhere near Nice, on the Côte d'Azur, and even if it was only because it might be good for business, he'd thought it wise to turn up.

A contemporary poet had described a vulgarian as 'one of the low, upon whom assurance sits as a silk hat on a Sheffield millionaire'. Tony Hill was the other side of that particular coin: upon him assurance sat as easily, as naturally and as inevitably as a crown on the head of an hereditary monarch. It never occurred to him, even remotely, that anyone could gainsay him, that he could conceivably fail to have his way. Certainly, in his clipped, stiff-upper-lip, very English fashion, he was a charming man. But more than anything it was this total confidence, this complete belief in the rightness of his cause, that literally assured his success . . . especially with women.

The opening, when it came, was a natural. They were already in the Ritz bar, although Zita didn't quite recall exactly how – or why – she had agreed to share his taxi into Paris in the first place. In the second place, she had really had no intention of drinking champagne in the middle of the afternoon, before she had even checked into her hotel. But . . . here she was in the Ritz sipping 1928 Heidsick Dry Monopole (which must, she knew, be costing a small fortune).

'Honestly,' she said a little tipsily, 'it should be *me* buying drinks for *you*! After all, it was in a way my fault that you spilled yours when we were touching down – the company's fault anyway.'

'Forgotten all about it ages ago,' Hill said swiftly. 'Tell you the truth, old thing, the thoughts were running much more along the lines of touching *up*!' He flashed her his bashful, almost little-boy smile. And then: 'I say – why don't we whistle up a room and go to bed together *now*? Give us plenty of time for a spot of grub at Maxim's and then a show later, what!'

Zita opened her mouth, but before any words could come out, he had picked up her flight bag and his own valise and shot through the ornate archway into Reception. 'Wife's in the airline business, don't you know,' she heard him say to the liveried man at the desk who asked for their passports. He gestured vaguely back towards her uniformed figure. 'Sorry and all that, but she left her papers in the bally aeroplane.' A moment later, smiling conspiratorially, he was beckoning to her and a bell-boy was standing by the lifts with their grips.

The room was florid, with a heavily patterned carpet, swagged velvet curtains and a great deal of plush and gilt. An English hunting print entitled *Full Cry!* was framed in the centre of one of the silk-covered wall panels.

'Tony!' the girl said when the boy had gone. 'Really! I mean, honestly . . . what can have come over me? I don't know what I'm *doing* here!'

'That's all right, old thing,' Hill said. 'I'll soon put you right about that! Just leave it to me.'

'I can't think what can have got into me!'

He produced his crafty grin – the one that stopped short, just, of being a leer. 'As to that, sweetie, I'm more concerned with what's *going* to get into you. And I *can* think of that. Fact is, I can think of nothing else!' He held out his arms and Zita walked into them.

She was still protesting as she wrapped her own arms around his waist (it seemed at the time the most convenient place to put them, and the smile now was *very* charming). Her final protests were cut short when he kissed her, expertly but tenderly. He was one of those men with the particular kind of contained energy that appeared to make them kiss, as it were, with their whole body. The kiss developed, flowered, intensified, became suddenly a little feverish on Zita's part when she felt his need for her hard against the stuff of her skirt. When at last they parted, she was breathing very fast.

Hill held her for a moment at arm's length, looking deep into her eyes. Smiling, he flicked a glance at the hunting print. 'Tally-ho!' he said.

Although he was short, Tony Hill was extremely well proportioned: his neat body, hairless except for the dark thatch at the base of his tautly muscled belly, was a pleasing light tan all over, the skin glowing with good health and the flesh firm as an athlete's.

Lying on the wide, quilted bed, Zita looked at it with approval. What was it the girls in the Sixth used to say? When rape is inevitable, lie back and enjoy it! Well, this was no rape: she wanted him, and she was damned sure she was going to enjoy it. The hell with the morality of how she happened to be here, in this smart hotel, pretending to be the wife of a man she hardly knew!

His penis was fairly short too, but thick – sturdy would have been the best word to describe it – gnarled with thick corkscrew veins, the dark skin distended and glistening with the proof that it was bloated to the limit by the hardness within. She reached out a hand to fondle its rigidity.

Tony was stretched out beside her, supported on one elbow. His free hand traced sensitive arabesques along her slender body, across the swell of the abdomen, into the waist curve, brushing the top of a thigh, always approaching – but just avoiding – the ultra-sensuous triangle at the belly base. Cushioned fingertips circled the breasts she had always considered too small, nudging the nipples to quivering erection. His lips, every now and then, swooped momentarily down to kiss, to nibble, to lick, each movement punctuated, underlined with a soft-voiced barrage of complimentary comments: 'I say! You must be the prettiest girl ever . . . Gosh, what a super shape! . . . I never thought skin could be so soft . . .'

By the time that hand strayed finally to her secret, most sensitive part, Zita's entire body was tingling with excitement. When questing fingers gently parted the wet and eager lips, she felt as though the whole lower half of her body was ready to swallow him up.

A small gasp of pleasure escaped her mouth as the lingering caress probed and searched for . . . and finally found! . . . the pleasure bud in which all her nerve ends now seemed to be concentrated, stroking it to ecstatic awareness. Tony groaned aloud as her milking hand accelerated the massage of his own throbbing shaft.

He lay face down between her parted thighs, hands outstretched to cup and knead the small, pointed breasts, tonguing her almost to orgasm. And so exquisite (Zita thought later) was his timing and his expertise and his control of bodily movement that when at long last he did take her, she was scarcely conscious of precisely how it all happened . . . only that suddenly, inevitably, he was *there*.

It was not the first time Zita had been to bed with a man, but she had never, ever experienced lovemaking of this perfection; no man had ever given her such joy. He had said he was an engineer: she could imagine those hands busy with the servicing of delicate mechanisms, the fingers meticulous in the manipulation of tiny wheels and springs, making infinitesimal adjustments with a watchmaker's precision. The hell with the fact that, this time, there was no emotional attachment . . . Lie back and enjoy it indeed! . . . This was . . . Golly, it was *bliss*!

Such was the artistry of Tony Hill's devotion to the task in hand that he was able to stimulate in her the exact response necessary both to complement and heighten the excitement of his own endeavours, heart to hammering heart, thrust meeting thrust, fingers feather-light in their silky flight, so that the two bodies moved as one and the shared climb accelerating to the heights of mutual delight became a single fusion rather than a coupled glory.

And even then he was careful to make sure that he had brought her to the pitch of quaking release before he permitted his own tribute to her desirability to explode up into the darkness within her.

Zita remembered little of the Maxim's dinner and nothing of the show at the Casino de Paris – only the joys of the bedroom when they returned. And those after breakfast the following morning, before he said goodbye to her at the Gare de Lyon, thrusting a handful of bills into the cab driver's hand and telling him to take her at once to the aerodrome at Le Bourget.

'It takes that plane seven days to fly to Batavia,' she said to a fellow stewardess at the terminal, with a wave at a Royal Dutch Airlines Fokker, 'but this damned engineer managed to take me to heaven in less than an hour!'

The Baron

Baron Johannes Eckbergh de Groet, known to his friends and certain intimates as Johnnie, was obliged at the age of nine to harness himself each weekend to a baby carriage, suffer himself to be equipped with reins and a bit, and drag his twelve-year-old brother around the perimeter track circling their father's estate in the Belgian part of the Ardennes.

'Boys,' said the Baroness when the practice was discovered, 'will be boys; it would be unkind to interfere with their childish games.'

Her husband, a colonial administrator, was assassinated by a political agitator in the Belgian Congo in 1901; the Baroness did not survive the 1911 influenza epidemic; the elder brother, six years later, flew his Nieuport Scout unexpectedly into a circus led by another Baron, with the name of Von Richthofen. The encounter was not to Eckbergh de Groet's advantage.

Johnnie thus succeeded to the title at the age of forty-four, But since his mother had neglected to add to her original aphorism the corollary that boys, while they might properly be expected to be boys, were not necessarily expected also to be work-horses, he retained in adult life his attachment to the science of harnessing and its use in the drawing of wheeled vehicles.

There being no elder brother any longer available, the Baron was now constrained to import help from outside: there is, after all, little point in a horse with no rider, a carriage without a driver. Originally most of this talent came from Berlin (the perambulator of course had long vanished, but among the industrial interests left to Johnnie by his wealthy father was a manufactory of farm implements and he was able himself to fashion from the wheels and seat and chassis of a lightweight harrow a small chariot to which he could be chained and driven around the familiar perimeter track). Eventually, however, tree-felling exposed much of the estate to public view, and the German ladies with their high-heeled boots and their black leather riding breeches and jockey caps had to be renounced in favour of a single driver and a more discreet course.

Because the Baron had business interests in the City, this happened to be in London. Intensive research, with the help of a dozen obliging estate agents, finally uncovered a first-floor Edwardian mansion flat in Sussex Gardens with a central corridor that was long enough and wide enough to enable the chariot to be used, and turned around at each end. There was an additional advantage in that the ground floor was occupied by the shop and warehouse facilities of a firm specializing in the production of outsize female boots, shoes and underclothes for male transvestites. There was thus little chance of awkward questions being asked if an occasional rumble of rubber-tyred wheels, the pounding of feet or the crack of a whip filtered through from the floor above.

It was here that the Baron installed and kept Romany Field, a woman of indeterminate age with long dark hair and a face like a flower. Romany, who came from Newmarket, was no leader in the glamour stakes – her figure had once been compared by an unkind comedian to a sack of cats being carried to the river – but for Johnnie she had two indispensable attributes: black leather looked well on her, and she was crazy about horses and their accoutrements.

For ten years the couple were paddock familiars at horse

shows, *dressage* events, show-jumping championships and steeplechases not only all over England but also in Ireland, Italy and France. The minutest details of reining technique, saddlery, gag bits, blinkers and harness accessories unfailingly held their attention, while such arcane devices as leather spoons, testicle nets and penis corsets to ginger up stallions excited them to a point it would have been imprudent to reveal. Anything new, inventive, or capable of modification – a patent, quick-release snap for a check-rein, for instance – they at once ordered, bought and adapted to the Baron's personal requirements.

By 1930, when Romany 'went for a drive' along the Sussex Gardens corridor dressed in the ritual leather jodhpurs and peaked cap, the horse-man strapped to the chariot's single shaft was virtually invisible beneath the weight of equipment – corsets and collars, blinkers and buckles and bits – linking him to the web of restrictive harness. A soft neigh was the only response she could expect to her rapped-out commands.

And then, at a loose end one day when a City meeting had ended early, the Baron went to a late afternoon performance at a cinema in Curzon Street. They were showing a film, the first, by the new American discovery, Lorraine Sheldon. When he came out, suitably impressed by the amount of flesh on view, it was already dark. But leaning against a nearby wall, clearly outlined in the light from a street lamp, was a young woman wearing boots and a three-quarter-length leather topcoat. The Baron's pulses quickened. He approached. Did the black coat, he enquired, signify what he hoped it did?

'But of course,' the girl replied – she had a German accent; her face was plain, the dark hair drawn tightly back into a bun. 'You will not be disappointed. I have much equipment.'

'Such as?'

'Oh,' she shrugged, 'a rack and pillory. Stocks. A

branding iron. Coffins. A whipping stool. A cross. You know.'

Curiously, the Baron – whose thoughts had been running on purely equestrian lines – didn't know. Extensive though his knowledge was on the details of his own fantasy, he was ignorant of the wider field of male submission. He thought now – Romany was at the hairdresser's – that perhaps he should enlarge his experience; the litany recited had intrigued him. He accompanied the girl to an apartment above a public house in Shepherd Market.

His initial introduction to her top-floor torture chamber – which was indeed equipped with a collection of devices, implements, restrictive gear and clothing in rubber and leather such as he had never imagined – was relatively mild. The dominatrice – her name was Gerda – chained his wrists to a trapeze bar hanging from an arrangement of pulleys and hauled him up until his naked toes only just touched the floor. While he was suspended in that position, she drew an eyeless, mouthless helmet pierced with breathing holes over his head and then amused herself circling a glowing cigarette end near enough to scorch – but not actually to burn – his nipples. Later, among other recondite treatments, he was raped with a jumbo-sized *godemiché* which had been purchased in Amsterdam.

Mild the treatment may have been, but the Baron was hooked. From then on his London sojourns alternated between Romany and Gerda.

Once these wider horizons had been opened, the Baron's natural inventive ness came to the fore. He bought a great deal of equipment, designed and had made a great deal more. Unfortunately Gerda's clientele was so extensive and so faithful that she was not able to spend as much time with him as he wished; it was with a friend who occasionally helped her out that he eventually realized his latest fantasy.

Before his arrival in London, the friend received by registered post a timetable listing, in fifteen-minute periods, everything that was to be meted out to him, morning, noon and night, during a two or three day visit. And for the whole of this time the couple were to be staying as man and wife at one of the capital's great hotels.

The Baron found it titillating to be shackled and rolled beneath the bed when the chambermaid came in to turn dawn the covers and draw the curtains, or lie bound and gagged in the wardrobe when room service rolled in the trolleys bearing lunch or dinner. Clearly the risk of discovery – and the humiliation it would bring – was one of his thrills.

Among others, he liked to be chained up naked and made to eat his food from a bowl like a dog; to be made to swallow his own semen; and to stay all night in a bath half full of cold water, encased in rubber, after he had been forcibly fed diuretics.

The friend who had agreed – at a price – to perform these services for him was Dale Fairleigh's mistress, Sonia.

Nobody knew whether the staff at the Ritz, the Berkeley or the Carlton in Haymarket really believed that Sonia was a Baroness, but the porters in all those hotels could certainly confirm that the couple arrived with the heaviest luggage of any guests they knew.

Subsequently the Baron contrived to bring Gerda back into his orbit – or vice versa. Experiencing a sudden desire to enjoy his bondage without actually being bound, he designed a full double mattress in ten-inch-deep foam rubber – a substance that was just coming on the market – in the centre of which was spreadeagled a Baron-shaped cutout. When the mattress was laid on the bed in Gerda's 'punishment room' he was positioned naked in this scooped-out portion like a gem in a jewel case – and a second mattress with corresponding hollows fitted on top, after which the two were zip-fastened together around the edges. With a craftily placed tube to breathe through, the Baron was then left immured for the rest of the day in his clammy prison, while the bed was made up with the usual sheets and blankets and those clients who were strange enough to demand actual sex frolicked with their partners unknowingly on top of it.

'I reject uncompromisingly,' the Baron once said angrily to an acquaintance who had stumbled on his secrets, 'the premise that we are perverts! The active partners in so-called sado-masochistic practices are not the kind of sadists who pull the wings off flies, tie tin cans to the tails of kittens or rape small children at gunpoint in front of their parents. Reflex erotic stimulation of the partner features in the sex routines of all human societies. And in all cultures except our own – the bigoted Judaeo-Christian one – be they Indian, Chinese, Japanese, Latin-American, Arab or Polynesian, pain in varying degrees forms part of the lover's armoury, both male and female.

'Because those sharing our particular tastes, which affect nobody but ourselves, have chosen as it were to ritualize this aspect of erotic technique, I see no reason to label them perverts. It is after all no more than a matter of degree – as any man who has favoured his lady with a love-bite and any girl who has dug vicious fingernails into her lover's back should be able to see!'

'All right, Johnnie, all right!' soothed the acquaintance, whose name was Raymond Large. 'If that's the way you feel, I reckon you'd be a natural for a little house party I'm arranging at my place down on the Coast. Saturday, any time after seven.' He clapped the Baron on the shoulder. 'Bring a girl if you like . . . and keep your eyes open!'

Which was why the Baron and Sonia arrived at the Gare de Lyon at 9.30 one Saturday morning, carrying reservations and first-class tickets for the world-famous Blue Train.

PART TWO

The Blue Train

Gare de Lyon

The original Blue Train was put into service for the convenience of well-to-do British travellers – those sybarites who, following the example of Queen Victoria, had discovered that it was agreeable to flee southwards to escape the rigours of their own climate. Disembarking from the cross-channel packet at Calais, passengers were ushered aboard the luxury sleeping-cars and installed in panelled cabins – usually a suite of two singles separated by shared washing and lavatory facilities – equipped with blue silk sheets, blue pillowcases and blue Merino blankets. Each coach had its own conductor, impassive individuals in chocolate and gold uniforms who made up the beds in each compartment once the passengers had trooped to the Restaurant Car for their seven-course dinners. The train stopped at Marseille, where the conductors took aboard breakfasts to be served in the cabins. And after that the visitors could gaze out of the wide windows at the red rocks and parasol pines fringing the blue Mediterranean as the train steamed along the Riviera coast to Nice.

This, of course, was when it was fashionable to *winter* in the South and a bronzed skin was considered the badge of navvies, farmers and peasants. After the Great War, when the Paris fashion queens had decreed that a tan was *chic*, paid holidays had materialized, and the Côte d'Azur had been transformed into a summer playground, the Blue Train resumed its service. And since the French, too, had learned to savour what the English poet Keats described as 'a beaker full of the warm South', a supplementary service was started from the Gare de Lyon, the huge baroque railway station on the right bank of the Seine, a little way east of the Cathedral of Notre Dame.

Neither this particular Blue Train nor the descendant of the original which still linked Calais with the Riviera were quite as élitist as the pre-war model, but there remained something special about the service: to take the Blue Train was to be part of An Occasion.

There was an additional air of excitement on that Saturday, because a rich American had arranged for a private pullman, brought specially across from England on the train ferry, to be added to the Blue Train. The two-tone chocolate-and-cream luxury coach supplied by the Pullman Car Company was shunted on to the front end of the line of dark blue SNCF carriages half an hour before departure time. Each pullman carried a female name painted on its side beneath the silk-curtained windows, on a panel bordered by gold curlicues. This one was *Amelia*.

A number of English-speaking passengers stood with their luggage by the first-class section of the train, isolated amongst the swarm of elderly French couples, a few Belgians and late holidaymakers with children under school age. Blue-overalled porters with peaked caps shouted urgently, jostling the crowd with their loaded trolleys.

One couple in particular seemed especially anxious about the four white hide suitcases trundled by their sweating porter – an elderly man, quite short, who spoke English with an accent, and a woman some years younger, striking in her dark way, with piercing brown eyes and a prominent nose. Although it was a sunny day – and already quite hot beneath the station's enormous arched glass roof – the woman wore a shiny black rubberized raincoat, buttoned up to the chin.

Conductors had unlocked the coach doors and were

showing passengers to their reserved seats. The porter with the white hide cases was having trouble heaving them on to the luggage racks. They seemed extraordinarily heavy. An Englishman passing the open door of the compartment stepped in and offered to help. Although he too was quite short, he slung up the unwieldy valises with an ease that defeated the beefy porter – a slightly built man wearing Oxford bags and an RAC blazer. 'My God, what have you got in there,' he said jovially to the elderly owner, 'machine-guns?'

'We both feel the cold,' the woman in the raincoat smiled. 'You never know, these days. With the weather, I mean.'

Tony Hill glanced out of the window at the reflected sunshine splashing their thronged platform with gold. 'Quite,' he said.

'Very kind of you, anyway,' the elderly man said, handing money to the porter. 'Perhaps, if you are taking luncheon on the train, we could persuade you to join us for an apéritif?'

'Just twist the old arm!' Hill said. 'Be glad to. See you later then?' He picked up the holdall with the shoulderstrap that was his only luggage and left them.

'God, Johnnie, look at that!' the woman said. 'Imagine getting enough gear to keep you quiet in a bag that size! That'd be the day, wouldn't it!'

Someone on the platform was tapping on the window, a tall, lean man with crimped grey hair and spectacles. 'Raymond!' the Baron exclaimed. 'That's our host, my dear. I didn't realize he'd be on the same train. Come – you must meet him at once.' He ushered Sonia out into the corridor and along to the door at the end of the coach.

'My dear fellow,' Raymond Large said. 'So happy you could make it. Everything all right? Quite comfortable? Splendid.' He glanced towards the front of the train. 'Forgive me, Madame' – to Sonia – 'I must be off: they're waiting for me in the pullman.' He waved a languid hand and was gone.

At the head of the train a small group of travellers stood with the conductor at the entrance to *Amelia*. The engine, with a great hissing of steam and a clank of linkage equipment, had just backed up to couple with the brown and yellow coach.

Raymond Large advanced with outstretched hand to the man in the centre of the group. 'Mondy!' he enthused. 'How marvellous! I have been looking forward to this so very much!' His hand was seized and determinedly shaken.

Mondragon Roth, the American multi-millionaire Raymond Large hoped would invest in his Riviera vineyard, was himself a large man in every way. He was well over six feet tall, with a hairless moon face, an enormous fat body and legs like the trunks of Californian redwood trees. His interests in the United States were as outsize as the man himself. Controlling a nationwide telephone system, he shared with the notorious financier Samuel Insull the franchise for street-cars in Chicago and Detroit, as well as being a majority stockholder in such diverse concerns as General Motors, an armaments factory, shipbuilding and railways in South America. The four dark-suited men with him were a travel agent, his lawyer, a Wall Street consultancy expert and a foxy-faced press agent whose job was to see that Roth's name and photographs appeared as frequently as possible in the world's newspapers. Except on this particular weekend, when his duty was to keep them out.

The group was completed by two young women, one blonde, the other a redhead, with busty bodies, tight flowered dresses and too much make-up for that hour of a hot sunny morning.

'Ray!' the industrialist crowed, pumping Large's hand a lot longer than was necessary. 'Good to have you with us, boy! What say we hop aboard and get this antiquated heap movin', eh? Show can't start until the prodoocer's in the wings!' Releasing Large's hand, he seized a polished handrail and swung himself up into the pullman, followed by his retinue. The two girls were the last to board the coach.

A whistle blew. At the far end of the long platform, by the ticket collectors and the grilled entrance gates, a man and a woman with hand luggage and several brown paper parcels were having an argument with a uniformed official.

The whistle blew again, a longer, more piercing blast. Somebody waved a flag. The man seized the woman by the hand, skipped past the ticket collector, skirted a rolling train of empty baggage trolleys, and sprinted for the last coach. He reached for the handle of a door, twisted it open, and bundled the woman aboard as the Blue Train started to move. A moment later, almost falling in his frantic efforts to keep up with the accelerating blue rolling-stock, he jumped for the running-board, grabbed a brass rail, and was hauled up into the vestibule of the final second-class carriage himself. The door slammed shut.

With a deep-throated, pulsing roar of steam power, the huge 4-6-2 'Pacific'-class locomotive drew the pullman and twelve coaches out from under the station canopy, across the grey, swirling waters of the Seine, and then, faster and faster, through the suburbs and on towards the beckoning South.

In The Pullman

Mondragon Roth wore a silver-grey suit in lightweight flannel, a flowered Sulka tie and a cream shantung shirt. His shoes were fashioned from bleached crocodile skin, dyed white.

He sat in a padded swivel chair screwed to the carpeted floor of the rear portion of pullman *Amelia*, which had been transformed into a kind of stateroom. The chair, with three more like it, surrounded a large circular table. Panelling of birdseye maple covered the walls of the coach, and there were lamps on double brackets between the silk-curtained windows. Framed nudes – a Modigliani and a very early Dali – hung on either side of a door leading to toilets and a small galley. The forward half of the coach, partitioned off, was equipped in the normal pullman manner, with a central vestibule gangway and tables with armchairs on either side.

Roth's dark-suited henchmen were installed on a tapestry divan flanking the connecting door. The two girls slouched in armchairs by a desk on the far side of the doorway. Raymond Large stood looking out of a window.

Black smoke punctuated by wisps of steam boiled past the window as the Blue Train arrowed through the new ribbon developments scarring the undulating country south of Paris.

A steward in a white mess jacket appeared from the galley with an ice-bucket of champagne. He placed the bucket on a stand by Roth's chair and went away to fetch glasses and a silver dish of ratafia biscuits. 'All right, you guys,' Roth said to the four men, 'you can scram now. Vamoose into the front part and have yourselves a game of poker. Frank here will bring you cards and a stack of liquor. Mister Large and me have . . . business to discuss. He fished a cigar case from the voluminous folds of his suit, selected a half-corona, and peeled off the band.

The press agent sprang to his feet, producing a gold cigar-cutter. By the time Roth had clipped off the end, the man was ready with a lighted wax vesta. The flame rose and fell as Roth sucked and puffed, rotating the end of the cigar carefully so that the tip burned with an even glow.

The steward reappeared with a large tray bearing bottles of rye and bourbon, glasses, a soda siphon and two fresh packs of cards. Roth nodded. The four men, followed by the steward, filed into the front compartment. 'We need you, Frank, we'll ring,' Roth called after them. The door closed.

The rapid puffing of the locomotive slowed and deepened as the train climbed a gradient. Wind rolled the smoke away over a flat landscape of cornfields and white farm buildings sheltered by clumps of trees. 'Okay, girls,' Roth drawled, pouring champagne. 'Time to earn the money kind daddy put in your purses.'

He pushed a glass across the table. Large sat down in the swivel chair next to his. The girls got up.

Large looked at them more closely now. A little brassy, certainly, but – as Roth himself might say – they sure were stacked! The blonde was the bustier of the two, all bulges and pouting curves, looking in that tight flowered dress like an effigy which had been pumped up just a little too hard. The redhead was more the wiry type, with a dancer's calves, but the muscular quality of the lower part of her frame was amply compensated for by breasts which seemed to be struggling to free themselves from the constriction of a low-necked dress whose edges were laced together over the diaphragm.

'Meet Hetty,' Roth said in his high voice, nodding towards the redhead, 'and her . . . partner . . . Florette. It's not exactly a sister act, but I think its intricacies may amuse you.'

Raymond Large smiled, shifting a little in his chair.

'Mondy,' the blonde protested in a whining drawl, 'you're asking a lot, expecting us to perform cold in front of just two people in an empty room! Don't you have any music or something?'

'We happen to be in a railroad train, Florette,' Roth said, the voice hardening.

'Couldn't you at least have brought some kind of wireless set?'

'In a *train*?' the big man repeated. 'Be your age, baby. Now c'mon: you can get started, undressing each other, nice and slow. You don't need to get up on the table until . . . later. Okay?'

The girl pouted, tossing back her pale hair. 'Whatever you say,' she shrugged. 'You're the paying customer. But don't expect the Casino de Paris.'

'It's an act much in demand at private parties,' Roth said to Large. 'They have printed cards – *Double Trouble: The Same Again, Please!* – with their initials, H and F in a cute monogram fashioned from nude figures.' He giggled, a high-pitched *He-he-he!* 'Some people reckon it stands for High Frequency!'

The two girls were facing one another now, their features impassive, tilting slightly as the train rounded a curve. Florette's long fingers, with their scarlet nails, started to unlace the front of the dancer's dress, threading the ends slowly through the eyelet holes. Hetty was busy unfastening her companion's tightly buttoned top.

The swelling slopes of Florette's big breasts gradually emerged between the gaping edges of the flowered material. At the same time the resilient, smooth-skinned curves of Hetty's bosom bulged free of the lacing.

Purplish nipples rose like dark suns above the printed silk horizon.

Roth leaned forward, the tip of his tongue brushing his top lip. Raymond Large was swivelling his chair gently from side to side, his legs crossed, one hand toying with his glass. The pullman lurched as the bogies rattled over a level-crossing, splashing champagne on to his sleeve.

The train roared out along an embankment above the outskirts of a small town. More ribbon developments chequered the land on either side – row upon row of identical new houses in tiny plots, with here and there a chopped-off example with an even smaller garden, as though half a plot permitted only half a house. In the distance, three tall apartment blocks in silhouette gazed out like Easter Island heads over the ruined landscape.

The girls had now pushed each other's dresses down off their shoulders, exposing to the two voyeurs the full glory of their naked breasts – taut and tight and firmly jutting in the case of Hetty; fleshy, slightly pear-shaped, but still voluptuously firm above Florette's tiny waist.

The dresses they wore had clearly been expressly designed so that they could be removed as elegantly as possible, with no ungainly shoving down over the hips and no need to wrestle them awkwardly up over the head. The girls faced each other breast to breast, their arms around one another's waist. They kissed, the pliant mounds of flesh mashed together as their bodies met. There was a bustle of hands at the back of each dress . . . and the garments simply unwrapped and were cast away.

They stood bare to the waist, wearing wide-legged, lace-edged knickers in gunmetal *crêpe-de-chine* with suspender-belts, black silk stockings and silver court shoes with Cuban heels.

'Remarkable!' Large said in a low voice. He drained his glass. Roth nodded, sliding the ice bucket across the table towards him. Very slowly, Hetty sank to her knees and began peeling the knickers down over the blonde's hips. A curve of belly appeared. And then, below the dark arch of the suspender belt, a contrasting triangle of pale and springy pubic hair.

The *crêpe-de-chine* slid down creamy thighs. Large cleared his throat. Black smoke rolled past the windows on one side of the rushing pullman; on the other, there was a flashing glimpse of a man lighting a bonfire outside a house with green shutters, a rusted, windowless car perched on the roof of a truck in an automobile junkyard.

The train was hurtling along at its maximum speed now. Hetty regained her feet in the rocking pullman, clinging for an instant to her friend's naked waist as she rose. And then – the coach staggered momentarily as an express slammed past in the opposite direction – the two of them were thrown off balance, to end up clinging together, spilled onto the divan and shaking with laughter.

The incident, unimportant in itself, seemed by its very unexpectedness to release some tension, almost to break a spell. The atmosphere between the two girls, until then stiff, formal, verging on the ritualistic, all at once became conspiratorial, gay, even jolly – a game everyone could play.

Florette stepped out of the knickers which had tripped her up, and jumped on to the table, sliding to a halt in front of Roth. 'Undo these garters, Mondy, there's a dear,' she cooed. 'Then take off the belt for me and roll down my stockings, but only to the knee.' She arched her pelvis forward as Roth rose mountainously to his feet.

Hetty was sitting in front of Raymond Large, legs draped over the table edge, leaning back with her weight supported on her elbows. She was still laughing. 'You,' she gurgled, 'can remove the knickers first – but no touching underneath!'

Large swallowed; his fingers were already shaking slightly. He drew off the silky garment as the redhead lifted her hips from the polished table. The wiry ginger hair triangling her loins had been clipped but not shaved close. When he had unsnapped the suspenders and rolled down the dark stockings. Hetty unwrapped the belt, dropped it in his lap and slid to the centre of the table. 'Florette, baby,' she said, 'I guess your place is here with me.'

The blonde, who had remained standing, swaying with the motion of the train as Roth completed the strip, evaded his outstretched hands and stepped close to her partner. She lowered herself to the shining wood. They sat facing one another, legs tucked under in the Lotus position, like two nubile statues in an oriental temple.

The train ran out from a steep-sided cutting. Slanting down between cottonwool clouds, sunlight dappled an undulating patchwork landscape with a tall church spire needling through woods on the horizon.

The two naked girls were gazing into each other's eyes. A slight smile twitched the redhead's lips. And then, puppet limbs manoeuvered by a single string, four arms reached out, a quartet of eager hands cupped themselves, and four breasts were gently palmed.

Roth drew in his breath with a sharp hiss. Beads of sweat dewed Large's upper lip. The four hands weighed, stroked, fondled the breasts they held. Thick nipples tipping the heavy globes jutting from Florette's chest were already stiffly erect. Hetty leaned forward and the two girls kissed.

Softly at first and then with increasing force, the lips touched, clasped and clung, and then ground fiercely together as the two tongues speared out and laced together in the hot caverns of their lascivious mouths. Cheeks hollowed as they sucked and nibbled greedily. Florette's eyes were closed; the redhead stared emptily out of the speeding window. A wayside station flashed past.

For a little while longer the mutual massaging of those breasts continued, the swelling mounds of flesh over the blonde's ribcage moving easily under her partner's touch, Hetty's smaller, tighter tits reddening where fingers tweaked and tugged. The watching men could see now that, despite the fact that this was doubtless in part a rehearsed act, each girl was beginning to breathe a trifle fast. 'You know,' Roth whispered, 'I fancy that Florette like crazy: but it saves so much energy if you can get another girl to do the work!'

Raymond Large licked his lips. 'I just like to watch,' he said.

They were passing through a fair-sized town. The coach lurched – this way, that way – as the train rattled over a complex crossing at the entrance to a goods yard. The girls were shifted apart, gliding over the table top.

Hetty was the first to react. Springing half upright, she seized her companion by the shoulders and forced her down on to her back. The blonde's legs shot out involuntarily, spreading wide as her hair fanned out across the wood. Hetty grabbed the thighs, forcing them wider apart. The redhead sank between them, dropping until the auburn crown was mashed into pale pubic curls.

Florette's hips arched up off the table. Her mouth opened and she cried aloud. Her hands flew down to cradle the head bobbing at her loins. Hetty's hands reached up over her trembling belly to caress the breasts swelling from her rib-cage. Kneeling, the foxy redhead lipped and sucked and tongued her supine friend's vulnerable cunt.

Big hips writhed on the wood as that invading tongue forced inner and outer labia wet and wide. The blonde head, eyes still closed, twisted frantically from side to side. Florette's mouth was open, the breath sobbing in her throat.

And then suddenly the kneeling redhead separated herself. Moving rapidly, she gathered her knees beneath her, swivelled around until she was facing the other way, cocked a leg over Florette's body, and then lowered her own until her hips straddled the blonde's face. She resumed her explorations among the pale, damp hairs thatching the big girl's crotch – only this time her loins too were being attended to from below.

Florette's loose lips gobbled greedily at the ginger bush and the pink, already gaping lips momentarily visible as the redhead changed places. Her thighs clamped each side of Hetty's head; her arms raked the lower part of her back, easing the buttocks apart.

Twined together, the two girls rocked on the table. Low, smothered moans and open-mouthed grunts and gasps of joy punctuated the hoarse, choking breaths of the locomotive and the clicking of wheels as the train panted up a gradient. Beyond her own squashed, fleshy mounds, Florette slid probing hands between their bodies, reaching for the taut cones of Hetty's breasts. Alabaster against the dark wood of the table, the locked figures heaved and writhed.

'Look, look!' Roth was on his feet. 'My dear fellow, do look! What a composition! Magnificent! . . . A Mondrian come to life, the picture Dégas dared not paint, a Buckland-Wright wood engraving in three dimensions!'

Raymond Large was looking. His hands were buried in his trouser pockets; there was movement within the tightly stretched material peaking at his crotch. Roth, circling the table with bright eyes, seemed unaware of the dark stain spreading on his silver-grey flannel.

In the pullman, the light abruptly vanished as the train plunged roaring into a short tunnel. When sunlight flooded through the windows again, the girls had rolled over to change position. Florette was on top now, with her blonde head buried between Hetty's muscular thighs. From the other end of the table, the two voyeurs gleefully watched the fleshy lips of her cunt splayed apart and then lapped by Hetty's pointed tongue.

The redhead nevertheless was the first to climax. Unexpectedly, the wiry hips jerked up off the wood, carrying Florette's bobbing head. The belly contracted. And then the whole body convulsed, thumping the table repeatedly, legs scissored over the pale curls, mouth open to sob out the dwindling cries of Hetty's release.

The blonde was not long afterwards. The shuddering of that pliant body beneath her, the thrust of belly and breasts, the hot clasp of her friend's vaginal lips around her tongue triggered an irresistible series of spasms deep in her own belly. Her head broke free of the scissoring thighs and she uttered a shrill scream, rolling off Hetty to lie quaking on her back with her legs spread wide and both hands clamped over her crotch.

When his breathing had returned to normal, Mondragon Roth poured champagne. Black smoke from the locomotive rolled slowly across a landscape of terraced vineyards.

Soon the two girls were active again. There was a slight sheen of sweat in the hollow between Florette's big breasts. She stood astride fondling her own nipples while Hetty knelt between her ankles and tongued her pussy. They changed positions and Florette sucked the tight folds of the redhead's cunt. Hetty produced a long, fat dildo made of black rubber and strapped it on to mime a rape of the fleshy blonde, the glistening black shaft pumping in and out of her savaged, gaping vagina as she writhed and gasped on the wood with her wrists pinioned above her head.

Roth himself was lying hugely naked on the table when the train clanked through the echoing glass cavern of the station at Lyon Perrache, his vast belly bulked between the two nude girls, one squatting over his face, the other straddling his hips. Florette, impaled on the American's thick cock, was rising and falling slowly, dilating and contracting her vaginal muscles as the veined staff throbbed within her; Hetty squirmed and gyrated hot, wet loins, grinding down on Roth's lascivious, spearing tongue. The girls leaned over his great belly, each twisting a little aside so that she could suck one of the other's inflamed nipples.

Raymond Large, having politely declined physical contact himself, was consumed with delight, dividing his attention between the coupled trio on the table and the passengers crowding the platform – outraged, intrigued or simply astonished as the pullman, with its lewd tableau in full view behind one of the wide windows, was drawn slowly past them.

Soon afterwards – they had been stopped by a signal outside Vienne – Roth jerked and quivered into his own ecstatic and private orgasm. When the two nude girls at last released him from the grip of their thighs, he dressed quickly, giggling quietly to himself. 'My babies,' he said, 'that was *divine*. An encore, perhaps, before you leave us at Marseille? Meanwhile . . .'

He rang the bell. The door opened and the steward appeared. 'Another bottle, Frank,' Roth said. 'And then you can escort these two darlings into the saloon, where the guys can share out the pussy amongst themselves.'

'No sweat,' he murmured to Large when the three of them had gone and the door was closed. 'There's a couple holes bored through the panelling and concealed between the curlicues of those lamp brackets. While we crack this bottle, we can watch comfortably from the divan!'

First Class

The Vienne waterfront was all verticals, tall, narrow façades cross-hatched with iron balconies. A bridge, and then the wide, calm curve of the Rhône, sliding out of sight between wooded hills.

Baron Eckbergh de Groet pulled down the snap-up blind to cover the window of the first class compartment as the Blue Train gathered speed and left the houses behind. 'This should be about right,' he said. 'We pass through Valence flat out, and then there's nothing of any size until we get to Avignon.'

Sonia slid open the compartment door and looked each way along the corridor. Densely packed trees shut out the sun on that side of the track. There was nobody in sight. She closed the door and pulled the blinds down to cover the three windows on the corridor side. There was a 'Reserved' notice on one of the glass panes: the Baron had booked all six of the seats in the compartment. Five elderly passengers – three of them asleep – occupied the compartment behind their own; the one in front was empty. 'All right, Johnnie,' Sonia said, 'take off your clothes. Quick now. All of them.'

The Baron hesitated, looking dubiously at the door. 'Do as you're told,' Sonia rapped, the voice hardening. 'At once! Or it will be the worse for you!'

A sheepish expression creased his features as he removed his jacket and loosened his tie. He stripped off shirt, tie and string vest, then unfastened the braces holding up his trousers. Sonia sat back in the blue-flowered corner seat, her dark head resting on the white lace antimacassar. She lit a cigarette and fitted it into a long ebony holder tipped with gold. She was still wearing the black rubberized raincoat. The train rattled across an iron viaduct.

When the Baron was completely naked – a pale, short, slightly paunchy figure looking if anything pathetic and over-vulnerable amongst the silk lampshades and brocade and rich panelling of the compartment – Sonia blew out a long plume of smoke and stubbed her cigarette in a polished brass ashtray. 'Now bring down the suitcase,' she ordered. 'You know which one – on the right, nearest the door.'

He had to climb on the seat, defenceless in his nudity as a frog on a dissecting table, to manoeuvre down the heavy white hide valise.

'Now stand over there, facing the door . . . *Stand straight!* . . . and don't move until I tell you to.'

Sonia unlocked the case, opened the lid, and removed half a dozen items from the esoteric collection of leather, rubber, straps and chains within. She packed the Baron's discarded clothes into the valise and closed the lid. In the corridor outside, footsteps approached. Facing the drawn blind, the Baron shivered. The footsteps grew louder, passed, faded away.

'Come here,' Sonia said. She picked a leather garment shining with buckles from the equipment on the seat.

'Sonia, I've been thinking . . .' the Baron began nervously.

'Don't,' she cut in. 'You are here to obey. What we are doing isn't illegal; you are a consenting partner – *aren't you*? If you are discovered, there's nothing anyone can do. It may be embarrassing, but there's nothing they can do. Except laugh.'

'Yes, Mistress.'

The garment was a strait-jacket. It was fashioned like a

hip-length tunic with extra-long sleeves, closed at the ends, and a divided strap passing between the legs and fastening behind. She eased him into it, laced up the high collar at the neck, and crossed his arms on his chest, drawing the sleeve extensions behind his back, crossing them there, and then carrying them back around to buckle tightly in front of his waist. She strapped up his genitals, drawing them painfully back between his legs, and bound together his thighs and ankles with thick cord. Finally she drew a black rubber bathing helmet over his balding head, buckled it under his chin, and wound a three-inch strip of adhesive tape several time around his head and over his mouth to make an effective gag.

'It's not one of the most complicated tie-ups we've done, Johnnie,' she said cheerfully, 'but I have to think of the time. We never know who might look in, do we?'

The Baron mumbled something behind his gag.

Sonia tested the buckles and bonds, tightening the strait-jacket a couple of holes, and pushed him down on to his knees. 'Lie flat on your face,' she commanded. The Baron folded forward and then flopped face-down along the blue drugget carpeting the floor between the seats.

With the toe of her boot, she tipped him over on to his back. For a moment she stood looking down at him, an enigmatic expression on her face. Then she rolled him out of sight beneath the seat.

She sat down above him and lit another cigarette. A few minutes later, she snapped up the blind over the wide window. The train was running beside the river. A tug drew a string of barges loaded with coal past a wooded island. Above a thicket of factory chimneys on the far bank, white quarries scarred a steep hillside.

The compartment door slid open. A blue-uniformed man with a peaked cap stood there, a pencil behind his right ear, a clipboard in his hand. 'Tickets, please,' he intoned.

Sonia opened her handbag, took out the two tickets and reservations. 'My husband's in the toilet,' she said.

The man nodded. He took the pencil from behind his ear, made a mark on the chart clipped to the board, and handed back the tickets. 'And the other four people?' he asked. 'Holding his hands in there, maybe?'

She smiled. A comedian already!

She said: 'A family of four. Our friends. We were going on holiday together. Unfortunately they had to cry off. A death in the family. You know.'

The inspector nodded again. He restored the pencil to its resting place. 'A vacation in the South? Where are you heading?'

'In the hills behind Nice.'

She was sitting a little sideways on the seat now, idly swinging one leg . . . and letting the heel of her boot thud against the body of the bound and gagged prisoner beneath the seat on each back-stroke. 'Do you . . . inspect . . . the whole train?' she enquired.

He shook his head. 'Just the first class.'

'Drop by again when you're through. My husband has business with folks in the next coach. It would be nice to have someone to talk to for five minutes,' Sonia said.

'I'll do that,' the ticket collector said. There was a protesting movement from beneath the seat. She drove her heel hard back into something soft.

The man smiled, backed out, closed the door.

Five minutes later a handbell rang in the corridor. 'Luncheon in the Restaurant Car,' an approaching male voice announced. 'Reservations for the first service . . . Luncheon is about to be served . . .'

Sonia stood up, opened the door, stepped into the corridor. 'A ticket for one, please,' she asked the steward swinging the bell.

Before she left the compartment, she leaned down to

push the Baron even further out of sight. 'You can lie there, Johnnie,' she said, 'wondering if anyone's going to come in and use those empty seats while I'm eating and drinking!' She heard a muffled noise – it might have been a groan, it could have been an entreaty – from beneath the seat. Sonia smiled. She took off the raincoat and draped it over the white valise. Without another word she let herself out and closed the door.

The train was going fast. Telegraph poles, a platelayers' hut, the banks of a cutting purple with valerian streaked past the windows. She found it hard not to lurch against them as she made her way towards the Restaurant Car.

The head-waiter wore dark trousers and a white mess jacket with gold epaulettes. She was aware of a pleasing tinkle of glass and cutlery on the white-clothed tables, a subdued hum of conversation all around, as she took the menu he offered.

Paired seats faced one another across the tables on one side of the central gangway, single seats on the other. The waiter showed her to a single seat at an unoccupied table. She lit a cigarette. The chef, she read, was Auguste Demorin, late of the Crillon Hotel in Paris. A savoury smell of wine cooking drifted from the galley. The train rocked around a long curve, swashing the water in a carafe on the table. In the distance, a huddle of pepper-and-salt tile roofs clustered beneath a conical hill crowned by a tiny chapel. Soon, they would be nearing the South.

Monsieur Demorin offered a choice of soup, asparagus or avocado pear salad, followed by poached brill with Sauce Hollandaise and roast duck or Tournedos Rossini. And there would, of course, be a cheese board and dessert.

'I say,' a well-modulated English voice asked beside her, 'would you mind dreadfully if I joined you . . . that is to say, sat at your table? Been a bit of a scrum, finding a place at the first service today. Everyone seems frightfully peckish all of a sudden.'

Sonia looked up. He was short, goodlooking, clean-shaven and youngish. Wearing a blazer and slacks. It was the man who had helped them with the luggage at the Gare de Lyon. She smiled. 'Do please sit down,' with a wave of the hand at the vacant place opposite.

'Most kind,' he said. 'Obliged to you, Ma'am.' And then, sliding into the seat: 'Name of Hill, Tony of that ilk. Perhaps you'd allow me to order a bottle for the two of us? You know – a lady no scandal doth have while she dines, if there be honest talk and wholesome wines.'

'That's a quotation, isn't it?' Sonia smiled again.

He nodded. 'Guilty. Poet chappie in the peerage: Tennyson, Alfred Lord. You will let me, won't you?'

Gazing at his eager face and the calm assurance he radiated, Sonia felt there could be a number of situations in which she might be happy to 'let him'. 'I think that would be very nice,' she said.

'What-ho! A splendid decision!' Tony Hill raised an imperious hand. The head-waiter appeared at their table instantly. 'Bottle of the Calvet claret,' he ordered. 'The twenty eight St-Julien if you have it. And I'd like it opened now, give the old elixir time to breathe a shade.'

The man bowed obsequiously. 'Very good, sir. At once.'

Hill was an amusing companion, and interesting when he talked about his work at Vickers and the expanding air-liner traffic which, he was convinced, would before long put anachronisms like the Blue Train out of business. They were halfway through Monsieur Demorin's duck before they discovered they were on their way to the same house party. 'What luck!' Hill exclaimed. 'Meeting on the train like this! I mean to say, gives us a chance to get matey, what! Before the madding crowd moves in.'

And she would, he realized now, be worth getting to know – especially if boozy old Raymond had hand-picked her for this weekend jaunt. He looked at her with new eyes: nice figure, not too young, interesting face with that prominent nose and the right amount of make-up. The mouth too. There was a certain wry twist there that spelled out . . . what? Experience perhaps.

But what about the elderly cove she'd been with at the station? Husband? Father? Elder bro? He put the question delicately.

'My husband,' Sonia replied, 'didn't feel up to lunch. He's not in a position,' she said truthfully, 'where he can eat what he wants, when he wants.'

'I'm so sorry,' Hill said – rather less truthfully.

'But – my God, *I'm* so sorry: I only just remembered – *we* should be paying for *your* drinks. He asked you to join us for an apéritif! He didn't realize, then, that he wouldn't be having lunch himself.'

'You don't want to worry about that, old thing,' Hill said.

'Tell you what, though' – Sonia was suddenly smiling – 'we *can* offer you a liqueur. There's a bottle of Hennessy VSOP in my hatbox. Why don't you come along to the compartment and have a brandy with us?'

'Love to,' said Tony Hill, beckoning the waiter. 'My bill, please – both lunches together.' No doubt about it, he thought: there *must* be more to this young woman than met the jolly old eye.

There was.

Noting the empty compartment, the blinds drawn on the corridor side, he asked: 'Where's the old man? . . . That is to say, no offense, the guv'nor, your better half?'

'Talking business, probably. There are people he knows in the next coach. You know how it is,' Sonia said carelessly.

'Quite.'

'Perhaps you'd like to get down the hatbox for me? The smallest one. With the rounded corners.'

While Hill was reaching for the case, pretending to pull up a stocking, she bent down and stole a glance beneath the seat. The Baron, motionless in his leather bondage, was still safely there, facing the compartment wall. The situation, she knew, would be absolutely up his street. But they would have to sit on the seat he was under: from the other, he wouldn't be invisible at all.

One of the three places opposite was occupied by the valise containing their s-m equipment. Hill was now lowering the white hide hatbox to the seat by the door. She picked the black raincoat from the top of the valise and dropped it into the place between them.

She snapped open the hatbox lid and took out the brandy bottle. The red leather pochette beside it contained six small silver goblets, fitting one inside the other. The pochette was closed by one of the new zip-fasteners. She slid this open and removed two of the goblets. The train was speeding along an embankment above apple orchards stretching as far as the eye could see. In the distance, the humped hills of the Auvergne stood against a cloudless sky.

Sonia was pouring brandy, balancing bottle and goblet expertly against the rocking of the coach. She handed Hill a drink and sank into the window seat, patting the cushion beside her.

He sat, raising his goblet. 'Down the hatch!' – and then, thinking of the husband: 'To absent friends!'

They both drank.

The conversation was general. But there was something – Hill was increasingly aware of it as he drained the goblet – that was lifting the atmosphere in the compartment out of the ordinary, some quality investing the banal with significance. What was it? An indefinable tension in the air, a sense almost of expectation. A feeling of suppressed excitement perhaps, identifiable in the half smile she tried to conceal, the humour lurking in her eyes?

Sonia was pouring again. When the second drink was finished, she placed her silver goblet on the narrow shelf jutting out below the window. She held out her hand for his, and then – holding him with her enigmatic gaze –

lowered it very slowly into her own. 'Very well,' she said in a level voice. 'Shall we start?'

'Start?'

'Undressing. We can't very well get at each other if we still have all our clothes on, can we?'

'Un . . . *dressing*?'

Hill stared at her. For once in his life he was completely nonplussed. She nodded. 'Removing our clothes,' she explained.

He gaped. 'B-but what about . . . ?' He gestured around the empty compartment.

'My husband? He'll be with them all afternoon. And if not – too bad.'

'And other . . . I mean the corridor and that kind of thing?'

'There's a large label that says "Reserved". Aren't you game?'

Hill swallowed. And then, his assurance regained: 'Oh yes. I'm always game.'

The Blue Train thundered through Pierrelatte and Bollène and Mornas as the first course of the second service was brought to the tables in the Restaurant Car. In Baron Eckbergh de Groet's reserved compartment, Tony Hill, naked from the waist down, was kneeling on the two arms of the central seat on the Baron's side, facing the framed watercolour reproductions of the Mediterranean coast on either side of the mirror. He was maintaining his balance by holding on to the empty luggage rack above his head.

Sonia sat sprawled in the seat. The cinnamon-coloured shantung silk blouse she wore was open to the waist. She wore no underclothes. She too, except for black silk stockings, was bare from the waist down. Her two hands cradled Tony Hill's testicles. His cock was in her mouth.

Hill was adapting the rhythms of train and track, the rocking of the first-class coach on its springs and bogies, to the thrust and withdrawal of his own strokes. The sturdy cock plunged in and out of her mouth with a compelling, almost syncopated, insistence.

Once he had got used to the piquancy of the situation – fucking a married woman half nude in a railway train, when who knew when the husband might not walk in or what passenger traversing the corridor might not risk a peek inside the blinded compartment – once he had accepted that, there was nothing much out of the ordinary in the relationship. Except maybe the dialogue.

Or, more properly, monologue. For the woman was far more vocal than most of the partners he had encountered. It was almost as if she was giving a running commentary on every detail of their lovemaking.

'That's fine, that's marvellous! . . . I love to lick it there, just at the tip! . . . Rub your cock between my tits . . . Let me squeeze it between them . . . Oh, those lovely balls! . . . Give it to me, sweetie . . . Mmmm, that's *goooood*!'

And when they had folded the arms up against the seat back and stretched out along the cushions, she was even more descriptive: 'Put your hand right inside . . . Yes, I love to feel your finger there – just *there*! . . . This is a splendid cock, stiff as a plank and hard as iron; I can feel those throbbing veins even when it's right inside my cunt . . . Give it to me, fuck me hard, hard, *hard*, with your beautiful rigid prick: I want to feel it up there, in up to the bloody hilt! . . . Yes, of course, lover – suck them until they bleed . . . Let me hold your balls as you put it in again . . . Yes, do it: it sends me when you suck down there . . . Oh, that dreamy *tongue*!'

She had good breasts, slightly dropped but full and firm. Her belly was flat and firm too; she had educated vaginal muscles which could grip and relax. They were in fact very well suited physically. And later, when her knees were drawn up almost to her breasts and she jerked repeatedly to the thrust of his inflamed shaft slamming between the hot lips opening amongst the black hairs at her loins, she said: 'You do this awfully well, you know.'

Inside her now for the third time, Hill was rolling them both from side to side as he plunged and withdrew, adjusting his strokes again to the swing and roll of the train. He grinned. 'You make me feel like the boy in the story!'

'Oh, really? What – *Aaaah*! Do that again! – what story is that?'

'At least it's short,' he said apologetically.

'Tell me.'

'There's this boy in bed with his sister, you see. And she tells him, "You do this better than Father does!" And the boy says, "Yes, that's what Mother says".'

Sonia laughed. 'You're a right card, you are!' she said.

'And you, darling' – Hill was panting a little now as he accelerated towards the climax – 'you honestly are the most frantically marvellous fuck! I only hope your husband appreciates that.'

'Oh,' Sonia said, thinking of the speechless Baron pinioned below them, 'there are things about me that he appreciates all right!'

Soon after that, with a series of almost total withdrawals followed by very slow, very deliberate and very hard penetrations, he brought them expertly to a shared release that left them both gasping on the seat as the train roared on, past Orange, through Avignon, towards the shady streets of Aix-en-Provence.

When he had dressed again and gone, Sonia dragged the Baron out from beneath the seat, allowing him to see that her breasts, reddened by love bites, hung free under the open blouse, that the pubic hair, dark above her dark stockings, was matted and damp. 'You'll never know who that was, Johnnie, will you?' she taunted, smiling her most seraphic smile a few inches above his staring eyes. With the tip of one booted toe, she rolled him back under the seat. She poured herself another brandy.

And then, emptying the goblet in a single gulp, she leaned down towards the seat and said softly: 'But that, my darling, my dove, was only the *hors d'oeuvre*, as you might say. Just wait until the ticket collector joins me after we leave Marseille . . .

Second Class

All eight seats of the compartment had been occupied, but five of the passengers had left the train at Marseille, and the old woman with the lapdog had moved to an empty compartment further along the coach as soon as the Blue Train backed out of the St Charles station. Maguy and Michel Blondin were alone for the last leg of the journey, along the coast past Toulon to Nice.

The omens were not good. Maguy, a petite blonde wearing a blue wool jersey suit that was going to be too hot for the Coast, had been staring stonily out of the window as the train crawled around the winding curves skirting the craggy mountains east of the city. Sitting opposite him, crowded in the centre of the compartment all the way from Paris, she had scarcely uttered a word. She had refused lunch. Now, clearly, whatever it was that provoked such a fury within her was about to boil over.

The train gathered speed. There were olive trees beside the line. A triangle of blue sea showed between two hills. The compartment door was open; Michel stood in the corridor, resting his arms on the wooden rail that spanned the wide window – a fair man of medium height, with a small toothbrush moustache. He was wearing a lightweight tan sports jacket with grey trousers and a white open-necked shirt.

'Dragging me along the platform like a naughty child!' his wife said venomously. 'Humiliating me in front of all those people!'

Michel turned around. 'Maguy! That was over four hours ago! If you wanted to complain about the fact that we almost missed the train—'

'And whose fault was that?' Maguy shouted. 'Who lost the tickets? Who kicked up a fuss with the controller when—'

'They weren't lost. I'd forgotten I'd put them in my hip pocket: there's no breast pocket inside this jacket.'

'Who "forgot" that it was impossible to find a cab in the Sixth *Arrondissement* at half past eight in the morning? Who said there was no need to reserve seats this late in the season? Who was so sure that we—'

'Maguy!' Michel came into the compartment and sat down. He shut the door. 'All right,' he said reasonably, 'it was my fault that we were late. I understand why you were cross, scrambling to make the very last coach like that. I'm sorry we couldn't find better seats. But that was a long time ago. Surely, if you wanted to get it all off your chest, you could have—'

'And drag out my private affairs in front of these ghastly people? Sitting squashed up against that dreadful old man who stank of garlic? Thank you very much!'

'I would have changed places if only you had asked.'

'From you, Michel, today I wouldn't even ask the time. You're hopeless.'

He said nothing. For some time there was silence in the compartment. The train rattled across points at a junction, passed a small station with the name *Cassis* spelled out in white stones on a grassy bank. Maguy was staring out of the window again.

'And another thing,' she said over her shoulder. 'These damned parcels!' She glanced at the brown-paper-and-string packages on the luggage rack. '"We must travel light," you said. "It's only a weekend, and I can't bear being lumbered with a whole lot of separate things." So who agrees to carry enough crap to make us look like trippers on a char-a-banc outing?'

'What could I do? My cousin knew we were coming south. How could I refuse when she asked me to bring the stuff? Ghislaine will meet us at the station and take it from us.'

'You could have said no.'

There was another short silence. And then she said: 'I can't think, anyway, why you agreed to come in the first place. This man Large and all his rich friends. I shall feel like—'

'He *is* my employer, Maguy.'

'So you have to suck up to him by demeaning your wife in front of his ritzy friends? A clerk in one of his offices?'

'I do happen,' Michel said mildly, 'to head the finance section of one of the most profitable firms in the Large Corporation. He may want me in on discussions with this American he hopes will invest in the vineyard. I expect he thought a weekend in the South would make a pleasant break for both of us.'

'You should have refused again. But you can never say no, can you?' Her hands were clenched in her lap, the knuckles showing white. 'Except of course in bed. When it comes to that, weak little Michel is all at once the strong man, the negative champion of the North!'

'Maguy . . .'

'When did you last see your father? – that's the title of a famous painting in England. The French version is: When did you last fuck your wife? If, indeed, you have a wife at all in that sense,' Maguy said viciously. 'Not, I imagine, that that stops you fooling around with secretaries and suchlike at the office which seems to keep you away from home so late.'

Michel said nothing.

'I saw you staring at those two flashy tarts who got out of

the pullman at Marseille. That's more your kind of thing, I daresay.'

Still he remained silent.

'Come to think of it,' his wife pursued, 'whores would just about be right for a man like you. Let someone else do the work and you wouldn't have to lift a finger. If your fingers are strong enough to lift. Have you ever heard of the Japanese No Theatre, Michel? You'd do well as a romantic lead there!'

'Maguy!'

'My masterful, resolute, positive husband!' she jeered. 'Vanquisher of railway officials – "Oh, please, Monsieur ... I'm so sorry, Monsieur ... I know I had them somewhere, Monsieur . . . If you would be so generous as to allow us through, Your Eminence!"'

'Would you stop this please, Maguy?'

'You're always the last one served at a bar. You can't even flag down a taxi in central Paris, and we have to get trampled in the Metro with all this—'

'Shut up!' Michel had had enough. He sprang to his feet. 'Shut up, shut up, shut up, shut *up*!' he yelled. 'Keep your mouth shut for once, you loathsome cow!'

He seized her by the lapels of her jacket and dragged her to her feet, slamming her against the window. 'I'm sick to death of your whining and carping and complaining,' he said through clenched teeth. 'Sick to death, do you hear? You want something "masterful", do you? Well, how about this for a start?' He drew back his arm and slapped her, hard, across the face.

Her eyes, which had opened wide at his initial outburst, blinked rapidly and filled with tears. Her mouth dropped open.

Before she could say anything, he slapped her again, forehand, backhand, leaving angry red weals on her pale skin. 'If it's sex you miss,' he seethed, 'try this for size.'

He tore the jacket violently open. A mother-of-pearl button flew off and hit the window; another split the inner edge of a buttonhole, leaving a long tear just inside the seam of the blue material.

'Michel!' Maguy squealed. 'What the devil—?'

'Shut up!'

Beneath the jacket, she was wearing an organdie blouse, of a darker blue than the suit, with a ruffled jabot at the neck. He ripped that open too, yanking her bust bodice savagely down to her waist to expose small pointed breasts. Then he grabbed her by the hips, picked her up bodily and threw her down on to the seat.

She lay staring up at him, her mouth still open, for once at a loss for words.

Michel leaned over her and dragged the jersey skirt up until it was concertinaed around her waist. He grabbed the elasticated waistband of her midnight-blue satin knickers and pulled them down to her ankles – feeling, rather to his surprise, a quite extraordinary hardness and urgency at his loins.

He gazed down at the half naked figure of his wife sprawled on the seat. She was still dazed by the suddenness, the ferocity and unexpectedness of his attack. Her breasts, the nipples raised, were lewdly revealed between the wrenched-aside remains of her jacket and blouse. One leg was drawn up, the knee pointing at the arched roof of the compartment; the other was draped over the edge of the seat, held in position only by the tightly stretched loop of the knickers shackling her ankles.

Michel jerked off the undergarment, throwing it on to the opposite seat. The leg sank lower, until the heel was resting on the floor. Now the whole hairy furrow between her legs, with the sliver of pink flesh at its centre, was obscenely unveiled below the ruched-up skirt.

Quite slowly, without taking his eyes from her face, he unbuckled the belt at his waist and started to unbutton his fly. He pushed dawn his underpants until they came up against the trouser crotch. Above the wrinkled, hairy sac of his testicles, his penis nosed aside the bottom of his shirt.

It was quite rigid, long and fairly thick, tilting up at an angle above the horizontal with a tiny pearl of moisture glistening at the tip.

Maguy lay without moving, still sprawled where he had thrown her.

He exploded then into sudden action. His two hands shot out, clamping themselves to the inside of her thighs. He wrenched them roughly wide, then doubled the legs back and up until the knees were almost touching her chest. The puckered ring of her anus was now visible below the untidy hair covering her vulnerably exposed vaginal cleft.

Michel knelt up on the seat. He freed one hand to smear the liquid welling from his cock over the tip and upper portion of the shaft, lubricating the distended skin until it glistened. Maguy breathed hard, the naked breasts heaving beneath her torn clothes. She was glaring fiercely at him now, lips compressed into a thin line.

He seized her wrists, forcing them above her head. Panting, breath hissing between locked teeth, she squirmed and writhed beneath him, fighting to free herself. He lowered himself between her thighs, once more freeing a hand to grasp his cock. He shoved the tip against the entrance to her cunt, stirring the wand among the folds of vaginal flesh, moistening the dry lips until they opened enough to admit the bulbous head. Then he flexed his hips, positioned the shaft . . . and drove into her as hard as he could.

Maguy yelled. 'Michel! *Michel!* . . . Stop! . . . You're hurting me!'

'Good.' He was smiling. He slapped her face again. Hard. 'Now shut up, or you'll be hurt a lot more.'

'Michel—'

'I said shut up!' Another slap. 'You're complaining

again. As usual. You're always complaining.'

His cock was swallowed in the hot throat of her vagina, clamped between the muscled walls where he had forced it in, throbbing against the clasp of her unwilling flesh. Buried to the hilt, he moved it a little, this way, that way, back and forth, until he sensed her own juices, involuntarily stimulated, flood warmly around it – a quivering staff sucked by a hungry, tight-lipped mouth.

Now he withdrew almost the whole length of it and slammed into her again. Once more Maguy yelled – more of a loud gasp, really – thrusting her body beneath his weight. He repeated the action, settling down to fuck her, in and out, in and out, in and out, each time a hard lunge down, battering her against the seat, a swift withdrawal from the wet sucking of her cunt, and then the next deep, rough penetration.

Outside the compartment, footsteps approached along the corridor, hesitated, broke stride for a moment as the traveller took in the dishevelled couple and what they were doing . . . and then moved on. The train rumbled over a viaduct spanning the mouth of a narrow valley. A stream ran out over a crescent of white sand stippled with sunbathers; children frolicked in the shallows by gaily coloured fishing boats moored to a jetty. The couple on the seat saw none of it.

Michel was shafting his supine wife with long, steady strokes. He had released her wrists and jammed the heel of one hand beneath her chin, forcing her head back against the seat cushion so that she was unable to look at him or speak. Her own hands were clenched into fists, beating ineffectually against the tan sports jacket as she jerked under his relentless, forceful assault. A continuous, low keening noise escaped from her closed mouth.

Michel found that he was actually enjoying himself. Turning at last on the waspish, backbiting venom that Maguy distilled had set the adrenaline coursing through his veins . . . and released his own aggression, now rapidly transforming itself into satisfied lust.

What had started, really, as a punishment, a getting-his-own-back revenge gesture – something that was more psychological than physical, basically – had metamorphosed itself into a pleasure for its own sake, a burning desire he was fortunately, happily, able to satiate.

He was talking to her again now, punctuating his words with smaller slaps as he plunged in and out of her defenceless body.

'Perhaps this . . . will help you . . . to understand . . . better . . . the difference between . . . positive . . . and negative . . . the two poles which . . . nevertheless . . . are opposite but *equal!* . . .'

He had no thoughts for Maguy. Or what she felt. This was his scene, his territory, his private scenario for once. He was going to fuck her until he came, and after that . . . well, the hell with her. Too bad if she didn't like it!

The sun had swung around to the west: it was behind them now. But as the train ran out around a rocky headland jutting into the sea, bars of bright light, slanting through the windows, swept across the compartment and the couple wrestling on the seat.

Michel was lost in a world of pure physical sensation. The exquisite agony inflaming his bursting cock, sliding in and out of Maguy as easily as a finger in an oiled glove, was urging him to increase his pace, accelerating the rhythm until his breath snorted through his nostrils in great gasps and there was nothing left but the aching shaft beneath his pounding hips and the hammering of the heart inside his chest.

And then, suddenly as a match flaring into flame, he was seized by the surge of an impending orgasm. At the end of a particularly deep stroke his loins seemed to explode. He was a shellburst, he was a missile, he was a rocket, lifting, soaring, to spatter the sky with a shower of stars.

His genitals convulsed, spurting a stream of sperm far up into the darkness of his wife's belly.

Perfect.

He levered himself up, glancing out of the window. They were skirting the mountains now: jagged red cliffs fell away below the line; the sea was there, aching blue between parasol pines.

But something strange was happening on the seat. The half-clothed blonde lying there had begun to moan. Her breath sobbed in uneven gasps. Her body arched momentarily up and her fists clenched. A faint trembling shivered her bared pelvis; her belly heaved; the trembling grew into a shiver, a shake, a shudder . . . and finally a series of violent spasms contorting her entire frame. With her mouth wide open, she uttered a strangled cry.

It was clear that she was experiencing a monumental climax of her own.

She reached up her arms, wrapped them around his back, and dragged him down on top of her. Small teeth nibbled the lobe of his ear. 'Michel!' she murmured huskily. 'Michel *chéri*, my lover, my honey-man – why did you never do this before?'

PART THREE

Château Material

Cocktail party

Raymond Large surveyed his guests – and what a curiously mixed bag they were! – with satisfaction and a certain amount of self-congratulation.

Apart from his employees, Séverine and Jean-Jacques Ancarani, and the two actors from the Opera House in Nice, the catch included a landscape gardener, a yacht skipper, an engineer, an accountant, a Belgian industrialist with a title, and a gardener of a more earthy kind – a middle-aged Italian stud whom the film-star woman had insisted on bringing. The females he hoped to circulate among them added two experienced and attractive whores to a notorious lesbian, a blonde suburban housewife, the star and a rangy English girl who was not averse to a spot of smuggling. The mixture, he was sure, would be stirred to greater effect by the Monte-Carlo journalist and his wife, who were reputed to be the most daring proponents of 'free love' on the Coast.

And one must not of course, Large told himself, neglect the rather special talents of the two Parisiennes acting as maidservants, whom he had been at such pains to educate in the ways of the sophisticated. He hoped – quite fervently – that the package, as the Americans called it, would appeal to the millionaire and fellow voyeur whose approval meant so much to him.

It was dusk when Séverine and the two Parisiennes started to serve the champagne cocktails which were to precede a lavish buffet supper in the château ballroom. A slight wind had risen, stammering the French windows opening on to the terrace, and clouds banking in the west threatened to blot out the stars later.

Large had been adamant that his guests were not to 'dress up' – the party was to be 'most informal' (in fact, if his plans were realized, the guests in the long run would not be dressed at all). That first gathering, nevertheless, was a colourful affair: the men, except for Seamus O'Reilly, in dark suits and most of the women wearing long frocks. Doll Jones was athletically seductive in a skintight, silver sequin creation with a fringed hem; Margot Fairleigh looked taller than ever in a high-necked red dress with no sleeves. Bella Cohen wore blue velvet and Sonia black.

The outrageous Seamus O'Reilly had chosen to flaunt a heather-mixture Irish tweed sports jacket with a red-checked shirt and no tie. Michel Blondin's wife, Maguy, who felt uncomfortable but looked fine in the only short skirt there, had attached herself to Seamus in the mistaken belief that he too would be embarrassed as the sole male nonconformist. In fact the simple black jersey frock she wore set off her blonde prettiness to admirable effect.

Mondragon Roth had been met at the station by a hired Delage limousine. He had been driven to the Countess van den Bergh's villa to bathe, shave and depose his seven suitcases and cabin trunk. And then, leaving his advisers behind on Cap Ferrat with Dagmar's other guests, he had brought his hostess to the château with Lorraine Sheldon. The Countess was resplendent in jade green taffeta. Lorraine wore a Hollywood confection fashioned from heavy, oyster-coloured *dupion* silk, which was basically a tight skirt slit to the knee on one side, with nothing above the waist but two straps, widening to accommodate her alarming breasts. Roth had not realized until they arrived that the man sitting beside the driver, a weatherbeaten Italian uneasy in a dark serge suit and a stiff collar, was a fellow guest.

Their entrance was not without a certain impact. The Baron, who was wearing a grey suede waistcoat with his blue pinstripe suit, stared at Lorraine in fascination. 'I'd been to see her first film the night I met Gerda,' he whispered to Sonia. 'My goodness me, I wouldn't mind seeing that bosom above thigh boots and a leather corset!'

'You can dream about that while you're under my bed tonight,' Sonia said. 'Personally, I find the lez more interesting. She looks topping for her age.'

Dagmar van den Bergh had homed in with unerring instinct on Margot Fairleigh. 'What a charming gown, my dear,' she said after introductions had been made all round. 'That dark red is such a stylish choice with your long pale hair.' She laid a gloved hand on the girl's bare arm. 'If you're based on Golfe Juan, you must sail round and spend a day at my place on Cap Ferrat. We have a little harbour of our own. With your boyfriend of course.'

'I'd love to,' Margot said. 'Actually he isn't exactly my boyfriend. More like my boss, really.'

'So much the better,' said the Countess, raising a dismissive eyebrow at Kirk Munroe. She smiled, as though the remark was a joke.

Margot's brother, Dale, was talking to Sonia. 'What an absolutely amazing coincidence,' he said, 'finding you here of all places! But I'd no *idea*' – with a sideways glance at the Baron – 'that you were married. And a Baroness at that!'

'We'll hear no more of that subject,' Sonia said quickly. 'Not another word, or you'll suffer for it.'

Dale grinned. 'Is that a promise?' he said.

The party had split up into several groups. Lorraine Sheldon, champagne in hand, was holding court before an attentive audience of Tony Hill, Ancarani, Kirk and Michel Blondin. Maguy was discussing house plants with Geraldo Porrelli, although her eyes never left her husband. The journalist, Dill Jones, was regaling Roth and Mark Harries with a lurid account of a serial murderer, the dismembered portions of whose victims were turning up in packages all over southern England.

'Frankly,' his wife said, shivering the sequins on her silver dress, 'I'd rather not hear the details of some of these sordid cases Dill picks up off the wire service. Either I'm squeamish, or else—'

'Or else,' boomed Seamus, passing with a champagne bottle, 'like the little girl in those *William* stories, you'll squeam and squeam and squeam until you're *thick*!' At his most boisterous tonight, in a well-meaning effort to make the party go, the Irishman declaimed:

I had a little suitcase
Nothing would it hold,
But the little lady
I met in Chiddingfold!

'Honestly!' Dale exclaimed. 'Any jingle or catch-phrase or funny, and the old bounder's spouting it before you can say Help! You can't take him anywhere!'

Five men in rusty dinner-suits had filed on to a small stage at one end of the ballroom and were setting up music stands and unpacking instruments.

Below the stage Raymond Large was discussing with Séverine and Bella Cohen the production the following evening of a scabrous and risqué skit on *The Importance of Being Ernest* which was to be put on with the help of Seamus and Dale. As the host, Large had permitted himself to disobey his own rules and wear a white tuxedo with a black tie. He glanced around the ballroom. It was not large – perhaps forty feet by twenty – but the separate groups somehow combined to emphasize the spaces between them. 'Make them circulate,' he murmured to Séverine. 'Mix them up a bit. Maybe we should eat now?' She nodded and moved away.

He watched her glide easily among the guests, handsome

and dependable, a tall figure in pale blue silk, offering a tray of brimming champagne glasses with a wide, welcoming smile.

'I don't know what I'd do without her,' he confided to Bella.

A long buffet table covered with a white linen cloth stood at the far end of the room from the stage. A line of opened Château de Courmettes wine bottles, red and white, occupied the centre of the table. These were surrounded by a profusion of local delicacies. Baked sea bass, cold with mayonnaise, vied for pride of place with lobster patties, dressed crab, garlicked *aioli*, Provençal lamb, black olive *tians* and Marseille *bouillabaisse*. Whole steak fillets in flaky pastry flanked a honey-roast ham and there were dishes of Russian caviar and raw salmon *gravelax* from Norway at opposite ends of the display. Huge olive-wood bowls holding a selection of salads – tomato with chopped basil, sliced raw mushrooms in a vinaigrette sauce, savoury rice with peppers – completed the collation.

An enormous board covered with local sheep and goats' cheeses stood on a side-table with crocks of butter and baskets of long French bread. The two Parisiennes, wearing black dresses, white aprons and lacy caps, waited behind the buffet table, dispensing knives, forks, plates and glasses. Both of them were dark, with sallow Latin complexions, one slender with unusually full lips, the other heavily built and – to put it politely – well endowed.

'We call them Lusty and Busty,' Large told the American. 'I leave you to work out which is which!'

Roth chuckled. 'A work-out with those two would be a pleasure,' he said.

Séverine had artfully – but apparently at random – separated the guests into the most unlikely groups, seated at half a dozen occasional tables around the dance floor. Thus Margot found herself with Dill and the Baron, Dagmar was with the two randiest men in the party, Kirk and Tony Hill, Lorraine was flanked by Dale and Mark Harries, and so on. Raymond Large and Roth remained together, and Séverine herself took care of Porrelli, because he was clearly ill at ease in company he considered to be outside his normal social orbit. The musicians – a fiddler, drummer, accordionist, double-bass player and a man at the piano – were tuning up. And soon, as the level of wine in the Indian-club-shaped Provençal bottles dipped, so that of the conversations rose, until the ballroom was loud with laughter and the chatter of the well-fed.

Mondragon Roth was toying with two quails in aspic. 'What exactly,' he asked, stripping the flesh from a tiny drumstick with his teeth, 'do you hope to . . . achieve . . . bringing this, shall we say unusual, collection of folks together?'

Raymond Large smiled, the thin lips creased beneath his blade of a nose. He passed a hand over his crimped silver hair. 'First of all and most importantly, my dear fellow, to amuse *you*. We do after all have more than one taste in common. Secondly, and linked of course with that aim, to render these good people so bereft of their inhibitions that their animal instincts will surface and they will be seized by such carnal desires as they normally suppress.'

Roth frowned, a second small bone halfway to his mouth. 'Say again?'

'I want them stoned out of their minds so that sex can take over.'

'Now that,' the American enthused, 'is a really worthwhile aim!'

'You and I,' Large said, 'will stand a little outside this scene of debauchery. But although we may be outside, we shall be looking in! Three of the bedrooms have two-way mirrors, there are concealed peepholes in several others, and one or two beds are equipped with hidden microphones relayed to wireless loudspeakers in my study.'

'That's my boy!' Roth beamed.

'There are more men than women, as you see. This is deliberate. It could lead, hopefully, to interesting situations. Particularly as some of the ladies present prefer their own kind. And Dagmar will hope to recruit more still.'

'The tall girl in the red dress?'

Large nodded. 'Séverine thinks there's a definite possibility there. And, as you have evidently noticed, our dear Countess clearly shares that opinion.'

'The woman with Baron Eckbergh de Groet looks interesting – the one in black velvet.'

'She is not, of course, Johnnie's wife,' Large said. 'She is in fact a professional dominatrice: the Baron is a dedicated bondage fan. But what adds a touch of piquancy here is the knowledge that Dale Fairleigh – the good-looking young actor sitting with Lorraine and my landscape gardener – runs on the same sexual track. He's a fetishist too, mainly hooked on rubber, I gather. And the mistress ministering to his masochism is that same Sonia who's with Johnnie!'

'I did say interesting.'

'Quite. Harries of course, my gardening expert, is just a plain stud. And so are the yacht skipper and the English engineer, Tony Hill.'

'What about the Irishman?'

'Seamus?' Large shook his head. 'Well, Seamus is what you might call heavy relief!'

'I'll buy that. You sure got yourself a varied bunch there!'

Nodding again, Large refilled both their glasses. 'Add the ones I just mentioned to the more "normal" guests, stir well and season with a judicious amount of weed, and we should see a fine example of what the mathematicians term permutations and combinations.' He laughed. 'We might even prove the Binomial Theorem!'

On the stage, the musicians had started to play. Popular dance tunes like *Angry*, *Sweet Leilani* and the rumba *Cuban Pete* set the diners' feet tapping, and once Lorraine had hauled Mark Harries on to the floor to show off her rumba technique, other couples followed – Tony Hill with Doll, Kirk with Maguy, Dagmar leading a reluctant and embarrassed Margot.

Seamus jumped up on to the stage and started to sing, waving his arms about as he bellowed in a fruity tenor. Mark Harries stood helplessly by as Lorraine went into a speciality act of her own, the famous breasts bouncing in a rhythm even more complex than that of her feet. Before long the whole dance floor was heaving and only Large and his guest of honour remained seated.

The accordion player slipped out of the straps and lowered his heavy instrument to the floor. He produced a clarinet and then an alto saxophone as the band swung into a selection of jazzier numbers – *Hard-hearted Hannah*, a Charleston and a slow version of *Hot Time In The Old Town Tonight*.

'My God,' Roth said, 'they sure are hotting it up right here – and the hell with what goes on in the old town! Did you feed them the stuff already?'

Large shook his head. 'It's either anticipation – for those in the know – or alcohol added to the exhaustion of a long journey,' he said. 'We're saving the hard stuff for tomorrow.'

'I can't wait. Hey, but this is a neat little combo you got here!'

The band was in fact not at all bad. Once the accordionist started wailing on his alto, the fiddler forsook his one-two, one-two approach and demonstrated a totally unexpected talent for syncopation in the manner of Stephane Grappelly and the Quintet of the Hot Club of France. They had torn apart *Eccentric* and were halfway through an up-tempo *Dippermouth Blues* when Tony Hill, pump-handling Doll around the dance floor for the second time, stopped, panting, near Large's table.

'Hell's bells, old thing,' they heard him say, 'I wouldn't

mind a spot of the old Dippermouth myself – just you, me, and the bedsprings, dash it all.'

Doll's face was flushed. She looked him straight in the eye – they were about the same height – and said: 'That's what I'm here for.'

Large's eyebrows scaled the furrows of his forehead. He turned to Roth. 'See what I mean?' he murmured.

The excitement stimulated by the music was contagious. Swirling, jumping, clutched together or flung apart, the dancers were transported. Kirk was kicking up his legs with Lorraine (the tight skirt was up around her thighs); Jean-Jacques Ancarani spun around the voluptuous Bella; Seamus was explaining to anyone who would listen that a pansy was a man who liked his vice versa; the Baron and Sonia executed a nifty foxtrot on the outskirts of the crowd. Even the two Parisiennes were snapping their fingers and swaying as they carried in fresh supplies of wine.

'What about those two?' Roth asked. 'The big one looks kinda sexy to me – and the other's a swell mouth for sucking, even if she is chickenshit thin. Do they have any part to play in your scenario for tomorrow?'

Large exchanged a glance with Séverine, drifting past dreamily with Geraldo Porrelli, held as delicately as if she were a porcelain shepherdess from Meissen. 'Lusty and Busty?' he said, blue eyes twinkling behind the horn-rims. 'Oh, my goodness, yes: they have a part to play all right!'

Morpheus Awake

'Jesus,' Lorraine Sheldon gasped, 'I never held a dick this big in my hand before! Where have you been all my life, lover?'

'Practising for tonight,' Dill Jones told her.

His work as a journalist and gossip writer brought him into contact with many women, a high percentage of whom, through boredom, divorce, widowhood or simple lechery, were happy in the right circumstances and at the right time to bestow their favours away from a marital bed. His experience, widened again after his own marriage to Doll and their mutual enthusiasm for the doctrines of free love, had taught him early on that the mere size and girth of his genitalia were in themselves enough to act as a *laissez-passer* – at least between the thighs of those ladies for whom sensation was more important than sexual subtlety.

He had unerringly picked out the film star as one of these, and craftily kept out of her way until late in the evening, when a great deal of wine had been put away. By this time, he hoped – although he had reservations about Ancarani and the Italian – the opposition would have been tried, tested and, hopefully, rejected as unsuitable. Or would be once his own claims were put forward. Eventually he cut in on the Frenchman, Michel Blondin, and eased Lorraine across the floor as the band swung into a slow-drag *Memories Of You*. He held her close, one arm clenched around her bare back with the fingertips stretched almost to the curve of breast loose beneath the moulded right shoulder-strap. She had just finished an energetic *Black-Bottom*, and a faint whiff of perspiration underlay the clouds of Chanel No 5 which still hung around her.

Dill was a good dancer. He swung into a lazy turn in the far corner from the band, one knee locked between Lorraine's legs, and manoeuvered his hips so that his prized equipment pressed into the silk sheathing her belly.

She was a little tipsy. 'Well, I'm flattered,' she said, 'to produce such a quick reaction, before we even made one lap of the floor!'

'I don't have a hard-on,' he said boldly, 'if that's what you mean. At least, not yet.'

Lorraine's mouth opened. 'You don't . . . ?'

She steered him behind a row of potted palms at one side of the buffet, and reached down a hand to grasp his crotch. 'My God, the man's telling no lie!' she exclaimed. 'This I must see!'

'As soon as you like.'

'Once the party's over, then, and I've said nighty-night to Ray and Mondy. Though as soon as I like, means like now.' Lorraine giggled. 'I'm in the Blue Room,' she said. 'Where else!'

It was after one o'clock when he sidled through the half-open door into the Blue Room – to see Lorraine already naked on the bed, lying with her shapely legs slightly spread, a tuft of pubic hair prominent at the base of her belly and the great breasts rising and falling as she breathed. Dill's hair was plastered to his skull. He wore royal blue pyjamas and a crimson silk dressing-gown. A six-inch cigarette holder jutted from his mouth. 'Thought I'd impress you with me Noel Coward set,' he said through clenched teeth.

She laughed, raising her arms to link hands behind her head. Her armpits were sculptured from alabaster. 'So I'm impressed,' she said. 'I'd hoped you might bring me something that would impress me even more.'

He moved closer to the bed. The red silk was thrust forcefully out below the belt knotted at the waist.

Lorraine extended an arm. She pulled one end of the silk belt to unravel the knot, then tweaked aside the edges of the garment. One of the pyjama trouser-legs peaked out sharply between hip and knee, but the material was too tight to permit Dill's rigid penis to rise to its full height. Fixing her eyes on his face, she slid her hand inside the pyjama fly, grasped the heavy staff, and hauled it out into the open.

She exclaimed aloud. Dill's cock was enormous. Freed now of constriction, it speared up from his loins, gnarled with veins below the empurpled, velvet tip, a tower dedicated to the celebration of lustful masculinity.

'Impressed is an understatement,' Lorraine breathed. 'Did you ever think of lending it to a horse.'

He grinned. 'All the mares turn into steeplechasers once I come into the field,' he said.

'Oh, my! Just how long is it?' she asked. 'And how far around? How thick?'

'That, madam, is classified information.'

'No, but really. Tell Lorraine. How long?'

'It depends,' Dill told her, 'on who is sucking it.'

She raised herself on one elbow. And then, with a challenging glance at his impassive face, patted the covers beside her. He sat on the edge of the bed. She leaned forward. The lush red lips, central point of a thousand lurid Hollywood movie posters, opened wide and then closed gently over the throbbing tip of his stiffened cock.

Dill caught his breath. The softly clasping lips, tightening imperceptibly as they oiled down the shaft, sucking with lewd insistence as the tip nudged the back of her throat and she could sink her head no further, drew every nerve in his body tingling down to his loins.

She withdrew her mouth, lips tighter, tighter, massaging

the distended skin over the hard muscular core of the cock, tongue flickering against the super-sensitive underside of the glans, until only the very extremity with the pearl of moisture dewing its slit remained between her teeth . . . and then plunged firmly down once more with cheeks hollowed, almost all of the throbbing staff engulfed in the hot depths of her deep throat.

For some minutes, breathing hard through her nose, she continued this steady, rhythmic pumping. Dill's heart was thumping; excitement rose in his chest, almost choking the air in his tightened throat; his pulse raced. He was about to lean over and try to reach her cunt with his own mouth when she abruptly raised her head and stared impishly up at him from beneath her brow.

'How long?' she asked.

'Longer than it's ever been,' Dill said hoarsely.

He slipped out of the dressing-gown, wrenched open the buttons of the pyjama jacket, tore that off, and pushed the trousers down to his ankles. He stepped out of the trousers. Naked, the great cock and bullish testicles seemed to weigh down his slight figure as he climbed up on to the bed beside her.

'In that case, baby,' Lorraine said, 'you can lay it on me. Come on – shoot it to Mama. I want that thing right here, right now!' She widened the spread of her legs, raised her knees slightly, and dipped both hands down to hold open the pink lips wrinkled in the midst of the springy hair at her loins.

Dill positioned himself between her knees. Taking his cock in one hand and supporting his weight on the other, he lowered himself until the cock-head was opposite those lustfully gaping lips. Moistened already in lascivious anticipation, the stretched folds of flesh glistened wickedly in the illumination of a lamp on the bedside table. He tensed the muscles of his hips and buttocks . . . placed the head at the pouting entrance to Lorraine's cunt . . . and drove in with all his force.

She cried out, jerking involuntarily as glans and shaft, thrusting past the wet labia, ploughed savagely up between clinging vaginal walls into the hot depths of her belly.

For a moment, Dill let the huge tool lie there, wedging apart the clasping tunnel of inner flesh. Then he started slowly to move, gently stirring the wand inside her, sliding it in, out, in, out with gradually lengthening strokes until more than half of the punishing shaft was engulfed each time he lunged forward to penetrate her quaking belly.

Lorraine shifted bemusedly beneath him, rolling this way and that, gyrating her hips, scissoring her legs over his back as her body flowered open to accommodate the fleshy spear on which she was impaled.

'That Dilwyn Jones,' a dowager reputed to be Monte-Carlo's 'Hostess with the Mostest' once confided to Dagmar van den Bergh, 'he's the original, the only cock-and-ball story! Instead of a guy with a stiffened prick, you've got a giant hard-on that happens to have a man attached!' Not, she had added, that that was necessarily a bad thing in itself.

Certainly Lorraine Sheldon voiced no complaints. 'Oh, God! Oh, Jesus!' she moaned, her head threshing wildly from side to side. 'This is dreamy, this is bliss! . . . With half the jocks who sock it to me, their dicks scarcely touch the sides. But you, lover – with you it's the biggest, the greatest!' She clenched predatory fingers on his upper arms. Her eyes stared wide. 'You fill me full, baby. I'm stretched to the limit; I want to cut it off and keep it in there forever!'

A little later however – Dill had just settled into a powerful rhythm employing almost the whole stroke with every thrust – she arched her pelvis up against him and held him there, buried as close to the hilt as he could get. 'Honey, this is sensational,' she said. 'And next time I'll let you go the whole way. It's a promise. In a half hour or so. But right now I'm just a tiny mite sore: you practically split me apart! Besides, this first time I want to *see* that wonder-wand while it jerks and squirts! I want to see you come, baby. Come sit on me here' – she patted the curve of belly between her hips – 'and jerk off over my tits!'

He was panting and there was sweat between his shoulder-blades. He felt like a king. Nevertheless, if Lorraine Sheldon was calling the shots . . . A little reluctantly, he withdrew, a sword dripping from its scabbard.

He straddled her hips, the cock still straight and stiff as a lance, and took the shaft between the thumb and first three fingers of his right hand. Slowly at first, and then with increasing speed, he began to masturbate.

His fingers skimmed the dark skin up and down the rigid core of his penis, passing every third or fourth stroke over the seeping tip to smear the colourless lubricating juice over the bulbous, engorged head and down around the glistening shaft. His balls, outsize in their hairy sac, rose and fell on the fascinated blonde's belly. His eyes were fixed on her splendid breasts, bouncing and bobbing with the reaction of the spring mattress to Dill's pistoning efforts.

His breathing, panting at first, then transformed into uneven gasps, was now reduced to a series of grunts and groans. His milking hand squelched faster and faster up and down the slippery, throbbing cock. And then suddenly his entire body seemed to convulse. He tilted back his head and cried aloud. At the same time his penis jerked out of his hand, the long, thick staff spewing forceful spurts of semen out over the swelling mounds of Lorraine's breasts in slowly diminishing spasms.

She gazed in delight at the gouts of hot, creamy fluid spattered over her satin skin, raising both hands to smear the stuff over her nipples. She turned her head to look into a large mirror above a dressing-table beside the bed. Pushing up a wet breast with one hand, she reached for his huge but now flaccid cock with the other. 'Boy, with what I've got and what you've got,' she told their reflections, 'that sure is a swell picture we make!'

On the other side of the mirror, Mondragon Roth and

Raymond Large clutched one another with manic glee. 'Magnificent,' Roth giggled. 'A triumph, my dear fellow – and a swell picture indeed!'

The Green Room – appositely enough, since she had once been in the entertainment business – was assigned to Doll Jones and her husband, although nobody who knew them would have had the remotest expectation that they would actually spend the night in it together.

'The door of this one is sculptured with Provençal-style panels,' Large told his guest as they stole along one of the tortuous corridors webbing the upper floors of the château. 'The crowning motif is a garland of leaves linking three separate rosebuds ... and the two outer roses have peepholes bored through their centres.'

'Remarkable,' Roth said.

Large took the massive American's arm and steered him around a sharp corner. He held a finger to his lips and pointed to the far end of a dimly lit passageway, where two pencil-thin rays of bright light pierced the gloom. Side by side, the two voyeurs tiptoed towards them.

Outside the door, each of them applied an eye to one of the cunningly concealed spy-holes.

The room was brightly lit. Green ivy leaves twined around a painted trellis decorated the antique-style wallpaper. Green velvet covered the easy chairs and the stool in front of the dressing-table. Cretonne drapes, an ottoman cover and a curtain drawn across an arch leading to the bathroom sported a tropical greenery design. A jade silk coverlet stretched smoothly across the empty bed.

Tony Hill and Doll were on the floor.

The engineer was kneeling up, his short, thick, sturdy cock jutting from the dark thatch at his loins which was the only hair visible on his body. Every plane of his tanned, healthy frame – the slim hips, the flat belly, his muscular chest – was tense with anticipation. In front of him, Doll, the ex-dancer and acrobat, stood poised, as naked as he was.

She leaned forward, placed her hands palm down on the deep-pile green carpet, and kicked her legs up into a handstand.

She balanced there, inverted, legs stiffly angled at the ceiling, the muscles of her outstretched arms trembling. Then, very slowly, she parted her thighs, bent her knees, and folded from the hips so that the legs draped themselves over her partner's shoulders, one on either side of his head.

Hill found the downy triangle of her pubic hair, at the base of a tight and tautly stretched belly, only inches from his mouth.

'Good Lord!' he exclaimed.

Doll shifted her hands slightly. She arched her back like a bow. Her throat shone in the bright light with muscular tension as she raised her head. Slowly, slowly the lips approached. She took the tip of Hill's cock in her mouth.

'Great Scott! What a wizard trick!' He was breathless with admiration.

Moments later – Doll's cheeks were hollowed as she sucked and his hips had begun to oscillate back and forth – he exclaimed again. 'By Jove,' he enthused, 'Mrs Hill's boy's going to have a basinful of this! I see what they mean by Dippermouth, what!'

He lowered his head until the tip of his protruding tongue could lap between the tight folds of flesh nestling amongst the dancer's pubic curls.

A slight tremor stirred the flesh of Doll's taut belly. A stifled murmur – of pleasure? of satisfaction? of surprise? – escaped from her busy mouth. Hill lashed the exposed cunt in front of him with his tongue, fastening his lips to her labia, sucking, exploring, probing until the quivering folds became wet and slippery and all at once he was licking the stiffened bud of her clitoris, and she grunted, accelerating the oral massage of his cock as her pelvis jerked and fluttered under his expert ministrations.

Beyond her stiffly arched back, his two hands had stolen around to fondle the breasts projecting from her bowed body. For a little while longer they remained like that, lost in the exquisite pleasures radiating from the subtly stimulated nerves of their genitals. And then the young woman freed her mouth. She took her hands from the floor and straightened her back. With agonizing concentration, she contracted her tense abdominal muscles, folding from the hips to raise the top half of her body to a horizontal position, to a canted forty-five degrees, and finally to the vertical. She was sitting on Hill's shoulders, the breasts heaving after that muscular exertion, her legs hanging down his back and the curve of her belly, relaxed now, pressed to his nuzzling face.

'I *say*, old girl' – his voice was muffled – 'that was an absolutely tiptop sporting performance! Do you have any more like that up your pretty sleeve?'

'Plenty,' said Doll.

She sprang nimbly away from him and knelt on the carpet, leaning forward to ground elbows and forearms, the hands linked and edge-on to the floor. She lowered her head until it was cradled by her hands, then raised herself slowly into a head-stand. In that inverted position, she parted her legs, sinking them in opposite directions until she was doing an upside-down splits.

Hill needed no invitation and no instructions. With a leg each side of her columned body, he straddled her crosswise. Taking his thick and glistening cock in one hand, he flexed his knees, lowering himself until he could stir the tip into the moist folds of her gaping, shamelessly exposed cunt.

He lowered himself further, sinking the shaft among the damp hairs between her extended legs, sinking it deep into the clasping heat of the vagina tunnelled into her belly. Alternately bending and straightening his legs, he ploughed his downward-pointing staff into her as she groaned and mewled below him.

On the other side of the bedroom door, Large and Roth could scarcely contain their excitement. 'A veritable tour-de-force,' Roth whispered. 'The *Kama-Sutra* was never like this!'

The couple in the green roam were running through a whole gamut of sexual variations. Hill stood, leaning slightly back as she impaled herself on his rigid penis, legs twined around his waist and arms around his neck; he thrust into her from behind while she was rolled into a ball, neat as a trussed chicken; they lay side by side on the bed, contriving to fuck, kiss and caress with their limbs disposed in a variety of positions unknown to the medical or orthopaedic professions.

'Can you actually suck yourself?' Hill asked after one of their more extreme contortions.

'Oh, yes,' Doll replied. 'But only on the outside.'

'I say! I'd certainly love to see that!'

'And so you shall,' she said.

Outside the door, Raymond Large laid a hand on Roth's arm. 'These two are experts,' he said. 'When they were making love on the bed . . . did you see? Did you notice her hands? Did you watch him? He was using his whole body, caressing not just with his hands, his tool, but with his hip, his toes, even his chin and his *calves*, dammit!' He shook his head. 'We can come back later if you like – they'll be at it all night, never quite coming to the point of no return – but just now there are other delicacies worthy of your attention.'

The American was still gazing through the peephole at Doll Jones's doubled-up figure. 'Jesus, what a picture!' he breathed for the second time. 'And what a waste, by God! If only we had a movie camera here . . .'

'Wait until tomorrow night,' Raymond Large said.

Dagmar van den Bergh had been driven home to Cap Ferrat before the party in the ballroom was over. 'Two nights running at my age,' she told Raymond Large as she settled in the back of the Delage, 'is more than these old bones can support . . .'

'You know perfectly well that you look gorgeous,' Large said.

'. . . but I'll be back for tomorrow night, and I promise I'll exert every wile that remains to me in an effort to make *that* party go!'

'And nobody,' Large said later to Roth, 'can mix it sexually more thoroughly than good old Dagmar. Even today. As of course *you* very well know.'

Making their rounds of the 'sabotaged' bedrooms, the host and his principal guest paused only a short while at the spy-holes affording them a glimpse into the private lives of Michel Blondin and Maguy. 'They are, after all, married,' Large said disapprovingly. 'I don't, to be honest, anticipate much of interest here.'

In this he was mistaken.

As Doll's room had been green, so the motif in this one was pink – down to a giant pink teddy-bear on the rose-coloured bedspread. But there was nobody under the covers. Pink as the figured curtains, Maguy's petite and shapely figure was in a kneeling position beside the bed, hunched over as if she might be saying her prayers.

If she was, it could only have been for clemency.

For Michel was close behind her, kneeling also, thrusting his iron-hard penis into her from the rear with savage force.

From time to time he drew slightly back, still with that rigid staff deeply embedded between the cheeks of her bottom, and slapped her viciously. The pale skin of the buttock nearest the door was already an angry red with the marks of his fingers.

After this he resumed his determined and forceful efforts, pistoning in and out of her defenceless body with increasing speed. Occasionally he leaned forward over her back to murmur something into her ear. The watchers behind the door were unable to hear everything he said, but the French words for 'bitch' and 'slut' and 'whore' filtered through more than once.

Later Michel picked his wife up and threw her on the bed. He levered up her legs, placed a heel on each of his shoulders, and thrust down once again, penetrating as ferociously as before while he stood beside the bed. This time he punctuated his rhythm with stinging slaps of his open hand on her breasts and belly and across her face. Maguy's face was turned towards the door. Her make-up had run and her cheeks were streaked with tears, but her expression was rapt and her smile radiant.

When he made her come, the choked cries were of joy rather than pain or humiliation.

'Good old Blondin!' Raymond Large enthused from his spy-hole. 'I didn't think the chap had it in him.'

'Well, she certainly had it in her!' Roth chuckled.

The next stop on Large's 'tour of inspection' – on a lower floor, in a different wing of the old château – was the Directoire Room. It was here that Mark Harries had been staying since he arrived from Paris at the beginning of the week. It was an elegant chamber with bow windows leading onto a balustraded balcony and an uneven floor of wide boards polished over the centuries to honey-coloured perfection. The furniture – chairs, commode, escritoire and *garde-robe* – was all subtle curves and tapering, straight-line legs. A canopy, valance and curtains of heavy amber silk framed the four-poster bed.

Harries was not alone in the bed tonight.

His companion was Bella Cohen, whose lush curves and hourglass figure looked as much at home among the lace and fine linen of the tumbled bedclothes as a Madame Récamier or Goya's scandalous Duchess.

They lay side by side, naked, with the covers thrown back, her voluptuously curving mounds and hollows admirably complemented by the uncompromising lines of his square, compact body, the soft sheen of her flesh set off by the hard planes of his muscular frame with its downing of dark hairs.

'She's a professional, isn't she?' Roth asked. 'I can always tell, even with the highest-class ones, like this.'

They were sitting side by side in a linen cupboard this time, the peepholes being concealed in the eyes of animals in a hunting tapestry on the bedroom wall.

'I prefer the term expert,' Large replied. 'Certainly Bella gets paid for her time and her . . . skill. But on this occasion that is entirely a matter between herself and myself. As far as the others are concerned – except my Séverine, of course, but she *is* exceptional! – as far as the others are concerned, Bella is just another guest. A lady of leisure.'

'Bully for you,' said Roth. 'I like a guy he should push out the boat for his buddies.'

So far as skill was concerned, Bella's expertise was certainly in evidence that night, although it would have been fair to say that she had found an ideal partner in Mark Harries.

Their lovemaking could have been used as a textbook illustration for a manual on how to get the best out of sex in a bed.

It started, like the words of the song, with a kiss.

This began gently, became more intense, involving tongues as well as lips, and stimulated at the same time that lazy, dreamlike promenade of the hands – touching here, stroking there – which precedes the mounting excitement of any meaningful exploration of an unfamiliar body.

The hands smoothed and sculpted, cradled and probed and tweaked, approaching in subtle arabesques, withdrawing, returning closer but never actually reaching those super-sensitive zones where a simple touch can trigger desire. As the hands dare more, trailing past the ear-lobes, the nape, the insides of the thighs, the nipples, the breathing quickens, limbs involuntarily stir, a pleasure band tightens around the chest and the pulses race.

And at last, the thudding of the heart pronounced now,

comes the breathtaking initial contact with the forbidden places . . .

Mark and Bella floated, sailed through these stages with an elegance at one with the style of the room, the cossetted four-poster. Their bodies moved imperceptibly closer as their kisses became more prolonged. They were face to face now the whole way down. A knee crept between Bella's knees; one of her feet rubbed catlike against his ankle. The foot curled, moved to his calf. The knee went in deeper.

Mark's hand left the swelling curve of a breast, travelled across ribs and scooped out a waist before resting on Bella's hip. His stretched thumb searched for and found the crease of her thigh, burrowing there among the outer fringe of her pubic hair.

She stroked the length of his body, inserting a hand between them to graze her knuckles across the top of his bush.

Now the scenario shifted towards its final phase. Flesh quivered here and there. Move and countermove succeeded one another in a progression as inevitable as the stages in a speeded-up chess game.

Mark's hand slid across the lower curve of her belly, a gold signet ring on his little finger catching the light when his palm closed over her pubic mound; a diamond in turn flashed from Bella's ring as her finger wrapped around his stiffened cock.

Mark's middle finger sank from sight among the dark thatch and her pelvis arched slightly off the bed when the finger moved.

His buttocks hollowed and his hips inched closer: the hand holding him had dragged him out and up, milking his tool with a stealthy insistence.

For some time they remained in mutual masturbation, bodies tensed as the caressing hands skimmed and probed. The wordless, moaning ecstasy of their shared delight was clearly audible in the linen cupboard on the far side of the hunting tapestry.

And then, as a more intimate contact relentlessly, irresistibly, imposed itself, their relative positions changed. The tenseness gave way to a lazier, more casual relaxation. Bella was lying more on her back. Her outer leg fell a little away, effectively parting her thighs to reveal among the damp, tufted hairs the dark red crevice in which Mark's fingers were so actively engaged. He was bent more enticingly towards her; the milking hand, encouraging his hardened cock to a glistening, slippery sheen, had settled into a steady, long-stroke rhythm.

She bent the knee of the leg beneath them.

In a single fluid movement, so natural in its execution that it seemed to involve no muscular exertion from either of them, he rolled over it and sank his body between her thighs. Her hips rose to receive him and the gleaming shaft of his penis plunged down and into her as easily and effortlessly as the piston in the cylinder of a well-oiled engine.

Within a moment they had established a reciprocating, rocking rhythm as perfect in its precision – again the mechanical symbol suggested itself – as the movement of a Swiss watch.

Mark's slim hips and tautly muscled buttocks rose and fell. Bella hooked her legs behind his knees and then wrapped them around his waist. Her arms were crossed over his back, hands clenched and fingers scrabbling in the resilient flesh. He removed his lips, which had been sucking a nipple up between his teeth, to Bella's mouth.

'Admirable!' Roth said. 'A remarkable performance. A little, well, *uncommited* though. A little lacking in passion, wouldn't you say?'

'You can't have everything,' Raymond Large replied.

The room which Sonia and the Baron had been given was one of the three fitted with two-way mirrors. The deceptive glass in this case was a large gilt-framed mirror, oval in shape, with a carved Victorian eagle at the summit of the curve, which was fixed to the grey and white striped wall at one side of the brass bedstead.

Sonia had been at work for some time when Large and Roth installed themselves in the broom closet which concealed the secret side of the glass. They sat on kitchen chairs between rows of shelves stacked with bottles of cleaning fluid, cans of wax, wadded floorcloths. Brushes and mops stood up-ended in galvanized pails and the airless cubby-hole was pungent with the odours of polishes, lysol and carbolic soap. The padlocked doors of what looked like a wall cupboard in fact opened directly on to the reverse surface of the glass.

'My God,' Roth murmured. 'What a view!'

They were less than ten feet from the bed; they could have been sitting in the room. 'Cost me a fortune,' Large confided. 'It used to be in Les Marroniers, one of the big-time houses in Paris. I was able to get hold of it when they changed from group sex to couples and trios, specializing in diplomats – so discretion became the watchword, and, of course, this kind of thing had to go.'

'Happily for us,' Roth said.

Sonia's white hide suitcase was open on the floor. An armchair and a writing table were strewn with garments fashioned from black mackintosh, straps, chains, lace-up punishment masks and lengths of pink rubber tubing. A thonged whip with a plaited leather handle lay on the bed. Sonia herself was dressed in high-heeled black boots laced to the knee, black satin open-crotch knickers, elbow-length kid gloves and a black leather corset. The nipples of her bare breasts were emphasized with scarlet nail varnish.

The Baron was roped to an upright chair with a rush seat and high back on the far side of the room. Skin-tight black latex clothed him from neck to wrists and ankles, except for two dollar-sized cutouts through which his nipples and the bright metal clips attached to them protruded. His genitals, hauled out through a hole at the crotch, had been crisscrossed with a fine chain and then drawn up high and tight when the chain was clipped to a ring at the front of a deep collar buckled around his neck.

When Large opened the cupboard doors to reveal the two-way mirror, Sonia was standing behind the chair, lacing a severe leather mask over the Baron's head. Clipped to the collar all the way round, the mask was without eye-holes. Two stubby breathing tubes, the inner ends of which had been plugged into the victim's nostrils, projected from the nosepiece; the corners of a chromed gag bit, fastened behind the head with a strap and buckle, emerged from a slit over his mouth. As they watched, Sonia attached a short length of chain to a ring sewn into the crown of the mask and dragged the Baron's head back until the veins in his neck stood out. She padlocked the end of the chain to a crosspiece in the framework of the chair.

Large's face was pressed to the two-way mirror. 'Extraordinary, isn't it,' he said without a trace of irony, 'what some people will do for a thrill!'

A muffled protest had issued from the interior of the mask when the final chain was fastened. Sonia slapped the leather where the Baron's cheek would be. 'Be quiet!' she snapped. 'You should be thankful I didn't thrash you first . . . Now that you're safely out of the way, perhaps *I* can start to have *my* fun.'

She twitched aside a curtain covering an alcove. 'You can come out now,' she said in a peremptory voice. 'Come here. At once. And walk *straight*!'

Dale Fairleigh shuffled from the alcove.

He was barefoot, his ankles chained together so that he could only take very short steps. He was draped in a shiny black mackintosh cape from neck to knee. The masculinity of his handsome features was emphasized by the black rubber bathing cap which flattened and concealed his springy hair, giving his head a more skull-like appearance.

At the same time a certain almost feminine aspect was lent to the ensemble by a thin rubber strap attached to the earpieces of the cap and buckling beneath the chin.

'Stand facing the bed,' Sonia ordered.

'Yes, Mistress.' Dale's voice was higher than his normal baritone, with a slight quaver – of apprehension perhaps? – on the affirmative. He turned, advancing until his knees touched the covers.

'And what will happen now?'

'The slave will be beaten by his mistress.' It was clear that Dale's words formed part of an often-rehearsed ritual.

'Yes indeed,' Sonia said. 'And why will this beating be administered?'

'To demonstrate the superiority – I beg your pardon – the dominance of the female; to underline the inferiority of the male.'

'Exactly.'

She pushed him suddenly, hard, in the small of the back. Dale staggered, then spilled forward over the bed. He lay face down on the mattress with his bare toes just touching the floor.

Sonia stepped forward, picked up the hem of the black cape and folded it back over his waist, exposing his naked buttocks. Between his thighs, the watchers could see that his wrists were handcuffed in front of him and locked to a metal circlet tightly enclosing his genitals.

'Twenty-five strokes, I think,' Sonia said. 'You haven't seen me for months and you must be punished for that neglect.' She reached for the plaited whip.

For the moment there was silence, broken only by Dale's heavy breathing. Sonia trailed the knot at the tip of the leather thongs thoughtfully across his bare flesh. The buttocks hollowed slightly, quivering with anticipation.

She measured her distance, backed off a little, and drew back her arm. 'The slave will count the strokes as usual,' she said.

The whip hissed through the air and cracked across Dale's bottom, raising an instant scarlet weal on the pale skin. His hips jerked violently and he caught his breath. 'One!' he said in a strangled voice.

'One what?'

'One . . . thank you.'

'One, thank you *what*?' Sonia snapped.

'Oh . . . one, thank you, Mistress.'

'That's better.' She raised her arm again. The leather whip whistled down – *Crack!* – across the bared body.

Another galvanic jerk. 'Two, thank you, Mistress.'

The third stroke was harder, a vicious cut which provoked a strangled exclamation from the man on the bed. 'Three . . . Aaah! . . . Thank you, Mistress.'

The three weals, ruler-straight, blazed red on Dale's buttocks. 'If you cry out, I'm going to have to gag you,' Sonia said. 'And then you won't be able to carry out your task later, will you? So you'll have to be punished again . . . *won't you?*'

'Yes, Mistress.' The voice was a stifled gasp.

The fourth stroke fell.

'*Fooouur!* . . . Thank you, Mistress.'

Between the seventh and eighth, noises of protest, half gurgle, half groan, manifested themselves from the far corner. Sonia strode across and released the chain forcing back the Baron's head. 'Very well,' she said. 'But if you utter another sound . . . !' The menace was underlined with a wristy flick of the whip across his exposed genitals. The Baron stiffened, writhing against the ropes. Sonia returned to the bed to continue the beating.

By the fifteenth stroke, Dale's entire bottom was inflamed and the network of raised weals crosshatched the surface with savage stripes. After the twentieth – he was biting the bedclothes, barely able to gasp out the required formula – tiny specks of blood outlined several of the heavier blows and the blue-black shadow of deep bruising already underlay the reddened skin.

'Oh, my!' Sonia laughed. 'We're going to be all the colours of the rainbow tomorrow – black and blue and yellow and purple and I don't know what!' She massaged the lacerated flesh with a gloved hand. 'Anyone would think you actually liked this, wouldn't they?' she mocked. 'After all, it's not as though you complained . . . is it?'

'No, Mistress,' he groaned through gritted teeth.

She stood back to survey her handiwork. 'I think, after all, that maybe that's enough for tonight,' she mused. 'But wait, though – we're on twenty, aren't we? What say we make you come of age, and give you a twenty-first?

Dale said nothing.

'Well?'

'Yes, Mistress, please – a twenty-first.'

She raised her arm high. The whip lashed down as his tortured buttocks clenched, fearing the pain. The leather thongs scorched across the most damaged area of his bottom.

Dale's body convulsed. He uttered a choked cry. He bucked off the bed and twisted completely around, falling onto his back with an iron-hard penis spearing out between his manacled hands.

'There, baby,' Sonia smiled. 'That was a nice little session, wasn't it?'

For the moment, Dale was unable to reply.

When his breathing had quietened, she seized him by the shoulders and dragged him entirely up on to the bed. He lay with his head just in front of the pillows, the muscles of his flanks still shuddering occasionally as an aftermath to the assault on his naked buttocks.

Sonia stripped off the black knickers and climbed on to the bed. She positioned herself with a knee on either side of his head, and squatted over his face. Very slowly, she lowered herself until the face disappeared from view. 'You know what to do,' she said.

For a while no movement was apparent. Then, below the

busk of the laced corset, her bare hips began almost imperceptibly to oscillate back and forth. Her hands vanished between her thighs.

A sudden trembling started within Dale's body. He gave a smothered moan. The trembling turned into a quake, and then a shudder which shook his entire prone frame. His rigid cock seemed virtually to explode.

It bucked and jerked between his handcuffed wrists, pumping out a stream of scalding semen in squirting spasms. By the time these pulsing spurts had died away and the deflated penis subsided, his belly, his chest, and even part of Sonia's back were spattered with the viscous fluid.

'That's a good boy!' she said, clambering off him.

Dale's sister had been given a room on the second floor. She was sitting up in bed, combing her hair, when Séverine, wearing a blue quilted robe, knocked on the door and slipped inside. 'Have you everything you need?' she asked.

'Oh, yes, *thank* you.' Margot's smile was a little wider than she meant. She had taken aboard a lot of wine. 'I'm very, very, very c-c-comf't'ble.'

'You have all the towels you want? Soap? You're warm enough?'

'Abs'lutely.'

'You know, we're awfully grateful. To you and Kirk, I mean. For bringing in the stuff and ferrying it up here. Especially to you – after all, you were the one who had to fall into the sea and all that.'

'That's all right. Not at all. Any time. It was a pl'sure.'

Séverine sat on the bed. 'I hope it will prove . . . more of a pleasure . . . when we use it tomorrow night!'

Margot grinned. 'I'm looking forward to see the . . . to sample . . . to absolutely feel the effects.'

'So am I,' said Séverine, looking her in the eye. She took the girl's hand.

For a moment there was silence. Margot looked away.

'Lovely party,' she said. 'Topping food, nice people. The band was lovely.'

'I'm glad you enjoyed it.'

'Your boss seems jolly nice.'

'He's a good man – an interesting man! – to work for,' Séverine said.

Another silence.

The fingers of Séverine's hand moved, absentmindedly tracing circles on Margot's palm. Without any conscious motivation – fingers are caressing my hand; I will caress them right back – Margot's autonomous response system reacted automatically, the way it always did. Her grasp tightened fractionally. Her thumb smoothed the skin on the back of Séverine's hand.

'I'd been hoping,' Séverine said, 'that we could become friends. You are English but I am from Alsace: I am almost more of a foreigner here than you are. You and I have much more in common than I have with the women in this village. I find I have nothing to say to them at all . . . or they to me. Besides, Margot, I *like* you.'

Margot leaned forward. She reached out her free arm. The comb was still in her hand. With a sudden impulsive gesture, she ran it through Séverine's pale hair. 'You're sweet,' she said.

Séverine caught her lower lip between her teeth. '*I* don't know,' she began. 'Perhaps tomorrow . . .'

'Yes?'

Séverine sighed. She shrugged, releasing Margot's hand. 'Never mind. Meanwhile I have my duties as a hostess to consider.'

'What do you mean?'

Séverine looked down at her lap. 'The Italian,' she said. 'The older man who's so goodlooking, who looks *such* a man—'

'You mean Countess Thingummy's gardener? He dances divinely.'

'Yes, him.'

'What about him?'

'He thinks you're very beautiful. You are very beautiful. But . . .'

'That's lovely. But what?'

'Well . . .' Séverine stood up. She cleared her throat. 'I don't in any way – in any way at all – want to seem as if I'm propositioning you . . . procuring you, I think it's called . . . I don't want to be part of any, well, of any *seduction*. But Geraldo would love to tell you that himself.'

'Then why doesn't he?'

'Because he's timid. A little out of his depth maybe. He feels that, just because this place is called a château, just because you work for someone with a title, he dare not presume.'

'But that's silly,' the English girl protested.

'Yes, it is silly, isn't it? That's what I think. I was wondering, therefore , if perhaps . . .' Séverine paused.

'Yes?'

Séverine swallowed. 'I was wondering if, perhaps, I could tell him it would be all right if he knocked on your door, the way I did, and . . . well, came in to see you?'

Margot shrugged. 'I don't mind,' she said.

Raymond Large and Mondragon Roth squinted through the holes bored in the rococo panelling on the walls of Margot's room, savouring the flowery blandishments with which Geraldo Porrelli declared his undying love . . . and the swiftness with which he slipped between her thighs once he was assured of her passive acceptance of it. In a way she was the perfect foil for his Latin *machismo*: she flattered his ego, she made all the right grateful noises, and she advanced no pesky ideas of her own to interrupt the rhythm of his conquest.

The two men had been drinking from a long-necked bottle

of Napoleon brandy as they made their rounds of the guest-rooms. Now the bottle was empty and they stood on a dark landing, watching – Large with a great deal of surprise – the vineyard manageress at the foot of the stairway leading to Jean-Jacques Ancarani's room. For a long time Séverine hesitated, standing like a statue with one foot on the lowest step. She bit her lip, staring up at the strip of light showing beneath the doorway at the top of the stairs. When the light vanished, she stole up and rapped softly on the panels.

There was no way of seeing into this room – or Séverine's own ('I dare not,' Large confided. 'Either of them would leave me instantly if they found out'). But it was possible to listen from the upper part of the staircase.

They listened.

There was a certain amount of low-pitched dialogue, the words of which were indistinguishable. But this was followed fairly soon by the familiar succession of *ooh*s and *aahs* and creaking bedsprings – an accelerating concerto of heavy breathing and smothered gasps, spiced with a cadenza of yelps and groans before the hectic final movement and the diminishing cries succeeding it.

'Splendid, splendid!' Roth whispered. 'Most refreshing. It's like listening to steam radio after going to the movies!'

Back downstairs, he put an arm around Large's shoulders. 'My dear fellow,' he said. 'How can I thank you? A magnificent evening, full of marvellous surprises! I find myself enormously stimulated.' He licked his lips. 'But if you don't mind, I think I really must get back to my own room now and retire to bed. My *fervent* thanks again.'

Large smiled. 'My pleasure,' he said truthfully. For the biggest surprise of all had remained a secret. This was that the third and last two-way mirror was above an antique dressing-table in Roth's own room.

Below stairs

Kirkpatrick Munroe and Seamus O'Reilly had missed out on the pairing – and indeed the coupling – which seemed, like a kind of natural osmosis, to draw the party guests upstairs once the band had stopped playing and been sent home. This was because the Irishman had roped Kirk in to play the Canon Chasuble part in the Wilde skit, and it had been necessary to brief him and explain the couple of handwritten pages detailing his part. Somewhat ruefully, the two men were now helping Lusty and Busty, the Parisienne waitresses, to clear up the buffet and transport used crockery to the kitchens.

'At least,' Kirk said thankfully, carrying in a tray loaded with plates and half-filled glasses and dishes of uneaten food, 'there's no bloody washing-up to do! Séverine told me a woman comes in tomorrow morning to handle that.'

'Washing-up, boyo,' Seamus said, 'is a state of mind. Think of it as a chore, and it takes for ever. Forget that, and it's quickly done, sure. Mind you,' he added, picking up a bottle with some champagne still in it, 'the state of mind's one I'm happy not to be in this minnit.' He raised the neck of the bottle to his lips.

Lusty and Busty – their real names were Agathe and Dominique – finished stacking plates in one of the deep stone sinks. 'Would you suppose,' Busty said conversationally to Lusty, 'that it was Monsieur the Irish or Monsieur the English who had been favoured with the most impressive equipment?'

'Impossible to say,' Agathe replied, looking over her shoulder, 'under the present conditions.'

'True. You would agree, though, that the speculation is an interesting one given that in all other respects – charm, masculinity, good looks and such imperatives – they are equal?'

'Undoubtedly.'

'It would be interesting,' the buxom girl said, 'if some means could be found to settle the question.'

'Indeed.'

'Pure measurement, of course – even if it could be effected – would be useless.'

'Naturally. It is not so much the *state* of the equipment that counts, but rather the manner in which it is used.'

'Precisely,' Dominique agreed, switching her gaze from the Irishman's robust figure to Kirk's slim hips. She untied the tapes of her white apron and removed it.

'You know something,' Seamus said to the yacht skipper, 'I have the feeling, just the tiniest wee hint of a suspicion, that these dear ladies *might* just conceivably be after makin' – what shall I say? – certain suggestions not unconnected with ourselves.'

'That's odd,' Kirk said, deciding to play in the same key. 'I was beginning to arrive at the same conclusion myself. What a coincidence.'

Seamus grimaced and set down the bottle. 'Flat,' he announced. 'Which is more than I can say for herself here,' glancing at the expanse of bosom the loss of the apron had revealed.

'Such matters,' Agathe, the slender one, continued as if the two men hadn't spoken, 'must necessarily be resolved pragmatically. Empirically would perhaps be a more suitable term.'

'Exactly. Such judgements can at best be subjective.'

'There is of course one method which would permit us to form at least an interim evaluation,' Agathe said.

'You mean . . . to transfer this of the equipment from the realms of theory to those of the practical?'

'I do. Such a course, however, would require the cooperation of these gentlemen. If,' Agathe added with a neat use of the subjunctive, 'the gentlemen were to be so inclined.'

'As an idea, that is admirable,' Dominique said warmly. 'There is nevertheless a possible flaw.'

'Namely?'

'For the comparison to be truly representative – as nearly impartial as it would be possible to get . . .'

'Under the circumstances.'

'. . . under the circumstances – it would be necessary, even vital, that each of us should have knowledge of both of them.'

'Or, to put it another way, that both of us should have knowledge of each of them.'

'I was under the impression that this was what I had said.'

'Perhaps. In any case your stipulation can be met – and a status of *primus inter pares* thereafter established – by the application of simple mathematics.'

'If the gentlemen were so inclined.'

'If indeed the gentlemen were so inclined.' Agathe, followed by Dominique, turned and looked inquiringly at the two men.

'Inclined? I'll shag the fuckin' arse off you, you saucy bitch!' Seamus said to the busty one.

'Provided there's a mirror,' Kirk told Lusty.

'There's a pier glass you can turn any way you want,' she said.

Kirk looked at Seamus. The Irishman nodded. 'We're in business,' Kirk said. 'If you ladies would be so kind . . .' He gestured towards the open doorway.

The maidservants' room was above the old coach-house. It was effectively two enormous alcoves, each containing a bed, a dressing table and a wardrobe, separated by a partition pierced by a wide archway. There was therefore a certain amount of privacy, although conversation in low voices was perfectly feasible between the two parts. A fairly modern bathroom had been built out above the stable yard on the far side of a passageway at the top of the stairs.

Neither Seamus nor Kirk was worried, by that time, about privacy.

Through an increasingly agreeable alcoholic mist, the yacht skipper lurched to the pier glass on its castored stand, turning that and then tilting the long mirror so that it reflected the best possible view of the bed. By the time he had it positioned to his satisfaction, Lusty was naked.

She had a strange but curiously sensual body. This was partly due to contrasts – wide hips and a fleshy bottom against very little bust; a dancer's muscular legs against slender, graceful arms – and partly due to her expression. Her angular face at first seemed inscrutable, the eyes virtually expressionless, neither warm nor cold, hard nor soft – as impersonal in fact as the formal, third-person 'butler's French' in which she and her colleague had so decorously suggested outrageous behaviour. There remained nevertheless a hint of humour in the wry twist to her thin-lipped mouth. And something else, deep in the unfathomable depths of those eyes, which was not at first apparent; some secret motivation responsible for the narrowed nostrils, the coiled-spring tenseness of the muscles on either side of her jaw.

The motivation, Kirk realised soon enough, was lust.

Of course it was! With that nickname, he should have realized at once!

She was already lying flat out, with her legs spread wide. Kirk ripped off his own clothes and climbed up beside her. The 'randy old goat' of the Golfe Juan yacht basin had drawn a high card. Ignoring as usual the niceties of foreplay, so-called, he found at once that he had been dealt a fellow enthusiast. It was evident the moment he dropped between her thighs and rammed it in: as he turned his head towards the pier glass, he saw that Lusty was already looking that way herself.

It was perfect, the beginning of a beautiful friendship: he loved to watch himself fucking; she adored to watch herself being fucked.

She wrapped her legs around him and, without taking her eyes from the mirror, favoured him with a satisfied, humming purr as he began plunging in and out.

Was there something just a little bit egotist and narcissistic about these two sophisticates hugely satisfied with their own reflections? The concept was as far away from Kirk's mind as the more extravagant, extrovert sounds coming from the other side of the archway.

Dominique had moved fast, and smoothly for such a large person, once she and Seamus were relatively alone. She ripped open his fly before he could utter a word, yanked his flannels down to his ankles, stripped off the tweed jacket and unbuttoned the red shirt. 'You can do the rest yourself,' she said, hauling the skirt of her black dress up over her hips.

'Remove me shirt and step out of me trews? All on me own?' Seamus complained blearily. 'Ah, well . . . into each life a little rain must fall!'

Dominique didn't hear him. She was pulling her dress over her head.

If Lusty had been accurately nicknamed, the soubriquet for Busty – which was based on characteristics that were somewhat more evident – was equally apposite. Her pear-shaped breasts hung heavily down as she cast away the dress and removed a tent-like undergarment. Her voluminous knickers were thrust out by a generous curve of belly, the wide, lace-fringed legs filled by impressive thighs.

'Yon Agathe hath a lean and hungry look!' Seamus misquoted in his stentorian 'theatrical' voice. 'Let me have women about me who are fat.' He moved, naked now, towards her with outstretched hands. 'If Julius can seize 'er, don't blame us if she's handled by Seamus!'

'Fat,' Busty said severely, 'is not a word that I accept. Big, yes; large if you like; buxom certainly; well-upholstered at a pinch – but fat no.'

'My apologies. Forgive me. I know not what I say,' Seamus boomed. 'See, I abase myself before your slender self.' He dropped to his knees and buried his face momentarily in the soft mass of her belly.

'Maybe you feel I come on a little too strong,' she said, smiling down at

He shook his head. 'Better by far,' he said, 'than the brozen flonde on the ictic arse.'

'*Pardon?*'

'The frozen blonde on the arctic ice,' Seamus explained. 'A private version of Middle English – only quoted because that's my chore, sir.'

'*Pardon?* I do not quite . . . ?'

'Let's fuck,' Seamus said.

He tore down the knickers, picked her up, and threw her on the bed. As she laughed, partly in surprise, partly with pleasure, he slapped her playfully on one buttock, palmed the insides of her thighs to spread her legs wide and lowered his husky body on top of her.

The engorged tip of his stiffened penis parted hair and nosed aside flesh. He flexed his hips, pushing hard . . . and caught his breath as a fiery heat slid along the shaft, swallowing it whole.

Dominique rotated her belly slowly, stirring herself with his wand. Slowly she lifted her hips as he began moving in and out of her with long, purposeful strokes. The mounds of flesh squashed beneath his chest moved sexily between them each time he lunged and withdrew. Rivulets of sweat ran from her breasts to her belly as they clasped and squirmed.

'That's my girl!' Seamus said thickly, slapping her again. 'Himself in there will have a hard job of it, following this!'

The big girl giggled, thrusting up at him more forcefully each time he pinned her to the mattress.

From the window of his den in the château tower, Raymond Large looked down, across the yard and in through a window of the apartment above the coach-house. A gap between the curtains allowed him to see the two naked bodies, the two moving bodies, locked together on the bed. He smiled. A most successful evening: everything, but everything, was now going exactly according to plan.

The picnic

Sunday morning in the vineyard, only a week before the vintage, was as busy as any other morning – the workers occupied from first light among the neatly planted rows, the tall tractor rumbling from terrace to terrace, harvest carts being readied outside the *chais*.

Séverine and Jean-Jacques were down there early. They had slept soundly, if only for a short time, after the hectic bout of lovemaking on which Raymond Large and his most important guest had eavesdropped. Large himself and his invited friends did not appear until later.

A Mistral had sprung up not long before dawn, stammering the shutters all over the château, tossing the branches of acacia trees in the park, blowing leaves and flower heads and spirals of dust skittering across the terrace. Swept clear by the blustering wind, the sky was a burnished blue by the time Lusty and Busty served breakfast outside the open French windows of the drawing-room. Below the balustrade, gnarled Roman olive trees leaned away from the powerful gusts.

Over coffee, orange juice and fresh rolls from the village, the members of the house party planned their day. Seamus, Kirk and Dale Fairleigh were to remain indoors with Bella and Séverine, rehearsing the Wilde skit which was to open the evening's festivities. Mark Harries, who by now knew the property well, was to take the others to the far end of the estate for a picnic lunch. First, though, he and his employer had business to discuss, with Mondragon Roth as an interested observer.

Mark produced a series of sketches and plans on a large clipboard. 'If you were to do away with the wall and these gates,' he said as he led them out of the yard, 'you could have a vista, a grassy ride leading across the flat parkland and up that slight rise to a baroque pavilion on the skyline. We'd have to cut down a few trees and add some more, but once it was done the eye would be led to that focal point from every window in the ground-floor reception rooms.'

And later: 'This is all secondary woodland, a mess of thickets and copses adding nothing visually. If you scrap the lot and clear the ground, here where the stream turns east and you have a north-facing bank, we could design a white garden like the one at Sissinghurst – facing the orange grove on the other side of the water.'

He was equally positive on the vineyard side of the château. 'A walled Dutch garden on this terrace . . . a tropical shrubbery on the southern slope . . . a summer-house – wood, I think – looking out over a rose garden here. Below the balustrade, classical figures and urns, with a double-S herbaceous border planted so there'd be flowers all the year round.'

Large was impressed. 'I think you'll find you have a contract to sign here,' he said. And Roth added: 'Once the roof's done and the walls are fixed, you got yourself a show-place here, Ray. Shit, you could charge folks to come in and look around!'

When the tour was finished, the three men strolled down to see Séverine and Jean-Jacques Ancarani and explore the business side of the property.

'It's always been a bit of a mystery to me,' Mark said to Séverine, '*exactly* how wine is made. I mean everyone knows wine is fermented grape juice, but how it ferments and what happens between picking and bottling, frankly that's a closed book to me.'

'If you have the rest of the day to spare,' Séverine smiled, 'maybe I could explain at least some of it to you! Basically, though, what happens is that once the grapes are crushed and the skins broken, yeasts living on the outside of the fruit start to *work*, as we call it, converting the sugar in the pulp to alcohol and carbon dioxide. When that process is over, presto! – you have wine. Of a sort. But it needs a lot more treatment before it's drinkable.'

'Yes, that explains the fermentation chemically,' Mark said. 'But what do you actually *do*, here in this plant?' He looked around the yard.

'Once the grapes are picked,' Séverine said, 'we feed them into a machine called an *égrappoir*, a crusher and stemmer, which separates and rejects the stalks. The juice is then pumped into fermenting vats.' She indicated a long, low building behind them, with huge cylindrical containers visible through an open door. 'When the sugar has all been converted, what we call the "free run" wine is siphoned off and the skins crushed once more in a hydraulic press. This produces about a fifth of the whole quantity, a dark, rather harsh wine which is added to the original run-off. Finally the mixture is transferred to cement *cuves* – in that shed with the shallow roof – where it remains all winter.'

Séverine turned to point at the first-year *chai*. 'The wine is moved there early the following year, after it has undergone a secondary fermentation and lost its sediment. We store it there for twelve months in oak hogsheads. Then it's moved again to make room for the next vintage. In the second-year *chai*' – she gestured to the far side of the yard – 'the wine is racked in *barriques* holding the equivalent of twenty-four dozen bottles. The actual bottling takes place after that second year, some here, some by shippers in Nice or Marseille.'

'That's just an *outline*,' Raymond Large said. 'There are many complex intermediate stages, most of them concerned with the quality of the final product. You know – sugar content, alcoholic strength, sulphur dioxide as a disinfectant, pumping of the fermenting juice over the floating skins, all these have to be constantly controlled. To say nothing of the actual taste!' He smiled. 'That's where our *Maître de Chai*, Jean-Jacques here, comes in with his hydrometer and his gauges and his racking techniques.'

'Maybe you'd like to make a tour of the different installations?' Ancarani suggested. 'Then I could explain the function of the gear as we come to it.'

Roth and Mark Harries nodded. 'Lay it on me,' the American said.

Later, after a ceremonial tasting of the new wine in the second-year *chai*, they returned to the château.

Séverine had gone back earlier to supervise the packing of the picnic lunch, which was to be carried by the men in the party in wicker anglers' creels converted for that purpose and supported by shoulder straps.

Mark led the party away just before midday. Including him, there were twelve of them, the Baron having cried off with the excuse that he was feeling fatigued (which was hardly surprising, considering that he spent much of the previous day bound and gagged beneath the seat of a railway carriage, and most of the night tied into an upright chair).

Dill Jones, Geraldo, Michel, Tony Hill and Roth himself completed the male contingent. The distaff side was represented by Doll, Margot, Sonia and Maguy Blondin, with Lorraine and the Countess bringing up the rear.

By the time they left the Mistral had settled down to a steady pressure blowing relentlessly from the west, flattening the meadow grasses, tilting the serried ranks of vines on their terraces, and whining through the telegraph wires between the château and the village. Beneath the trees, when they reached them, there was a continuous surf of windblown branches and creaking boughs.

On the far side of the wood, a narrow path zigzagged

down a steep, scrub-covered slope to the stream, half hidden here below banks of shingle washed down from the limestone bluffs inland. 'I'm trying to persuade Mr Large to have this bank cultivated,' Mark said to Roth. 'A cherry orchard, perhaps. It would be picturesque in the spring, when the blossom is out and there's more water in the brook.'

'I guess so.' Roth looked around, shading his eyes against the glare of the sun. 'Yeah, I reckon you got something there. Is there no way you could make use of the stream itself? I mean like a water garden or whatever?'

Mark nodded. 'Nearer the château, down below the orange grove. There's a wide bend with an ox-bow that could be turned into an ornamental pond with fountains and a water-clock and maybe some statuary. Further upstream, where we shall be having lunch, there's a series of spectacular natural pools, which we shall leave just the way they are . . . except perhaps for an arbour and a stairway cut from the rock, leading down from above.'

It was another half hour before they reached the pools – thirty minutes of fairly hard going, beneath overhanging willows, across a swampy patch where the path vanished, and along a slant of bare rock at the foot of which the water had carved out a channel for itself.

There were satisfactory exclamations and gasps of pleasure when the party broke through a final screen of broom and found themselves face to face with the chosen spot. The site was impressive. The stream, flowing more swiftly here, tumbled over three rock ledges in delicate cascades, swirling afterwards into four pools hollowed from the limestone, the last of which was still, clear, quite deep and about twenty yards across. A natural amphitheatre bordered by acacia trees surrounded the place, and there were areas of flat rock between the pools where it would be easy to lay out a picnic meal.

Out of the wind in the limestone-floored depression, the sun was very hot. Roth and the Countess preferred to sit in the shade, so Mark organized the party around a horizontal outcrop which could serve as a table, on one side of the largest pool. Here the American and his hostess could install themselves beneath the acacias on comfortable, water-smoothed boulders while the others lay around on the rocky shelf nearby.

The men unpacked their creels. Bottles of wine were lowered into the water on lengths of string; wafer-thin slices of mountain ham, duck and hare pâtés, stuffed eggs and a terrine of guinea-fowl with apricots covered the improvised table along with the cheeses, butter, green *roquette* salad and bread rolls at the shady end of the outcrop.

For a long time, as the guests ate and drank, the conversation was desultory. The upper branches of the acacias stirred in the wind. Water splashed and gurgled. Birds sang. A vivid blue-green dragonfly darted from pool to pool in the shafts of sunlight penetrating the glade.

After the thermos coffee, however – and a particularly delicious selection of feather-light *friandes* specially baked by Séverine – the party, sated and happy, livened up considerably.

It was Lorraine who set the ball rolling. She was lolling beside the water, resting on one elbow, a large percentage of the famous breasts visible between the edges of a striped ticking shirt open almost to the waist. From there on down, she was hidden by the voluminous folds of jade-green beach pyjamas. 'Hot, hot, hot!' she murmured drowsily. 'This pool here is broadcasting an invitation little Lorraine ain't gonna be able to resist!' She levered herself to her feet, undid the last button of the shirt and shrugged it off. The brassière beneath it was cut very low.

'But, honey,' Dagmar ven den Bergh protested in mock horror, 'you *don't* have a swimming costume with you!'

'One hundred and forty million movie-goers all over the world have already seen all but three percent of me,' Lorraine said. 'And those are folks I don't even know, for

God's sake!' She looked around the glade and smiled. 'Shit, what's three percent among friends?' she said. She unclipped the brassière and took it off. Then she stepped out of the pyjama bottom and kicked away her sandals.

For a moment she stood at the edge of the pool, naked as the day she was born – rather more naked, if the truth were to be told, Tony Hill thought, eyeing the prominent breasts and the lush swell of her hips and bottom – and then she dove in, leaving scarcely a ripple on the surface. She emerged on the far side, treading water to shake the drops from her hair. '*Icy!*' she gasped. 'But, God, how refreshing! Now, who's going to join me?'

'I'm game,' Doll Jones said at once. 'I could do with a dip after the walk and all that delicious food!' She stripped off her own skirt and halter top, pushed down a pair of tight-fitting knickers with elasticated legs and waist, and walked unconcernedly to the water's edge. She turned her back on the pool, threw herself into a handspring and executed a back somersault which landed her smack in the centre with a splash that reached everyone in the glade.

Amid the feminine shrieks and male guffaws following this, Lorraine shouted: 'Swell. But what about the guys? Come on kids – are you men or mice? Ain't nobody gonna keep us gals company in this here bath?'

Mark Harries and Tony were already stripping off. Michel Blondin glanced at his wife, who shook her head firmly. Dill Jones appeared to be asleep, and Geraldo, the Italian gardener, was repacking the remains of lunch and affected not to hear.

'I suppose we could go in wearing our underpants,' Michel began doubtfully. But he was shushed by a basilisk glare from Maguy and a shout from the Countess: 'Don't be bloody silly! There's nobody here, I promise you, who hasn't seen a man's cock before! Go on, Michel: let's see what you have to offer.'

The young Frenchman nevertheless remained hesitant,

glancing once more at his wife. Mark was sitting on the edge of the pool, with his feet in the cold, still water. As Tony Hill, naked now, prepared to dive, he lowered himself slowly in. They swam across to the two girls.

Mondragon Roth, enormous in a lemon-yellow silk shirt, white duck trousers and a panama hat, was leaning across to whisper in Dagmar van den Bergh's ear. The Countess laughed, nodding her russet head. 'Margot, dear,' she called, 'you're a wet-bob, aren't you? Why don't you cool off and join the girls too?'

Margot looked up from the creels she was helping the Italian to pack. She shrugged. 'I don't mind,' she said. She began to unbutton her blouse.

Dill Jones meanwhile had woken up, undressed and moved towards the pool. 'Oh, no!' Lorraine screamed. 'Not that! If you bring that weapon in here, the pool will overflow and we shall all be drowned!'

Dill grinned. He took his huge penis in one hand, ran to the water's edge, wrapped his free arm around his knees as he leaped . . . and landed, in a sitting position, showering all the bathers and most of the others with sheets of white water.

There was a lot of laughter and splashing now as the naked bathers frolicked from one side of the pool to the other. Lorraine was giggling continuously, the big breasts buoyed up by the current. Dill sat like a Buddha beneath the waterfall in the pool above. Michel had wandered off among the trees.

Some time afterwards – curiously, nobody seemed to have noticed the actual passage of time – the components of the party had re-arranged themselves once more. Sonia was lying on her back asleep, with one arm shielding her eyes from the sun ('My profession,' she had confided to the Countess, 'is a tiring one if it is to be followed with any kind of integrity or pride in the work.' 'I know, dear,' Dagmar had replied. 'All those knots have to be *un*tied as well, don't they? No wonder you welcome a rest!').

Mark and Lorraine had remained in the pool long after the others had emerged to dry themselves, standing very close together, each with hands on the other's hips, bobbing up and down in an oddly compulsive rhythm. There was a lot of laughter, and from time to time they kissed in a lazy, languorous fashion, with much probing of tongues and the sucking of lips into eager mouths. Now they had moved to the first and shallowest of the pools. Half hidden in the iridescent spray blown by the Mistral from the cascade, Lorraine stood at the edge, her legs spread and the water up to her knees, leaning forward to rest her chin on arms folded along the rocky lip. Mark was immediately behind her, knees slightly bent, hands cradling the big, wet, pendant breasts below her ribs. The muscles of his sturdy bottom contracted and relaxed as he drove his thick cock in and out between the buttocks quivering beneath him.

Geraldo Porrelli, who had finally been persuaded to undress and bathe, sat naked on a grassy bank ten feet away, quietly masturbating as he watched the lascivious antics of the couple in the pool. 'Don't waste it all, lover,' Lorraine called suddenly, raising her head to glance at the hairy torso above his moving right hand. 'I may have use for you again when this sexy beau has shot his delicious load!'

Roth was standing at the downstream limit of the depression. He was holding a pair of Zeiss binoculars to his eyes. 'I can't imagine why you want to weigh yourself down with those,' Dagmar had said when he slung the heavy leather carrying-case over his shoulder before they left the château. 'The picnic place, according to Séverine, is in a hollow, completely surrounded by thickets of birch and willow and acacia.'

'Ah,' the American had replied with a sly grin, 'but it's what may go on in *among* those trees that interests me!'

Both the interest and the forethought were now being rewarded.

Between a nimbus of out-of-focus leaves, a small grassy clearing assembled itself with stark precision in the circular field as Roth adjusted the knurled control between the twin barrels of the instrument. The scene revealed could have illustrated a Greek pastorale – a naked nymph with two attendant fauns.

To be more precise still, the characters involved in this sylvan idyll were Doll Jones, her husband, and a slightly reluctant Michel Blondin. The young Frenchman's clothes lay in a discarded heap at one side of the glade.

Roth uttered a soft crow of delight. He would have been happier still if he had been able to hear the dialogue in this particular scenario.

'Come on, old fellow,' Dill Jones was saying. 'We all do it . . . and I'm not exaggerating: I do mean all. We live a very free existence, the wife and I. All our friends too. Why confine yourself to a single joy when so many are – if you'll excuse the phrase – at hand?'

Michel looked confused. He spread his hands helplessly, sharing guilty looks between his half-erect penis and the nude figure of Doll, who was sitting on the grass. 'I don't know,' he said. 'I mean . . . well, of course, naturally I would want to . . . would love to. But . . .' This time he looked over his shoulder.

'There's no reason why she should know,' Dill said swiftly. 'In any case, she is being . . . well looked after, I can promise you!'

Michel bit his lip. 'Well . . .'

'You can see Doll wants you to,' her husband pursued. 'Wants both of us, in fact.' He flicked her a meaning look. She rolled half on to her back, supporting herself on her elbows, with one leg slightly bent. Between her thighs, the tuft of dark pubic hair was gashed by pink labia, partly open already and crowned by a translucent pearl of moisture. She smiled, gazing fixedly at Michel's tumescent prick. The tip of her tongue appeared, wetting her upper lip. He stared wordlessly at the husband. In spite of himself, he was growing harder every second.

'Anyway you, the French, have a word for it, a proverb indeed! *Jamais deux sans trois*, isn't that right? Never two without a third!'

'I thought that only applied to disasters,' Michel said with a flash of humour.

'There'll be no disasters here, only joys. Won't there, darling?' Dill assured him. She nodded, reaching a hand out towards Michel's genitals.

On the edge of the wood, Roth swore. The unfocused leaves were threshing violently, blurring the view of the glade. A large bird, which had just taken off from a nearby branch, flapped heavily away among the treetops.

By the time the image in the disc shown by the field-glasses was clear again, Michel was lowering himself between Doll's legs and Dill was bent over, straddling her head with a knee planted on either side.

Roth saw the young woman's body stiffen and then arch up off the grass as Michel plunged his now rigid staff into her. He began easing himself in and out of her belly in a slowly accelerating rhythm. Her legs scissored over his back; her hands reached for her husband's balls and her mouth stretched to its widest extent to close over the tip of his giant penis.

Roth watched for a few minutes and then moved away. He was smiling. He strolled to the opposite side of the hollow and himself moved in among the trees. Between the young trunks of saplings, about thirty yards higher up the steep bank, a screen of low bushes was moving. He could hear the rustle of dry undergrowth, the snap of an occasional twig and the sound of laboured breathing. He soft-footed towards the bushes, treading carefully on dead leaves.

'That's right: push them down, right down!' The hoarse voice was Tony Hill's. 'Over the knees and down to the ankles. Now step out of them . . . Pull up the skirt. Up over your hips and hold it there . . . Now turn around, bend over – further than that! – and let me look at your hairy cunt and the little arsehole between the cheeks of your bum.'

There was a short silence. And then Hill's measured tones: 'Now I'm going to shove this into you, right up you . . . *now!*'

A sharp intake of breath. A stifled gasp. Roth parted two small branches. Beyond the screen of bushes, Margot Fairleigh, naked from the waist down, was bent double like a croquet hoop, grasping a tree stump with both hands as her contorted body shook to the repeated assaults of Hill's pistoning cock. Hill leaned back a little from the hips as he fucked, his hands spreading the blonde girl's buttocks wide, his eyes fixed on the lewd spectacle of his own dark-fleshed staff vanishing and re-appearing between the lips of her shamelessly exposed cunt.

Roth sank soundlessly down on to his haunches behind the bushes. He was too near to use the field-glasses, but he was unwilling to risk being seen by one or the other if he continued to peer at them through the leaves. Now that he had the image fixed in his mind, he would content himself with the sound effects so generously contributed by the hardworking, breathless couple.

In the glade, Dagmar called across to Maguy Blondin, who was lying some distance away on the far side of the pool: 'You're losing the sun there, my dear. The shadows of all those leaves blowing in the breeze! Why don't you come over here where it's still hot?'

A little reluctantly, Maguy pushed herself to her feet, skirted the rock basin and jumped across the stream running out of it. She was, if the truth was told, a little afraid of the Countess, with her age and experience and socialite sophistication. And of course her reputation. But although she would really rather have kept her distance, she wasn't herself sufficiently strongwilled to cross the older woman.

The Countess was still sitting on her smooth boulder. The

only place in the sun that was flat enough to lie on comfortably was a stretch of bare rock at her feet. Maguy lay down and closed her eyes.

'Such a blessing, the warmth,' Dagmar said. 'One does so miss the sun in Paris. I remember, when I lived there, how much I used to look forward to my visits here in the South.'

Maguy nodded.

'You want to let it get to you as much as possible,' Dagmar pursued. 'Especially when you are here for such a short time. Sunshine is such a tonic for the skin.'

Maguy smiled, without opening her eyes. She said nothing.

'You have such pretty legs. Why don't you allow the sun to see them all? Even a little tan is better than none. If you pulled that skirt up around your hips . . .'

Maguy caught her breath. Her eyes flew open. The Countess had leaned down, grasped the hem of her flowered cotton skirt and twitched it up in a single fluid movement as far as her waist. The back of the flared skirt was still anchored to the rock by her buttocks, but the front was now raised as high as a can-can dancer's, exposing her pink silk knickers.

'There!' the Countess said. 'That's better, isn't it?'

Her eyes, glinting green in the afternoon light, smiled warmly. The wide mouth curved into a conspiratorial smile. Maguy knew she ought to protest. The woman, a person she hardly knew, had no right – no right at all – to . . . but somehow the words never came out: the tingling warmth of the sun, a certain light-headed, almost dizzy feeling which was nevertheless curiously reassuring, the sudden heaviness, equally comfortable, of her limbs . . . all these things combined to make it seem, frankly, well hardly worthwhile to speak at all, let alone complain.

'You have such a shapely bosom,' said the Countess. 'Why not let that, too, enjoy the warmth of this splendid afternoon?' Once more she bent forward. In a trice the buttons of Maguy's cream blouse were undone.

'No, not a word!' – Maguy, half sitting up, had opened her mouth this time to remonstrate – 'Let us not be sidetracked by false modesty. You show much more of yourself than this every time you go on a beach to bathe. Who, in any case, is going to complain? Your husband? Where is he at this moment?'

'He . . . he went for a walk with the English journalist and his wife.'

'Exactly. Sonia is fast asleep. Lorraine and the landscape gardener are still behaving outrageously around the topmost pool. To all intents and purposes we are alone here until the others return from their explorations. So why this sudden timidity?'

Maguy's bust bodice fastened with a clip between the two cups. Before there was time for a reply to Dagmar's question, she leaned down for the third time and swiftly undid this. The blonde Parisienne's breasts sprang free.

'You have no need, none whatever, to feel shy,' the Countess said with severity. 'You are a very attractive young woman. Concealing your charms lessens you in the eyes of everyone – not least yourself. No, let me continue' – Maguy had started again to speak – 'the first and most important step on the road to self-assurance is *knowledge* of the self. And knowledge of the self, so the psychologists tell us, starts with knowledge of the body. How well do you know yours, my dear?'

Maguy lay silent and wide-eyed, staring up at Dagmar as if mesmerized.

'You will of course be aware,' Dagmar said, 'of the exquisite pleasure which can be derived from these delectably firm little mounds' – Maguy repressed a shiver, a thrill of excitement as the back of the Countess's hand brushed against one of her bared nipples – 'but do you realize the *extent* of the pleasure, the self-determination, the built-in satisfaction you can experience through open, deliberate attention paid to those parts by your own loving self?' She paused for an instant and then added very softly: 'Or to those . . . other parts . . . lower down?'

Maguy's mouth opened again, but no words emerged.

'Put your hand on your belly and slide the fingers under the waistband of your knickers,' the Countess said.

'Oh, no, Madame . . . really. I couldn't. Don't make me – I couldn't!' Maguy's inhibitions found a voice at last.

'*Do what you are told!*' Roth's voice thundered from behind them.

He had appeared unexpectedly at the edge of the wood. And, as happens so frequently when a direct command is made with sufficient authority, the subject of the order obeyed instantly, automatically and without question.

Palm flat on the smooth curve of belly, Maguy lifted the elasticated waistband with her fingertips and slid the whole hand then beneath it.

'Reach down into the pubic hair,' the Countess said. 'Touch yourself. Feel the lips. Are they tender? Are they soft and folded? Creased? Stroke them, part them, lower your middle finger between them. Are they *wet*?'

Roth said: 'Open those lips; stretch them wide. Plunge one finger, two fingers, *three* fingers inside. Bunch those fingers together and push them as far up your hot vagina as you can. Now bring them back and find the little button. Is it stiffening, is it erect like a tiny cock? Then frig it with your own fingers. Massage it, caress it, feel it sliding, slippery, wet and lovely. Go on – touch yourself, feel yourself, finger yourself, *love* yourself!' He paused, breathing heavily. And then: 'That's right, you slut, you dirty little bitch – *toss yourself off!*'

Maguy squirmed and writhed on the smooth, hard rock. She rolled her hips from side to side, the knuckles of her slaving, salacious hand thrusting out the thin stuff of the knickers as she probed and stroked. Small mewing groans escaped from her lolling mouth. Her rubbery nipples were swollen and stiff. A dark patch stained the silk at her crotch.

Soon, without being told to, she moved her other hand in under the waistband, down through the damp hairs to her voracious, blazing cunt.

When Mark Harries and Lorraine, dressed now and decent, made their way down from the upper basin, the sun had vanished behind a sinister cloudbank blowing up from the west and the trees threshed as noisily as waves on a reef under the furious onslaught of the wind.

Maguy's knickers had been dragged down to her knees. The knees were raised and tilted apart. At the base of her naked belly, tense fingers held wide the flaring lips of her cunt, lewdly gaping amongst the matted hair furring her loins. And between those lips the Countess's expert fingers worked frenziedly at the girl's exposed clitoris, mashing it against the pubic bone while her hips arched ferociously up to meet that raping, masturbating hand.

Roth was squatting down behind the girl's head, leaning over her, tweaking her inflamed nipples, pulling them up and out to shift the taut, firm breasts on her heaving chest. 'Come, baby,' he crooned. 'Let yourself go and come, come, come . . . You're being violated, you're being finger-fucked: these hands are punishing your tits and your cunt to make you come whether you want to or not . . .'

Maguy no longer knew where she was – or who she was. She was lost in a world where nothing existed but sensation. Her hands clenched and unclenched, stretching the labia wide, wide. The mewling groans had changed into sobbing grunts. Saliva ran from a corner of her mouth.

'Aaaaaah!' she screamed as the shuddering, quaking spasms started to convulse her somewhere deep inside. 'Oh, God! Oh, Jesus! Oh, Christ, I can't . . . I don't want – *Ohhhhh!*'

Sonia, wakened by the noise, had strolled up to watch. 'I rather think,' she said, exchanging a glance with the Countess, 'that I may have another client for tonight!'

A Night to Remember

Afternoon tea was served a little late that Sunday. The party returning from the picnic had been caught in a sudden heavy shower while they were crossing a stretch of rocky hillside covered only by a *garrigue* of heather and cistus with an occasional clump of broom. By the time they scampered back through the château gates still full of good humour and giggles, they were all soaked to the skin. When they had queued for one or other of the château's three bathrooms, washed off the rain with hot water, changed and returned to the big drawing-room which opened on to the terrace, the high spirits seemed more pronounced than ever. Only the Blondins appeared a little reluctant to join in the general merriment – Maguy for once remaining at a distance from her husband with a certain unwillingness to meet his eye; Michel for his part renouncing, at least for the moment, his new-found dominance.

Mondragon Roth and the Countess were perhaps less effusive than the others, but their sly, secretly exchanged smiles were charged with a wealth of complicity.

In any case, the overall atmosphere of barely contained hilarity was in no way diminished during the tea party – the Lapsang Suchong accompanied by more of Séverine's prized *friandes* – or the drinks in the ballroom which followed. The savoury cocktail canapés here were especially well received.

Seamus O'Reilly's all-star production of the Wilde skit was scheduled for seven thirty and designed to bridge the gap between cocktails and a formal dinner served by Lusty and Busty in the château's heavily panelled baronial dining hall.

'Ideally,' Raymond Large had told Seamus, 'I'd like it to last around half an hour. Just enough to start their minds working along sexy lines, but not long enough to make anyone restless. You can go as far as you like, be as outrageous as you wish . . . verbally. But I don't want any fucking on stage. The idea is to titillate, to start the fantasies forming, but no more. The action, if there is any, should then arise naturally after a good dinner in the more intimate atmosphere of the baronial hall. There's too much space, and it's too impersonal anyway, in the ballroom.'

He had said nothing to the Irishman about the laced canapés and *friandes*. Nobody but Séverine, Margot and Kirk, who had supplied the hashish, knew anything about that aspect of the party, not even Roth or the Countess.

There were no curtains to close off the small raised platform on which the band had played the previous night, but Séverine had produced two Chinese tapestry screens and these had been unfolded to act as wings on either side of the stage. The other performers were already concealed behind them when Seamus strode forward to introduce his creation.

'Once, when I was touring,' he began, 'I had a canary in a cage which I took around with me. For reasons which will not be hidden from those familiar with the Good Book, I christened this bird Onan.'

'What does he mean?' Margot whispered to Séverine over the laughter.

'It's in the Bible. Onan was the man . . . he "spilled his seed on the ground".'

'You mean he tossed—?'

'That's right.'

'Old Oscar, as we all know,' Seamus continued, 'was a fellow who preferred his vice – er – versa, so to speak.'

More laughter.

'But we do not, here, intend to follow the author along that particular primrose path; we shall tread, instead, until something better comes along, a more solitary route. Ladies and gentlemen, allow me to present to you – *The Importance of Being Onanist*.'

Seamus bowed, then vanished behind one of the screens to a patter of applause and a comfortable burst of merriment.

The skit – it was no more than an extended sketch really – was full of scabrous dialogue, awful puns and heavily underlined innuendo. The plot, such as it was, borrowed from the Wilde play the mistaken-identity-deceived-heroine storyline – but instead of the original happy ending with everything working out for the best, here the female characters refused to be reconciled with their lovers, leaving them by inference to justify Seamus's new title.

Most of the lines were adapted from Wilde originals. The inserted copulatory and masturbatory scenes were suggested by graphic orgasmic sound effects voiced by characters behind the screens. The character of Algy, now known as Bulgy, was played by Dale Fairleigh with a rolled-up handkerchief in his left-hand trouser pocket; John, now known as Big Dick, was played by Seamus himself, with an even larger handkerchief in his pocket. The hired help had been reduced to a single manservant, a Russian emigré named Tossov (Kirk), and the two recalcitrant heroines, Vagina and Vulva, were impersonated by Bella and Séverine. The Lady Bracknell character, often quoted but never seen, was referred to as the Vice-cuntess Ina Labia.

The most dramatic – indeed the most impressive – moment in the production came five minutes after the beginning. Seamus and Dale were on stage alone. They were wearing the formal, high-collared, tightly waisted Victorian clothes they wore on stage at the Nice Opera House. The set was dressed simply with a chaise-longue, a table and two leather-seated chairs.

BIG DICK: Like virtue itself, vice earns its own reward. My special virtue is that I leave my vices untouched – except of course by human hand. My reward is therefore twofold, since, vice becoming a virtue, that virtue of its own nature translates into the vilest of vices.

BULGY: And the sin-drome, of its nature, is self-perpetuating?

BIG DICK: Self-perpetuating too, old lad. Like that organ whose gratification is its aim, the system is in a constantly expanding state.

BULGY: You have of course no intention of arresting the – shall we say – development of this propitious and priapic progress?

BIG DICK: Certainly not. It would be most inconvenient. I have been discovering all manner of hateful qualities in my nature. Women love us for our defects. If we have enough, they will forgive us everything, even our gigantic intellects.

BULGY: And especially our gigantic—

BIG DICK: *(interrupting)* In any case, I do not approve of anything that tampers with natural immodesty. Like lust itself, immodesty is a soaring, delightful bird: set it free, and heaven is its destination; imprison it, and the song is ended.

BULGY: But the malady lingers on.

Enter TOSSOV, *carrying a tray of tea things.*

TOSSOV: The Misses Vulva and Vagina are leaving the Dutch Garden, sir. They will be here shortly.

I have ventured to bring in the tea and comestibles they requested.

BIG DICK: Setting their Dutch caps at a windmill, no doubt! . . . Very well, Tossov, you may leave the room.

BULGY: *(aside)* Not in front of the audience, I trust!

TOSSOV: Very good, Milewd.

Exit Tossov.

BULGY: Very *bad*, I fear. As the Cuntess has remarked, women – all women – become like their mothers.

BIG DICK: Yes, that is their tragedy. No man ever does. That is his.

BULGY: She has also remarked that the happiness of a married man depends exclusively upon females he has not married. But what if one is actually in love?

BIG DICK: One should always be in love. That is why one should never marry. When one is in love one begins by deceiving oneself. And one ends by deceiving others. That is what is called romance. Talking of which . . . Oh, here they come now!

Enter Vagina *and* Vulva.

It was this dual entrance that provoked the dramatic surprise. For while the three male characters were not only fully dressed, but dressed in formal attire, both the girls were stark naked. That was the surprise. The drama factor was supplied by the fact that none of the males affected the slightest notice of this: the play continued exactly as if the females had been wearing clothes of the same style and period as the men. No reference at all to the girls' nudity was made throughout the remainder of the performance.

'It was my own idea, basically,' Raymond Large explained to Roth. 'Seamus and I worked out the details together. The point was to underline, to *emphasize* the difference between men and women, already made much of in Seamus's Wildean dialogue, in a satirical way. This drove the point home literally. With a jolt!'

'And the fact that the guys don't seem to notice the nakedness?' Roth queried.

'In a sense,' Large replied, 'the nakedness is noticed only by the audience. The male characters ignore – or choose to ignore – that aspect of the male-female differentiation . . . just as they choose to ignore all the other, less physical, differences.'

'Well, it sure made an impact,' Roth said when the skit, enthusiastically applauded, was over. 'I was a mite surprised, though, that your Irishman didn't include any hanky-panky. Not even a hot kiss. Just those slurping, ooh-aah jerk-off noises in the wings.'

'Oh, but the play was never intended to offer anything more than *verbal* pornography,' Large said. 'Restraint is the name of the game. Keep 'em waiting, keep up the expectation and the suspense. If we'd had people playing *soixante-neuf* and shafting all over the stage, it would have jumped the gun completely; there'd have been nothing left for later. Don't forget that more than half the guests have to be coaxed and nudged and *willed* into action: they're not actors – not even amateur actors – who have been rehearsed, who know what they are going to do. The aim here is to build the sex atmosphere, to lodge the *idea* of sex in all their minds, so that if anything happens, as I hope it will, the motivation will be entirely spontaneous, an expression of their own fantasies and not something imposed from outside. The play was just one of a series of titillations we planned, leading hopefully to that end.' Large laughed, tapping Roth on his fat knee. 'You'll see!' he said.

Titillation of a different kind was provided after the sumptuous dinner – a gastronomic poem of many stanzas, with courses ranging from *pâté de foie gras* to truffled ptarmigan, from stuffed sea-bass to wild boar with chestnuts. Sated by featherlight desserts of fruit and cream and flaky pastry, the guests were pushing back their chairs when Large rose to his feet at the head of the table and announced: 'Before we move to the drawing-room for coffee, I have a little surprise . . . something in the way of a cabaret turn from the good old days!'

He sat down. Abruptly, music filled the room. Lusty and Busty had placed a record on an electric cabinet gramophone which stood near the double doors: a full symphony orchestra playing the progression of Chopin waltzes, preludes and nocturnes scored for the ballet *Les Sylphides*.

Séverine and Bella, who had not dressed again after the play was over, dining unconcernedly nude among the long frocks and dark suits, rose suddenly to their feet and jumped up on to the table.

Breasts and buttocks and bellies fringed with pubic hair swayed above the astonished guests. There was a burst of laughter. Somebody clapped.

The two maidservants hurried forward and handed each of the naked girls a wicker basket with a lid. As the music swelled to the first crescendo, each one opened her basket and took out a black silk stocking.

With a sly smile, gyrating her bare hips as she trod carefully between the dishes, she made a circuit of the long table, wafting the flimsy stocking in front of the expectant faces below.

Then, holding it up to view one final time, she bent down, inserted a toe . . . and, slowly, lasciviously, rolled the stocking *up* her leg.

A second stocking, waved enticingly in front of the guests, followed the first.

First Bella, and then Séverine, plunged a hand back into her basket – to withdraw it holding a filmy pair of black, lace-edged knickers.

More laughter. Some applause.

Equally slowly, with the same mocking expressions, the young women drew the knickers up over the sheer sheen of the dark stockings, past the pale statuary of their thighs . . . and then bent double, turning around to offer a lewd view of the hairy furrow between their buttocks before they straightened and slid the garments up over their hips.

Black brassières with cutaway cups were next on the list.

Effectively, the performers parodied an entire strip-tease *á la* Gypsy Rose Lee . . . in reverse! Starting totally naked, Séverine and Bella completed their 'negative' version of the raunchy burlesque routine fully dressed, wearing sequinned evening gowns with high-heeled shoes.

The act, lasting the time it took to play the two sides of a twelve-inch 78rpm classical record, was an unqualified success.

Among the vociferously applauding guests Mondragon Roth, who knew the real thing better than any of them, was laughing immoderately. 'Jesus,' he wheezed, the tears running down his cheeks, 'that really takes the biscuit! I never thought I'd see . . . Two broads putting *on* their clothes to make a sexier show than the burleycue queens stripping off: now I guess I've seen everything!' He shook his head. 'Hey, Ray! The rest of the party goes that way, you got yourself a sell-out, boy!'

Raymond Large smiled. The eyes behind the horn-rims gleamed. 'As your fellow-countrymen might say, you ain't seen nothing yet,' he promised.

It was Lorraine Sheldon, the extravagant and lusty Lorraine, who set the ball rolling, as Large had hoped she would. Setting down her empty coffee cup, she drained a brandy balloon and said: 'Well, we had stage sex and we had cabaret sex and this afternoon some of us had *al fresco* sex . . . so who's game now for some real-life indoors sex?'

The guests, some of whom, in other circumstances, might have raised a supercilious eyebrow, remained unshocked.

Dazed with fine food and wine, high on the hashish they had unknowingly consumed, they saw nothing unusual in the remark. Lorraine, who was perched on a piano stool, looked challengingly around the drawing-room. She was wearing a floor-length dress in heavy olive green satin, which was slit up to the thigh on one side. The back of the dress was slit too, from neck to waist, and the neckline in front plunged almost as far. The geography of the famous Sheldon bosom was no longer a secret.

Tony Hill looked approvingly at the map of love. 'If there's a queue, old thing,' he said, 'bags I be the man in the number-one position.'

'I'll be right behind you,' Dill Jones said. 'And guard your rear!'

'I have room for three,' Lorraine called. 'One in front, one behind, and one – well, never mind about Number Three. Where's my lovely Italian, where has Geraldo gone?'

'He's not here, sweetie, he went home before the play,' Dagmar told her. 'He reckoned it was acceptable if he stayed – officially – at my place last night on account of extra work I invented in the evening and early today. But two nights away from the family was asking too much. You know Italian wives!'

'Too bad,' Lorraine said. 'Still . . . he was nice while he lasted.'

'You can say that again,' Doll smiled. 'And he lasted for *ever*!'

'Okay, since we have him in common, sweetie-pie,' Lorraine said, 'why don't you step up and join the boys? Like the song says: let you be my little dog, till the big dog comes!'

'All right,' Doll agreed. And then, with a wink at Margot: 'I don't mind.'

'That's the stuff!' Seamus said with a guffaw. 'Hell, what's the use of a Dill without a Doll, after all . . . though if you're as good as they say you are, the lady will not be after the requirement of a device of that type.' He turned to the Baron. 'And what about you sir? We've not heard the slightest peep out of your excellence since before the coffee was served. What would be your pleasure, sure, on this free and easy—'

'There are other Toms here who can peep,' Sonia cut in with a glance at Large and Roth, who were settling into armchairs. 'Johnnie's taste lies in other directions.'

'There are times, begob, when a lie's better than the truth,' said Seamus – who seemed to have appointed himself master of ceremonies. 'But yourself, ma'am, your svelte and sophisticated self? In what direction—?'

'Before anything else,' Sonia said, 'I must punish Johnnie for chickening out of the picnic this afternoon. But for that I need to fly upstairs and change.' She turned to go, but Seamus caught her arm.

'I've a young friend here a mite shy,' he said confidentially. 'I observe that it's already too late' – with a glance at a panelled alcove where Lorraine and her admirers whispered together – 'for you to go, so to speak, up Hill – but there's nothing on this earth to prevent you going down Dale!' He nodded towards his young colleague, standing a little hesitantly near the entrance doors.

Sonia flashed him a brilliant smile. 'We shall see,' she said. And then, with a meaning look at Dale himself, 'I may already have . . . plans . . . for young Master Fairleigh.' She turned again and hurried from the room.

There were giggles now, punctuating the murmurs in the alcove. The skirt of Lorraine's satin gown was up around her waist. Several hands were visible around her thighs and the lower part of her belly. Doll Jones was unfastening the clips behind the film star's neck. 'No, no, silly,' Lorraine's drawl emerged from the busy group. 'Not yet anyway. It's more fun to start dressed – or at any rate partly dressed.'

'Yes, old thing, that's all very well' – this was Tony Hill – 'but where, actually, are we going to go?'

'Go?' Seamus boomed, striding across the room. 'You're

not supposed to be *going* anywhere, dammit! It's coming we're interested in. You stay right there and arrange yourselves the best you can on that blasted chesterfield.'

There was more laughter as Dill, his wife, Tony Hill and the actress subsided. Dill sat on one of the arms and unbuttoned his fly. Lorraine was on her hands and knees facing him, her bare and generous bottom shining in the soft light. Hill, his trousers around his ankles, knelt behind her, and Doll wormed her way, face upward, beneath the voluptuous blonde's heavy body. An arm and a hand appeared to drop a pair of silk knickers on the floor.

Roth nudged Raymond Large, leaning forward in his chair. He licked his fleshy lips. The remaining guests were scattered around the big room. Seamus walked over to Bella as Lusty and Busty cleared away the coffee things. 'Tell me, Madame Cohen,' he said, 'do you have any Scottish relatives?'

'*Scottish?*' Bella was surprised. 'Well, it's a funny thing, but I did once have an uncle in Belgium who was married to a dancer from the Moulin Rouge called McTavish. Would you call that a relative? Why do you ask, anyway?'

'Because it's Sunday,' Seamus answered gravely, 'and anyone with Scots connections should surely be going to Kirk?'

'Oh, Seamus, oh God!' moaned Dale, covering his face with his hands. 'Can't anyone stop him?'

But the yacht skipper – who had for some time been eyeing Bella's seductive curves with unconcealed interest – had already walked up to her. Taking her hand and brushing it with his lips, he murmured: 'Lady of the lyrical shape – will you be my evensong?'

Dale was deep in conversation now with the Baron. Seamus, switching to a personal approach, had one arm around Séverine's waist. Dagmar was perched on an arm of Raymond Large's chair. Four guests were still 'unoccupied'.

Michel Blondin realized instinctively that any kind of

intrigue with his own wife, at least as a simple couple, would be frowned upon. So he raised an eyebrow at the sole alternative candidate, the slim, blonde, longhaired English girl. He smiled invitingly. 'I don't mind,' Margot Fairleigh said.

That left Jean-Jacques Ancarani and Maguy, who had at first looked askance at the lustful group in the alcove but now, sitting on the edge of her chair, offered the world an expression that was simply a trifle dazed.

The *Maître de Chai* could gauge with an expert eye the best approach to use with a given type of woman. Fixing Maguy with his burning gaze, he said peremptorily from the far side of the room: '*Come here!* At once.'

Maguy came.

When Sonia returned to the château drawing-room, the party had separated into a number of different components which together formed a tableau resembling a *quattrocento* sketch for a mural depicting *The Cities of the Plain* or a censored plate from *The Rake's Progress*.

On the alcoved chesterfield, Lorraine Sheldon lay face down on top of Doll Jones, with the ex-dancer's face buried between her thighs. Tony Hill, hips fiercely oscillating, was firmly plugged in behind the star's heaving bottom. Dill Jones still sat on the arm, his great cock jutting from his open fly. As Sonia came into the room, Lorraine was raising the top half of her body to that level, supporting herself on her elbows. 'I always was a big mouth, baby,' she said to Dill, 'but whether I can take in that artillery piece . . . well, in more ways than one, it's in the lap of the gods!' She advanced her wide-stretched lips to the suffused tip of the oversized shaft.

Sonia looked around. There were four other couples amorously entwined within sight of Dagmar, Roth and their host.

Jean-Jacques Ancarani had placed Maguy on her back in a

deep leather easy chair. Her little black dress was around her waist, her knickers were on the floor, and her legs, spread wide, were hooked over the arms of the chair to expose the maximum amount of her pale, bared loins with their blond thatch. Jean-Jacques himself was naked, the hairs furring arms, legs and his muscular chest wiry in the light from a standard lamp behind the chair. His knees rested on the outer edge of the cushion, his hands grasped the chair back, and his hips splatted ferociously against the young blonde's uptilted thighs as he ploughed his stiffened prick in and out of her shamelessly gaping cunt. She lay motionless except for the slight quiver of her belly each time he thrust into her, wide eyes staring up at his rugged face. He was talking to her as he fucked, savagely, almost brutally, but his voice was too low to be heard by the others.

Michel and Margot were more decorously positioned in their chair. She was sitting on his lap with her arms twined around his neck and her cheek against his. They both appeared to be fully dressed, but a closer inspection revealed an unexpectedly wide spread of skirt over his knees ... and the fact that his hands, apparently resting in a friendly way on Margot's hips, were raising and lowering her in a continuous, gentle rhythm. Clearly, beneath the artfully draped skirt, her bared underparts were impaled on the young Parisian's cock.

Seamus and Séverine were on the floor behind a sofa. Nothing could be seen of them, but the Irishman's rumbustious chuckles and occasional spurts of laughter from Séverine implied that whatever they were doing was mutually agreeable.

Kirkpatrick Munroe and Bella had decided upon the same *modus operandi* as Michel and Margot. But they had both stripped naked and the chair was an upright wheelback. Kirk had found an eighteenth-century folding screen, one side of which was mirrored, in the far reaches of the big room, and they now sat contentedly regarding their several reflected images – front-view, side-view, near-back-view, the upright cock swallowed in the fleshy slit amongst pubic hair, her spread thighs rising and falling and the full breasts bobbing as he strained upwards against the moving weight of her lush and nubile body.

It was strange, Sonia thought – unaware of the doped *friandes* and their effect – how the dress-undress/undress-dress alternations before and after dinner, added to a certain amount of intoxication, had totally expelled normal inhibitions and so veiled the distinction between the done and the not-done that a group of strangers had begun quite spontaneously to behave in a way most of them would customarily consider outrageous.

Not only to switch partners, but to do so without any overt coaxing, virtually *in public* – that was the astonishing thing!

Sonia herself, nevertheless, was the source of a certain amount of astonishment – among those not too involved to notice – on her second entrance.

At dinner she had been wearing wine-red velvet. Now she was dressed in a skintight, floor-length gown of polished black rubber. The high-necked, gleaming garment was plastered to her body as closely as a glove, outlining her uncorseted breasts with the nipples evident; sheathing her hips and thighs, and then falling from the knee in soft folds. The hem at the front of the skirt was raised six inches to show black patent leather boots laced at the front.

Thin black rubber gloves reached above the elbows on her bare arms. In one hand she held the plaited whip which Large and Roth had seen used the previous night; over her other arm she had draped several lengths of rope and a number of silver chains ending in leather wrist and ankle cuffs.

Those who were aware of the apparition reacted in different ways. Dale and the Baron shrank back into their chairs – though their eyes were bright with excitement. Large, Roth and the Countess looked eager. Dill Jones knew the score and grinned lopsidedly. His wife was busy with her tongue and couldn't see anyway. Bella flashed a sisterly smile Sonia's way. Lorraine was aware. She freed her mouth and drawled: 'That too? My God, this is some scene you got going here!' To the others the costume was no more than some kind of fancy dress.

Half an hour later, the scene had radically changed. A curious sub-conversation that the worldly Sonia had noticed – a susurrus of breaths and gasps and quasi-groans choked from the coupled guests – had either subsided or peaked in cries of release. The party, dressed, half dressed or nude, sprawled around the drawing-room apparently at ease and eager to go, sipping fresh drinks served by the indefatigable Lusty and Busty. Dagmar van den Bergh thought it was time she took charge.

Uncoiling her languid length from a tapestry-covered Louis XIII armchair, she rose to her feet and surveyed her fellow guests – a stately figure in jade green tussore, still slender and upright despite her sixty years. 'We've all been entertained, royally entertained, by our host,' she said. 'We've been wined and dined and excited and amused; more recently we've been – shall I say stimulated? – partly through Seamus's suggestions, partly by our own choice. Now I think it's time *we* started to entertain *him*.' She glanced at Raymond Large.

'The first principle of entertainment is pleasurable surprise,' the Countess said. 'And surprise means the unexpected . . . and the unexpected often comes through experimentation. In this case' – she paused and looked around her audience again – 'the experimentation must come from us. Are you with me?'

The guests, still on their artificially induced high, had reached that warm, comfortable, giggly stage when almost anything suggested seems *fun*. 'Lead on, Lady Duff,' Seamus called in his sepulchral theatre voice. He was sitting cross-legged on the floor, wearing nothing but blue-and-white striped underpants. 'We only wait who also serve and stand!'

'If the experiments are to succeed,' the Countess said, 'and not remain simply repetitions of existing experience, there must be an element of surprise in them for us too. So the order of events must be as nearly random as possible. That is to say, decided by third parties. And to make this decision truly arbitrary we must resemble one another as closely as possible, to become as anonymous as we can.' She clapped her hands. 'The first step, then, is to have *everybody* naked. So come on – off with those clothes, all of you!'

Dagmar was in the driving seat, imperative, ordering things the way she used to do at her notorious parties in the Avenue Kléber mansion now owned by Raymond Large. 'In this case,' she said, 'I am the third party; I will decide who does which, and with what, and to whom!'

'Shouldn't it be "who does *what*, and with which, and to whom"?' Seamus protested. 'The limerick about the lesbian and the nancy-boy, I mean.'

'Not when I'm in command,' Dagmar said briskly.

She gazed around with a satisfied smile. Apart from Large and Roth, those still wearing garments of any sort were now obediently stripping them off without the slightest hesitation or any sign of prudery or dissent. Once the authoritative voice had uttered, they became like kids at a birthday party. *Now, children, I want you all to get down on your hands and knees . . . There! . . . and when the music starts, I want you all to count out . . .*

There were exceptions, of course, but the Countess hadn't been talking to them. They were installed in the second of the big room's alcoves, on the far side of a huge, hooded mediaeval chimney-piece – Sonia with her two 'slaves', Dale and the Baron.

The deep leaded windows at the back of the recess were covered by heavy drapes hanging from wooden rings threaded on to a stout pole fixed to iron brackets near the ceiling. The curtains had now been pulled back, and the two men stood facing out through the windows, into the night. The wind had risen again, moaning through the chimney, and large raindrops spattered against the glass.

Sonia had fastened leather cuffs around her captives' wrists, and looped the chains attached to these up over the curtain pole, stretching their arms wide, and so high above their heads that they were forced to stand on tiptoe. As the Countess turned towards the alcove, Sonia was fixing the chains in position with small brass padlocks.

Dale and the Baron were already bare to the waist. Now she wrapped her arms around the hips of each man in turn, unbuckling belts, unbuttoning flies and then jerking each pair of trousers and underpants down below buttocks by now quivering with uneasy anticipation. The garments were unable to be dragged further than that because each man's knees and ankles were lashed together with lengths of the rope Sonia had brought down from her room.

Now she prowled up and down behind them like a panther in a cage, running the plaited thongs of the whip through the fingers of her left hand while she pondered her next move. Highlights from the room's illumination slid oil-smooth over the contours of the black rubber tightly clinging to her hips and buttocks and thighs as she moved; wrinkles at the wrists of her long gloves and in the leather sheathing her ankles shone in the diffuse light.

She stopped pacing and stood square. Nodding to herself twice, she drew back her right arm and slashed a stinging blow with the whip across the Baron's bare flesh. The whip cracked diagonally from the right shoulderblade to the left buttock, raising a livid weal darkening instantly to angry red. The Baron uttered a stifled cry, at once bitten off.

'Don't you dare cry out!' Sonia snapped, hitting him again. 'It will upset the other guests. You will take your punishment in silence. Both of you. Each . . . time . . . I hear

. . . a noise . . . the number of strokes . . . you have to take . . . will be doubled!' She punctuated her words with separate, alternate lashes, forehand for the Baron, backhand for Dale, positioning herself precisely between them, a couple of yards to the rear. This time there were no cries, only a series of smothered gasps each time the whip fell.

Dagmar van den Bergh turned her own back on the alcove as the whistles and cracks of the leather whip continued. The 'children' were all naked now, looking at her expectantly. As it was in its way with Sonia and her willing victims, so now, once the ascendance, the dominant rôle, had been established, the players in the game waited only to be told what to do.

'Experiment and experience,' the Countess said with a smile. 'Kirk, I think it's time you experienced what we might call the lower hand – playing the underdog, so to speak. Lorraine, darling, perhaps this time *you* can show *him* a thing or two?'

'My pleasure,' the big blonde said. 'He likes to watch, doesn't he? Well, this time *he* can watch *me*!' She led the yacht skipper to an ottoman strewn with silk cushions and a white bearskin rug.

'Margot,' the Countess said, 'I want to keep you out of this in the early stages. Just relax on that *chaise longue* for the moment. Séverine – perhaps, you'd keep her company?' She turned to Maguy. 'Madame Blondin, I believe it is time you enlarged your foreign interests. Shall we see just how *cordiale* you can make an *entente* with our English friend? I am sure Monsieur Hill will be happy to oblige.'

'Absolutely,' murmured Tony.

Dagmar turned to Michel. 'You on the other hand could profit from further experience on your own home ground. Bella certainly has enough for the two of you! . . . And as for Doll – well, wouldn't it be a change to forget the acrobatics and simply lie back and let a *man* take over?' She seized the muscular, deep-chested, dark-haired Jean-Jacques

Ancarani by the elbow and whispered: 'Take her over there and show her how it *should* be done, all right?'

From his chair, Raymond Large was holding up both hands and silently miming applause. Dagmar inclined her head and smiled. And then, affecting all at once to notice that there were still two men standing rather sheepishly alone, and no unaccompanied females left to be assigned to them: 'Oh, my! *Quelle tragédie!* ... but take heart, gentlemen. All is not lost. You can still work in the cause of science and the orgasm! You see . . . ?'

She clapped her hands. The first alcove, the one in which Lorraine had been accommodating Tony Hill, and Doll and Dill Jones, had for some time been curtained off. Now the drapes were pulled back again to reveal the original chesterfield.

And seated in it, each snuggled up against the cushions in one corner, were the redoubtable, concupiscent maid-servants, Agathe and Dominique, better known to the initiated as Lusty and Busty.

Each of them, although nobody had noticed the transformation, was now sitting, legs apart and arms outstretched, as naked as the other female guests.

'Thank goodness!' the Countess breathed. 'For a moment, I was afraid I was going to have to ask you two chaps to make love to each other, failing any suitable feminine company! As it is . . . well, why don't you rush over there and make up for lost time?'

'Ah, well,' Seamus said, clapping Dill Jones on his bare shoulder. 'It's true enough, I guess, what they say: a miss is as good as a male any day!'

Taking the journalist by the hand, he hurried towards the alcove.

'I don't like to think of her hurting Dale,' Margot Fairleigh protested. The sounds of the whipping, and the choked, indrawn explosions of breath still punctuated the groaning symphony of sex filtering from every corner of the drawing-room. 'I can't think why he allowed himself to be talked into such a thing. Especially with that dreadful little Belgian, who never says a word. What can have got into him?'

'Margot,' the Countess said – she was perched on the arm of the easy chair in which the English girl sat – 'there is something I have to tell you about your dear brother.' She exchanged glances with Séverine, who was sitting on the other arm, with one of her own bare arms draped casually along the chair back, just above Margot's head. 'But first let me make a guess – an impertinence, perhaps, but it may be important – about your background. You were brought up in a country vicarage, I believe, in which case evidently your father was a priest, a pastor?'

'Yes, but I don't see what that has to do—?'

'Wait. Would I be right in saying that your father was a strict man, if a kind one – the kind of person who has a rigid code of conduct from which you depart at your peril – but who has nevertheless some difficulty himself in disguising, shall we say, a preference for a daughter over a son?'

'I suppose so. But—?'

'And a kindly, maybe fussy, perhaps over-protective mother, possibly only subconsciously aware of this, who compensates by indulging the son?'

Margot stared up at her and said nothing.

'Your brother,' the Countess pursued, 'probably went to one of those boys-only English boarding schools where behaviour is as rigorously conditioned as the rules laid down by your father, and initiative is discouraged or even punished. And since then, despite his talent, he has displayed a certain . . . how can I put it? A certain indecisiveness, a lack of direction in his life?'

'How can you know all this?' Margot burst out. Séverine lowered her arm to rest a friendly hand on the girl's shoulder.

'Because it's a classic recipe among the English,' the Countess said. 'Such a background produces leaders or the led. And with a home life like yours, it's going to be the led – most of whom will turn out to be either homosexuals or masochists. Your brother's not a queer; he wants relationships with women. But his upbringing has conditioned him, subconsciously, to renounce the imperative, so called *masculine* rôle; psychologically, he wants the decisions to be made for him. So although he *wants* a woman, he *needs* her to be the dominant member of the couple. What you see here is merely an *exteriorization* of that conflict: a literal illustration of a psychological truth.'

'Are you telling me that my brother *likes* to be tied up and beaten?'

'I'm explaining that he *needs* the situation in which that can happen. The details are due to the other person. That's what I mean by decisions.'

'Well, I think that's the most extraordinary thing I ever heard of,' Margot said.

'If you think about it,' Séverine put in, 'the situation is no more extraordinary than your own, you know.'

'What do you mean?' The girl was immediately on the defensive.

'She means,' said Dagmar, 'that we have been watching you. Forgive me if I am frank – but, unlike the rest of us, you don't really enjoy sex, do you?'

'Well . . .'

'We get the impression that you allow men to make love to you, not because you want to, not from any desire on your part, but simply because . . . well, because it's so much easier to say Yes than to say No. And because they can become such a bore if you refuse. Am I right?'

'I suppose so. In a way.'

Séverine's hand had taken up a strand of Margot's long blonde hair and was threading it through her fingers, brushing the curling ends against the girl's bare skin. 'And why do you suppose that is?' she asked. 'Could it be because of that very same background your brother shares?'

'I don't see how . . . ? I mean I wasn't at the same kind of school as . . .' Margot's voice died away. She leaned her head absently sideways, so that her cheek rested for a moment against the backs of the fingers playing with her hair.

'It's nothing to do with schools,' said the Countess. 'It's what they call a father fixation. Here you have an upright man, a man of principles, a person requiring a particularly strict code of conduct who is nevertheless subconsciously aware of an excess of love directed at his daughter. So what does the daughter do?' She picked one of Margot's hands from her lap and began stroking the palm.

'Once she has grown up' – Dagmar answered her own question – 'the daughter is prepared, like most children, to rebel against the code. She will certainly sleep around. But the men she chooses, or the men she allows to choose her . . . Ah, now there's the problem! Because what she is really looking for is what the psychologists term a father figure – someone to replace the father, with the same principles and an equal attachment, often an older man. But of course she won't find him, because nobody is going to come up to that childhood ideal, nobody is going to fulfil the exacting standards in her subconscious mind. With the result,' said the Countess, 'that she will place no value on the men she does find. None of them will come up to scratch. And as she has basically no respect for them, nothing they do will give her real pleasure; she simply won't allow it to.'

'To go back to your brother,' Séverine said, 'there's a story I heard the other day.' She was cradling the girl's head now in her hand, pressing a cheek against the swelling curve of her own bare breast. 'It seems there was some important function in the City to which both the Protestant Archbishop of Canterbury and the Roman Catholic Archbishop of Westminster had been invited. When it was over, there was a dearth of taxis and finally the two churchmen were obliged to share one. "It is, after all, only right and proper that we should share this conveyance," says Canterbury, "because when you come down to it, we *are* in the same profession; both of us live to serve Almighty God."

'"Indeed we do," the Catholic Archbishop replies warmly. "You in your way, and I in His."'

Séverine laughed. 'You may,' she said, 'think I'm descending from the sublime to the ridiculous. But all I'm saying is that your brother has arrived at a situation where he can find joy in sex . . . *his* way.'

'Yes, people are far too narrow in their view of sex,' said the Countess. 'One day someone's going to write a book called *The Joy of Sex*, explaining just how many ways there are of taming the beast! Has it ever occurred to you,' she said to Margot, 'that your own lack of joy in this particular field may be because you allow yourself to become involved in *the wrong kind* of sex?'

Margot opened her mouth to reply, but before she could get a word out, the Countess leaned over, lowered her head, and kissed her very gently on the lips.

'God, you got yourself some circus act here, Ray!' Mondragon Roth enthused. 'Best prodoocer of – uh – spectaculars I ever saw in my life.' He chuckled. 'If I don't mention Broadway, it's because I figure it might be misconstrued.' He jerked his head in the direction of Lorraine Sheldon.

She was lying flat on her back in a very deep armchair. Her arms were hooked behind her knees, drawing back her doubled-up legs to expose her entire anal-genital region in shameless abandon. She was singing happily to herself as Kirk and Seamus took turns to kneel and pay tribute with their lustful tongues.

Dill Jones was still on the chesterfield with Lusty and Busty, his face clamped between the big girl's thighs, his huge cock spearing up into the thinner one straddling his hips. The two young women, leaning forward over his prone body, were kissing chastely.

Tony Hill, traditional as ever, had commandeered the ottoman and was fucking Maguy in a businesslike way, in the old-fashioned missionary position on the white bearskin. Bella, on her knees, sucked off Maguy's husband in front of the mirrored Chinese folding screen.

Above the chorus of panting, groaning, inarticulate murmurs rising from these energetic couples, Lorraine's warm, fruity drawl chanted:

Herrings do it; kippers do it;
Actors, even, and cruiser skippers do it:
Let's beat upstream . . .

Shafting a supine and for once non-acrobatic Doll Jones on top of an ivory-coloured grand piano, Jean-Jacques Ancarani raised his head to call out tipsily: '*Chérie*, you must be the craziest of all Monsieur Ziegfeld's follies!'

Such pleasantries passed over the heads of the trio in the armchair nearest to Roth and Large. The three women there were totally immersed in one another. Dagmar van den Bergh's jade green evening dress was lying in a crumpled heap on the floor. Naked as the rest of them now, she was kneeling on the floor in front of the chair, framed by Margot Fairleigh's shamelessly spread legs, her hands on the girl's slender hips, her lips brushing the satin skin at the base of her belly, just above the blonde curls of pubic hair. The top half of Margot's body was slumped on the cushioned seat of the low, deep chair, hidden by the graceful curve of Séverine's back. Large's vineyard manager, still seated on the arm of the chair, had leaned right across Margot, supporting herself with an elbow on the other arm. Her free hand traced teasing arabesques between Margot's small breasts. They were kissing in a lazy, languorous, almost absentminded fashion.

Margot was lost; she was in another world. Since that first unaccountable thrill had tingled through her at the

Countess's unexpected kiss, time had stood still. She was dazedly aware that this heightened sensitivity, this curious intoxication expanding a limitless *now* into a fast-fading past and a dreamlike future, was at least in part due to the hashish which she, almost alone among the guests, had knowingly consumed. But there was more to it than that, more than the heady timelessness she had been led to expect anyway. 'It makes you feel good,' Séverine had told her when she brought the stuff up from Kirk's boat. 'There's no hurry, no problems; life's a big joke and you've all the time there is to giggle at it.' True enough, but . . .

How to explain the indescribable joy, that amazing sense of being *alive* at last, that flamed now through every nerve in her body, although she was lying still . . . just where? With whom? With two nude women in a crowded room!

Dagmar van den Bergh's lips were buried in her pubic hair. Her tongue, a small, soft animal with a warm life of its own, burrowed between the damp curls, seeking, twisting this way and that, finding . . . Ah! Homing on the interfolded labia, penetrating the hot, wet depths, lapping the long slit of her hungry cunt.

The Countess's hands left her hips, sculpting a curve of belly, hollowing out the crease at the top of each thigh, thumbs creeping inward to rest on those pouting, fleshy lips, drawing them at last lustfully apart.

The body sprawled in the chair jerked violently. The animal had come home: the moist, questing tip of Dagmar's tongue caressed Margot's quivering clitoris, now fully exposed with its protective hood drawn back.

And all at once she came. Deep down inside her the familiar shuddering commenced, rippling through her body with savage intensity as the Countess licked and sucked her clitoris, grinding it ferociously against her pubic bone with that muscled tongue. But although these first convulsive spasms, the outward, physiological signs of an orgasm, could be triggered by anyone, almost independently of her own volition, Margot knew that this was different, this was *real*. Her entire body rocked out of control. Her tongue speared hotly into Séverine's mouth; her two hands forced Dagmar's head more fiercely still into her crotch as ecstasy flamed through her in a way she had never experienced before. She heard a low, growling scream and realized that it came from the back of her own throat, her head now free and shaking wildly from side to side.

Even when that first titanic wave had released her, leaving her alone on a dark shore as the undertow ebbed away, successive combers curled back in with diminishing force to send still more ripples vibrating through her nerves.

When the last faint quivers had died away, the Countess gently stroked the girl's soaking mons and then rose to her feet. 'I knew it,' she murmured. 'I can always tell. And I knew it about you too,' smiling, she said to Séverine.

Séverine smiled back, a slow and rather secret smile. She had lowered herself into the chair and was cradling the English girl's blonde head against her breasts as if she were a baby. '*You* can always tell,' she said mischievously, 'but *one* never knows, does one?'

A sudden gust of warm wind swept through the drawing-room, blowing the alcove curtains to a glimmering curve. The French windows leading to the terrace had been opened. Outside, rain still pelted down and the dark shapes of trees threshed beneath low, scudding clouds yellowed by reflected light from the village.

Maguy Blondin lay spreadeagled on the wet flagstones, her drenched hair fanned out by the downpour, her small breasts pushed up by her two hands. She was staring up at Sir Kirkpatrick Munroe, who stood naked above her with his limp prick in one hand.

'Yes, go on, do it!' she sobbed. 'I want you to. All over me!'

The Countess turned to Séverine. 'My dear, you're absolutely right,' she said. She bent down to pick up the jade green dress. 'One never really does know, does one!'

It was 1.30 in the morning. The wind had dropped but the rain fell more steadily than ever, beating against the windowpanes and pattering down the wide chimney to spray the huge flower arrangement Séverine had positioned on the hearth. Raymond Large, exhausted perhaps by the success of his party, had fallen momentarily asleep, his head sunk on his chest and the hornrims displaced to the tip of his blade-like nose. Mondragon Roth, on the other hand, was more alert than ever, his small eyes glittering and his huge body quivering with excitement as he surveyed the lascivious tableaux surrounding him.

Dagmar van den Bergh had, on the suggestion of Dill Jones and his wife, organized a variation on a children's party game which resulted in a number of bizarre and arbitrary combinations in different parts of the drawing-room. The rules were simple. The players were obliged to move quickly around the big room in any direction they wished while the Countess played a record on the electric gramophone. The moment she lifted the needle from the disc and the music stopped, each person was to halt and stretch out both arms. Anyone they could touch was then expected – immediately and on the spot – to start some kind of sexual activity with them. Those who had not touched continued until there were no unoccupied players left. At that point there was a pause to allow the various combinations to explore one another to the full. And then the music restarted, the partners split up, and the whole process was repeated.

The records Dagmar had chosen – not without a sly appreciation of the results they would provoke – were the Josephine Baker hit, *I Have Two Loves*; a dance band version of *A Little Of What You Fancy Does You Good* and a robust rendering of the old music-hall favourite, *The Man Was A Stranger To Me*.

The first time the music stopped only two sets of players were 'in touch', and this produced two separate trios – one teaming Tony Hill and Michel with the voracious Lusty ('No problem,' she said, 'every house has two entrances!'); the other, perhaps unfortunately, throwing together Kirk, Dill and the Baron. 'Near the alcove and its curtain, thank the Lord,' Dill said piously.

Séverine and Margot cheated, circulating with their arms already linked, on the far side of the ottoman.

Mark Harries, who had volunteered earlier to run Geraldo Porrelli home in Ancarani's Delahaye, had watched for a while on his return but was now as naked as the rest of them. Dale, released some time ago with the Baron, was also playing, and Sonia, although the rubber dress had been discarded, was compromising by retaining her laced boots and corset. Despite the addition of the two masochists and the return of Mark, this nevertheless left the remaining males outnumbered by four to six: Dale, Mark, Jean-Jacques and Seamus versus Lorraine, Doll, Maguy, Bella, Sonia, and Busty.

Covertly, Dagmar watched their progress, hoping to lift the needle at the right time to promote couplings that would be 'interesting'.

Her first attempt placed Dale in an unholy alliance with Lorraine Sheldon, Doll Jones and Busty; the second effected a seemly partnership between Bella and Mark. This left only Maguy and Seamus unattended, so Dagmar switched off the gramophone and gestured them together. She moved across to the grand piano and set a metronome down on top of it. 'All right,' she called, 'whoever you are and whatever you're doing – this is the ten-minute critical period. I'm setting this machine at a reasonable speed. A bell will ring and it will stop when the time is up. Between now and then you are to time your movements, whatever they are, *exactly* to the rhythm it establishes. All right?'

She wound up the metronome, set the speed and time, and

switched it on. The pointer clacked rapidly across the machine's triangular face. 'Off you go, then,' the Countess ordered. 'One, two, three, four . . . *One*, two, three, four . . . Click, clack, click, clack . . . . *One*, two, three, four . . .'

The château drawing-room, which had been a disorganized chaos of flailing limbs and gobbling mouths and writhing hips, was transformed at the clap of the Countess's hands into a regimented, sensual ballet – an orchestrated symphony of flesh. In perfect time with the clacking machine on the piano, bottoms heaved, cocks thrust, hands groped, bodies arched all over the nakedly peopled floor.

It was an extraordinary sight.

Mondragon Roth nudged his host awake. 'Remarkable!' he enthused. 'Unimaginable!'

Dale Fairleigh was being virtually raped by his three women. He was lying on his back on the cushioned swell of Busty's voluptuous frame. One of her arms was clamped around his waist, holding him in position; the fingers of the other hand probed deep within his anus. Doll Jones was straddled across the two of them, her cunt grinding down on his frantically sucking mouth. And Lorraine, straddled again over his hips, was riding his cock like a horse, raising and lowering her big body to pound the breath out of him in rhythmic accord with the metronome.

Margot and Séverine, stretched out now on the ottoman, were sublimely unaware of the orgy around them, although unconsciously their movements had harmonized with the tick-tack-thwack of the metronome. Still riding high on her release – probably the first real orgasm she had ever had in her life – Margot had been avidly looking for more as they circled the padded, flat-topped oriental chest. And then, as the identical thought occurred to her companion, she reflected: four hands, four legs, four breasts – but only two mouths and two cunts: clearly there was only one logical way to arrange these components, and the ottoman was the ideal place to do it!

So now the English girl's feet were splayed out at one end of it, and Séverine's at the other. With the two-backed beast of breasts and bellies between them, the two heads bobbing, lapping, sucking while roving hands fuelled the fires of lust.

The Countess favoured them with an indulgent smile. Later she would join them, adding a little variety to spice their new life. For the moment she was concerned with a mathematical error. The last time she had stopped the music, only Seamus and Maguy had been left on the floor, so she had waved them together and moved to the metronome. But there were two other guests unaccounted for. What had happened to Jean-Jacques and the professional girl from London?

She found them sprawled on a pile of cushions behind an Empire sofa. They must have slipped away from the others during the first musical break. Perhaps they didn't like playing games. At the moment they were extremely conservatively coupled – Sonia lying on her back with her arms around the *Maître de Chaï*'s shoulders and her booted legs hooked neatly behind his knees while he shifted smoothly in and out of her with well-timed strokes. Perhaps too, each being normally a dominant partner, they had a tacit agreement to avoid excess?

Bella and Mark, the other Anglo-French pair, were equally circumspect, fucking in a similar position on a Persian rug in front of Séverine's flower arrangement by the chimney piece. How odd, the Countess thought, that the two 'business girls', certainly the most experienced of all the guests, and those bound as it were to be familiar with all the tricks of the trade, should in fact be the least sexually adventurous of all the players in the game!

There were certainly adventures under way behind the curtain in the alcove, where the Baron – to his great delight – was simultaneously being buggered by the yacht skipper and tossed off by Dill Jones. Lusty too was ringing the changes:

having been plugged behind by Michel and fucked by Tony Hill, she had effortlessly bent over to switch the engineer's penis to her mouth and transferred Michel to her cunt without losing a beat. Now she moved swiftly again to suck the Frenchman and take Hill in behind. Seamus, for his part, was for once at his most tender, shafting Maguy gently from the rear as she knelt forward in a chintz-covered armchair.

Alone amongst the men, he had just jerked into orgasm when the bell sounded.

The two young women entwined on the ottoman didn't hear it. Their newfound joy was a revelation to both of them. Margot's first orgasm, rather than slaking the sudden thirst for sensation, had only increased her desire, whetting an appetite for more and more and more. And for Séverine, experienced as she was with men, this fresher, gentler approach to sex was an irresistible turn-on. The exciting thing, the joy of it for each of them, was the total identification it provoked: the extraordinary, almost unreal sense of *knowing* precisely the effect of one's actions; the conviction that such and such a movement would stimulate such and such a reaction – because each of the bodies was the same and in any case the identical thing was being done to oneself!

Margot sucked, Séverine sucked. Margot took a quivering clitoris gently between her teeth, Séverine duplicated the action.

Séverine reached down between their squirming bellies to fondle the breasts squashed against her hips, Margot reached up to make the same gesture.

There were only two mouths but there were four pairs of lips. One girl used the moisture tongued from her partner's vagina to ease the passage of her finger through the tight ring of the other's anus . . . only at once to sense the mirror-image of that manoeuvre between her own buttocks.

The experience was near-magical. Doing was being done.

Sensing exactly what the other person felt at exactly the same time in a way doubled the thrill – but in another way it was as though one was making love to oneself. And this masturbatory concept increased the feeling in each partner that she was almost playing on an instrument . . . that she herself *was* the instrument . . . and finally that the instrument was playing her.

Action and reaction, say the scientists, are equal and opposite. It took no backroom boys to see the truth in this observation as it applied to Margot and Séverine. The music of their shared desire resonated through and through them, its harmonics vibrating so deeply inside that their mutual orgasm trembled to life in each of them at the identical instant. As they were seized by these first throes, every movement made by either of them was amplified in the other until their two bodies shook in unison with passion . . . and even that shuddering itself became an additional component in their ecstasy, swelling the music to such a crescendo that it spilled over into an experience neither of them would ever forget.

Raymond Large and Mondragon Roth had left their chairs and strolled over to watch this epiphany at closer quarters. Dagmar had turned over the music-hall record to play a song entitled *Every Little Movement*, but it was not until the spasms of the inverted couple embracing on the ottoman had finally subsided that she could cajole the players into a second round of her game. Before they started to circulate, there was a round of applause, but neither Margot nor Séverine heard it.

This time it was Seamus who contracted out. 'Me darlin' girl,' he said to the Countess with a downward glance at his limp cock, 'I'm after findin' meself so bloody flutered that I could not bare it any longer!'

He sank to the floor, pulling Bella Cohen down with him, and sat with his back propped against the wall. 'Would you look at that!' he said, gesturing towards the naked guests prowling around the room. 'A fuckin' orgy, begob! It puts me in mind of a limerick, but. I hate the ones that start, "There was a young man of . . ." and all that caper. This one's a cracker.' He frowned, trying to concentrate, then recited: 'A vice both bizarre and unsavoury, was that of the Bishop of Avery . . .' He paused, shaking his head. 'Shit! Now I've forgotten the rest of it!'

'Never mind, sweetie,' Bella said. 'Just watch the nice people fuck.'

The nice people were by now so dazed with drink and sex and the hashish they had consumed that half of them no longer really knew what they were doing.

The first music break had tumbled Michel, his wife and Dill Jones down near the Irishman. Sonia was slapping Dale's face in the alcove. The Baron was busy playing with himself as he watched. The others had started to circulate again.

Maguy was staring with apprehension at the journalist's enormous cock, rising like a thick pole from his slight, pale body. 'You watch yourself there, honey,' Lorraine called from the centre of the floor. 'That goddam ivory tower is big enough to *live* in, I'm telling you!'

The young blonde blenched, but it was clear that he intended to impale her on his massive weapon. 'Go on, give it to her,' Michel urged harshly. 'Make the little bitch take it!' He pulled her down on the floor, seized both her hands and dragged her arms up above her head. Dill grasped the inside of her thighs and spread her legs agonizingly wide. Smiling, he positioned himself between them, extended his own legs and lowered his hips. The bulbous, blood-engorged head of his great penis nudged the thatch of blonde pubic hair at the base of her belly.

Maguy caught her breath. She was lying helplessly spreadeagled between them, unable to fend off the assault of this stranger with his monstrous tool because Michel – her own husband! – had her arms pinioned; she was to be raped in front of all these people and he was actively encouraging it!

She didn't know that her eyes were shining, but she was aware that her nipples had unaccountably hardened. And she had an uneasy suspicion that she was already wet . . . down there.

Both the inner and outer labia, Dill saw, stretched by the intrusion earlier of other guests and her own titanic masturbation session during the picnic, were indeed moist and glistening. Kneeing the vulnerably exposed young woman's legs even further apart, he took his cock in one hand and stirred the head in among the warm folds of flesh. He flexed his hips, hollowed the muscles of his buttocks and thrust forward as hard as he could.

Maguy screamed.

She had always thought of her cunt as tight – a long, tight slit which could be prised open to let a man inside her. She knew it was less tight today because of the continuous attention paid to it here, during the picnic, last night in the bedroom . . . ever since Michel's extraordinary behaviour in the train in fact.

But this . . . ! My God – she remembered reading the phrase once in an erotic magazine story – this was like forcing open an oyster!

The thick, long staff was distending the labia unbearably, stretching wide the vaginal walls, penetrating deep, deep, deep inside the quivering flesh of her belly. She could feel that taut flesh giving way, opening to let him in as he lunged even harder. She thought she would split apart; her whole cunt was opened in a soundless scream, gagged by the stifling bulk of this stiffened shaft.

Dill withdrew, perhaps half the length of the weapon, then plunged in even further. Maguy gasped. Nobody and nothing had ever reached so far inside her, filled her so unimaginably full. His pubic bone ground against her clitoris to send waves of sensation flaming through her. Once more he withdrew and then rammed it back into her, faster now. She felt as if the night was swallowing her up.

After a few more powerful strokes – his hands were squeezing her breasts, the thumbs rubbing the hardened nipples – Dill raised his head. 'Come on in, squire,' he said to Michel. 'There's room for all.'

With a single powerful movement, he rolled over on to his back, pulling the young woman's slight frame, still impaled, on top of him. She stared down into his lustful face. He was smiling. 'I reckon you can make your own way in now,' he said to her husband.

Maguy bit her lip. She knew what was going to happen. It had never happened to her before, though she had often thought of it, dreaded it even. In any case Michel had never dared.

He was daring now. 'I certainly will,' he snapped. 'I've been waiting to give it to the bitch all evening!' She felt his hands on her back, the hard ridge of a cock dipping down against the cleft between her buttocks.

Her anus was already wet from the juices seeping from her cunt when she was lying on her back. She moaned as marauding fingers forced their way in, widening the tightly puckered ring for the brutal penetration she knew must follow.

Michel wrenched apart the cheeks of her bottom. He lay along her back. She felt the velvety knob at the head of his rigid penis against her most private, her most intimate and secret place. He flexed his hips and lunged.

Maguy yelled for the second time. The shaft slid in with surprising ease – but it was tight, tight, and now her whole pelvis, front and back, was on fire.

She was violated, sandwiched between two men; now there were two cocks piercing her body, Michel's cock thrusting up beside the great weapon buried in her cunt – the two of them, hotly pulsating, separated only by the thin and throbbing wall of flesh between her two passages.

Slowly, and then with increasing speed, they began thrusting in and out.

Maguy came almost at once, writhing her imprisoned frame between them as they bucked and plunged, quaking, shuddering and finally convulsing with a loud cry to greet the incredible orgasm storming through her.

Seconds afterwards she came again, when each man stiffened and jerked, squirting his load of scalding semen far up into her impaled flesh.

Later again she freed an arm to crush Michel's head against her cheek. Breathless murmurs streamed from her slack mouth, but the only words emerging clearly from the incoherent babble were 'darling' and 'love'.

Dagmar van den Bergh had been organizing another sex game on the far side of the room. A line of naked women knelt forward on the floor, their knees together and the hairy furrows of their private parts salaciously visible between their buttocks. The men stood ready some distance behind them. 'You run forward and plug into whichever one you fancy when the music starts,' the Countess told them, 'fucking again in time with the metronome. When it stops, each man moves one girl to the right, starting in again when the music resumes. And so on. Those who come fall out. Last pair in get the prize.'

Neither Large nor Roth was listening. They were still intently watching the lewdly coupled trio on the floor, each now with a darker patch staining the crotch of his dark trousers. 'Magnificent,' Roth said hoarsely, placing a hand on his host's shoulder. 'And look, even though they're all through, the kid still has both of those guys trapped like a vice in there!'

'Vice!' Seamus cried suddenly, starting up from his place by the wall. 'That's it: I remember now!'

'Remember what?' Bella said sleepily. 'Do sit down again, sweetie.'

'The vice of the Bishop of Avery,' he said. 'The bloody

end's come back to me, sure.' He quoted: 'With hideous howls . . . he deflowered young owls . . . which he kept in an underground aviary.'

'Shut *up*, Seamus!' Dale called from a far corner, where he and Sonia were engaged in some private vice of their own. 'Pack it in, man, do. I can't hear myself scream.'

But the Irishman was not to be deterred. 'While we're on the subject of the clergy,' he said, 'with herself acting the priestess over there' – he nodded at the Countess, who was conducting her game in the manner of an orchestra leader – 'while we're on the subject, by God, there's another one come to me that starts not with the dread words, "There was a young someone of someplace". Listen, you, to this.' He drew a deep breath and declaimed in his most theatrical voice:

An innocent virgin from Devon
Was had in a wood by seven
Itinerant priests.
Lascivious beasts!
Of such is the kingdom of heaven.

He smiled genially around at the assembled company, slid down to the floor again, and fell instantly fast asleep, with Bella's head cradled in his lap.

The Countess's game was over, though nobody had asked what the prize was. Most of the guests by now were too dazed and exhausted to remember there should be one. Lorraine however was still available – and there was a part she wanted to play.

'Something Shakespearean, no doubt?' a voice suggested acidly.

'Fuck Shakespeare,' the film star replied. 'Guy was too wordy by half. What's this he says in *Julius Caesar*: "Let me have men about me who are fat", right? In my scenario, I'd cut that to, "Let me have men about me". Period.'

She climbed up on to the closed grand piano. 'Come on, guys. Who wants to make sweet music with Mama?'

Jean-Jacques Ancarani was the first to jump up beside her, his thick cock spearing up from his black bush. 'Bully for you, handsome,' Lorraine approved. 'I'm gonna let you in the back way, okay? I feel like resting my shoulders on that hairy male chest!' She bent forward shamelessly, guided the hard shaft between her buttocks, and when he was firmly embedded in her anus coaxed him to lower the two of them to the polished piano lid. He lay on his back with Lorraine face-upwards on top of him, his strong arms around her waist and his crossed hands cupping the large and famous breasts.

The scene that followed was remarkable – and became increasingly bizarre.

Lorraine turned her head from side to side and looked around the room. Dale, Sonia and the Baron had retired upstairs; Maguy had passed out blissfully; Bella and Seamus were still asleep and Séverine held Margot in her arms on the chesterfield. There remained eight nude people, six guests and the two maids, staring expectantly at the piano. 'Yeah,' Lorraine said, 'with a little luck – and maybe a shoe-horn! – I reckon I can fit you all in.' She beckoned to Dill Jones. 'This way, Elephant Man. I know you've been like busy, but a guy with your talents should be able to get it up again, no?'

Dill walked up to the piano. 'Try me,' he said.

She reached for his mammoth cock, peeling back the foreskin and milking the shaft until it regained its normal impressive rigidity. She grasped the bullish, hairy pouch swelling below the huge organ and drew him gently closer. 'Drive up and garage that in here' – with her free hand she patted her cunt – 'I want to keep it under cover for now.'

Obediently, he clambered to the closed keyboard and then to the lid. He positioned himself between shapely legs invitingly spread, lowered his knees on either side of Ancarani's, and approached his giant tool to the scarlet-nailed fingers now holding wide the lips of Lorraine's cunt.

Thrusting down and forward to meet her upwardly arched hips, he slid the thick length within her.

Lorraine caught her breath. 'Christ!' she gasped. 'That's a custom-built model all right! I guess they don't build them like that any more.'

She caught Mark Harries' eye. 'Lover, you look tired,' she said. 'Come and rest your butt on these tits of mine. I'm told they're comfortable enough. But be sure to leave that dick within reach of my mouth, okay?'

Mark did as he was told, his buttocks squashing down the fleshy swell of her full breasts, the head of his stiff cock resting in the hollow of her neck.

Next on Lorraine's list were Kirk and Tony Hill 'I'm real sorry there's nothing left for you guys but manual labour,' she said, 'but walk up, walk up and see what Mama has to offer.'

'You bet!' Tony Hill said enthusiastically. 'My word, what a wizard sight!' He approached and stood by the piano as she reached down a hand, took hold of his erect penis, and began gently wanking the shaft.

In the curve of the piano, on the other side, the yacht skipper was similarly received. 'Just what the doctor ordered!' he said.

Four people were left: Lusty, Busty, Doll and Michel.

As Lorraine had promised, they were all accommodated, almost as though a blueprint existed for the neat execution of the party's finale.

Lusty and Busty jumped on to the piano and stood one on either side of Mark, facing outwards above Kirk and Tony. If they bent their knees slightly, their pubic triangles descended to the level of the Englishmen's faces.

That left only Doll and Michel. The journalist's wife was equal to the occasion. She went to fetch an upright chair, planted it at the narrow end of the piano, and climbed up until she was standing on the seat. From here she leaned forward until she could kiss Mark Harries – himself bent over the film star's head – on the mouth. Michel straddled the edge of the chair, facing backwards with his face buried in her crotch and his hardened cock caressed by the toes of one acrobatic foot.

Lorraine laughed aloud. 'Okay, guys and dolls,' she cried. 'Let's go!'

Suddenly the whole complex group heaved, thrust and gobbled into motion.

Dill and Jean-Jacques plunged forcefully in and out of the actress; she herself took Mark's cock in her mouth while tossing off Kirk and Tony on either side. They in turn tongued the cunts of Lusty and Busty as Michel sucked Doll and she kissed Mark. Apart from Dill and the *Maître de Chai*, who after all had the most enviable tasks, there was not a single participant who didn't have at least two separate and sensitive sexual areas under attack! Even Lusty and Busty, standing on the piano with their bellies thrust forward to meet the Englishmen's mouths, managed to lean the upper parts of their bodies back and turn their heads sideways so they could kiss one another.

'Regarding this of the equipment, its length and girth,' Lusty murmured, 'it would seem senseless now to pursue the matter of alternatives.' She glanced at the thick and glistening stem of Dill's cock as it ploughed between the inflamed lips of Lorraine's cunt. 'Clearly Monsieur of the unusual proportions must be adjudged National Champion in this category.'

'Clearly,' said Busty. She slid her tongue into her friend's mouth.

The phalanx of differentially united but uniformly moving naked bodies centred on the grand piano, with the receptive voluptuary from Hollywood as its nucleus, was an astonishing sight – a classic case of the whole being greater than the sum of the parts. For over and above the individual sucking and licking and shafting and rubbing – in which the parts indeed received their fair share of attention – the whole gradually established a corporate life of its own.

The mound of nude bodies with its heaving limbs and strangled gasps, the orchestrated chorus of squelching sucks and slapping flesh, punctuated by the grace-notes provoked by a myriad roving hands, combined somehow to form a single composite organism. An animate being with many mouths and multiple limbs, which could nevertheless, in the perfection of its impeccably reciprocating components, be regarded – perhaps even treated – as an entity.

An entity which, judging from the accelerating symphony of moans and groans and snorting gasps choking from its centre, was heading for one of the most monumental group orgasms of all time . . .

Mondragon Roth was beside himself with excitement, his huge body shaking as he literally danced with glee.

'Ray,' he crowed, seizing his host's hand, 'you got yourself a partner, man, and that's for sure. If the wine you make has this effect even before the modern installation's in place . . . well, shit, I'm buying in, daddy, and I want a piece!'